HOT POPPIES

REGGIE NADELSON

arrow books

Published in the United Kingdom by Arrow Books, 2006

1 3 5 7 9 10 8 6 4 2

Copyright © Reggie Nadelson 1997

Reggie Nadelson has asserted her right under the Copyright, Designs and Patents Act, 1988 to be identified as the author of this work.

This novel is a work of fiction. Names and characters are the product of the author's imagination and any resemblance to actual persons, living or dead, is entirely coincidental.

This book is sold subject to the condition that it shall not, by way of trade or otherwise, be lent, resold, hired out, or otherwise circulated without the publisher's prior consent in any form of binding or cover other than that in which it is published and without a similar condition including this condition being imposed on the subsequent purchaser.

First published in the United Kingdom in 1997 by
Faber and Faber, London.

Arrow Books
The Random House Group Limited
20 Vauxhall Bridge Road, London, SW1V 2SA

Random House Australia (Pty) Limited
20 Alfred Street, Milsons Point, Sydney
New South Wales 2061, Australia

Random House New Zealand Limited
18 Poland Road, Glenfield
Auckland 10, New Zealand

Random House (Pty) Limited
Isle of Houghton, Corner of Boundary Road & Carse O'Gowrie
Houghton 2198, South Africa

The Random House Group Limited Reg. No. 954009

www.randomhouse.co.uk

A CIP catalogue record for this book
is available from the British Library

Papers used by Random House
are natural, recyclable products made from wood grown in
sustainable forests. The manufacturing processes conform to
the environmental regulations of the country of origin

ISBN 0 09 9497824

Typeset by SX Composing DTP, Rayleigh, Essex
Printed and bound in Great Britain by
Bookmarque Limited, Croydon, Surrey

For Paulette Goldenhar
with love

With many thanks for telling me the stories
(and for being the good guys)
to Detective William Oldham
and Inspector George Lee

PART ONE

New York

1

The fresh cold snow slapped my face around and when I licked some off my mouth it tasted like a blast of gin right out of the freezer. It was the morning I found the snapshot of the dead girl near her body. In the picture she stood next to a big white Caddy convertible, wearing a hot pink jacket and grinning fit to die. In real life, if you could call it that, she lay on the floor of my friend Hillel's place in the diamond district, dead, naked and white. Not white like the snow; more the color of asbestos.

I'd been in bed with Lily Hanes when the phone rang around dawn. I groped for it on the floor—I hate the goddamn cellphone, always going off somewhere you can't see it, like your heart ringing—and Lily switched on the TV. She's an event freak like all reporters. Taking in the news of the blizzard, Lily smiled. "I love the sense of impending disaster," she said, then she kissed me, turned over and went back to sleep. I threw on my clothes and left, and Lily's tousled red hair and her bare freckled back were the last warm things I saw.

★

and it, Plaza, I could Rosa lot... You'd weaselness up his

It was like walking into a meat locker when I got to Hillel Abramsky's, or maybe like walking into hell, if hell froze over. Even before I got inside, a snake of chemical cold curled out from under the door, and I knew it was much worse than Hillel had let on when he called me at Lily's. Why would you put on air conditioning when it's snowing out unless there's something putrid in your place, something you figure is going to stink?

The cold made my skin pucker up like an old persimmon. The hairs on my arm went rigid. The thing on the floor made me hang back in the doorway. In my pants pocket, I scrabbled for cigarettes.

"I'm glad you're here, Artie. I need you."

I had to squint to make out that it was Hillel talking. Then I saw him. He was kneeling on the floor under the window. Black hat on the back of his head, beard spread over his shirt front, he was lit from behind like one of those Jesus pictures by the thick milky light that was coming up outside. From somewhere I could hear the grind and whine of the garbage truck eating bottles and a radio playing Frank Sinatra. "I've got the World on a String", Frank sang. I scratched the wall for a light. A fluorescent bar blinked on and made everything look hard and flat.

"You got to look, Artie. Please. It's why I got you out of bed. Please." Hillel said again and pulled back the coat to show me the body. She lay on her back, tiny and dead. The nakedness embarrassed me.

"She's Chinese." Hillel clenched his fists when he said it. "I got enough trouble. What's she doing up here

4

on 47th Street, anyhow? What's she doing outside Chinatown?"

She *was* Chinese, and her scrawny legs were splayed at skewed angles. Bruises covered her arms. Everywhere else, as far as I could see, there were lacerations, scratches, stab wounds. Rigor had set in and her tiny hands seemed to clutch at something: life, maybe.

I bent over. Her face appeared to have been slashed with some kind of rake, a knife with multiple blades. The flesh looked like rats had clawed it over and over.

"Jesus Christ," I said and sat on the edge of the cot in the corner to keep from shaking.

"Drink that," Hillel said, reaching for a paper bag and extracting a carton of coffee. He dumped in some sugar. "Drink it."

The coffee was cold and it tasted of cardboard, but the sugar and caffeine gave me the buzz I needed.

Hillel put his coat back over the body and I should have stopped him. It would contaminate the scene, but I kept my mouth shut and Hillel, nimble for such a tall man, got up and put his hand on my shoulder. He's forty like me, but the black clothes make him seem a lot older. Also, Hillel has seen a lot more of life. He already has six kids.

"You want to turn the air off, Hil. It's gonna freeze up and bust if you don't." I looked at the body. "It's OK. She's not going to stink or anything. Turn it off. You called 911?"

"I called you, Artie. I don't want trouble. This woman, she's Chinese," he repeated himself. Bullets of sweat seemed to freeze on his forehead and hang there.

5

"You have to call the cops, Hil. I'm out of it. I'm not on the job. They call this extended leave without pay, but it means it's over. I'm a civilian."

"You're the only cop I can trust," he said.

"I'm not a cop. I quit."

Hillel looked exhausted. "Fine. You're not a cop any more. You're an ex-cop. What's the difference? You're my friend."

He sat down heavily on the cot next to me. Bent over himself like a hollow giant, he sat on the edge of that cot and picked at the floor. He pulled up a wood splinter and examined it, then tossed it away and leaned his elbows on his knees. "Give me a cigarette, Artie," he said, then added sheepishly, "I was supposed to quit."

For a minute we sat and sucked at the cigarettes; the nicotine helped.

"I'm grateful you came." He gestured at the dead woman. "I don't want trouble with the Chinese. We already got plenty trouble in Crown Heights. We sold the place in Flushing because the Chinese came in. We sold the place on Canal Street when Chinatown ate up the neighborhood downtown. We were trapped, they had all these fights going on between themselves, different factions, different everything, Fujianese, Cantonese, what do I know from all this, except we got caught in the middle and these people are eating us up."

"I didn't know the Chinese went in for diamonds." I picked up the phone to call 911. Hillel took it away from me.

"Diamonds are big in Hong Kong. They got their

6

own set-up. Sources in London, Russia also. They don't play by our rules."

"What else?"

Hillel pulled on the cigarette. "There was a kid. Errand boy from one of my suppliers. He was OK. Then he gets nosy. Wants to learn the business, he says. I figure he wants a taste. I tell him, we're only family here. I tell his boss, keep him away, but they don't like it. He wants protection money. So I change suppliers."

"What kind of supplier?"

"Toilet paper." Hillel laughed without any humor. "Paper towels. Cleaning supplies. I told him to beat it."

"Anything else I should know about this kid?"

"He was a kid, nineteen, twenty. Gold necklaces. Petulant. Weak mouth. So skinny, he stooped like an old man. Weird hair. Red."

"What kind of weird?"

"More orange than red. You know, dyed. Like a lot of gang kids. And big in front. You know what I'm saying?"

"A quiff."

"Like that."

I went to the door. No one had touched the locks. Only Hillel has keys, it's practically a religion with him.

I've known Hillel Abramsky a long time. He helped me with diamond district stuff when I was on the job. In a few hours, he would have been running back and forth to his uncle's building next door; the men cut the stones there in a room where diamond dust seems to float in motes of sunlight. Once, Hilly showed me what good diamonds look like, made me look through his loupe at them, beautiful, icy, unfeeling things that people kill for. Hil is not a material guy but I had seen how much the diamonds excited him.

"What's your security like?"

He stabbed his cigarette into the coffee carton where it hissed and died. "I have first class alarms. But this office I only use for paperwork. Sometimes I come in early to catch up. Mo, the accountant, does the books sometimes. I read a little. Pray. Next door at my uncle's where they keep the stones they got locks from Fort Knox." He tried smiling, but all the gusto was gone.

"Then how did this girl slip through your door on a Sunday night, Hil? How? Talk to me."

"I don't know. I don't know anything any more." He was closer to despair than I've seen him in fifteen years.

"Call 911," I said. "I'll wait until they come. Call like you would if you just found the girl. What else did you see when you got here?"

Clutching the portable phone, he punched 911. I looked at the body shrouded in Hillel's black coat. I'd seen worse stuff. Much worse. I'd gone numb with seeing stuff over the years, like cops do, drinking too much, getting ulcers, telling competitive horror stories for the laughs. "You hear about the baby on the plane that never cried?" some detective would say in a bar after work. "It was dead, man, hollowed out, stuffed with cocaine. They don't put that shit on TV." Maybe being off the job, I had turned back into some kind of human being.

The radiator came on. The room grew suffocatingly hot and airless. Sweat trickled down my sides like ants.

So a Chinese girl was dead, I thought. It was tough, but it happened all the time. When I looked at the body, though, I had the feeling this thing would snowball, it would get bigger and bigger, I could run away but it would roll over me. Run me over, gobble me up. I didn't want it. I lit another cigarette.

"Take your coat off her. Someone's gonna get real pissed off if they think you messed up the scene."

Squatting on his heels, he pulled the coat back off the body then he got up. I crouched beside the girl. Lime green hairs from a sweater in a small pile of clothes next to it had drifted into the air and settled on her, stuck in the dried blood. I picked up the sweater. In the pocket was a stick-on label, an address printed in magic marker, like a kid going to camp. You could send her back if she got lost. Return to sender: one dead girl. No name. Probably never would have a name. I scribbled the address on a matchbook I had in my pocket.

Then I found the photograph—the girl in it fooling around next to the white Caddy. I looked at the girl on the floor, then back at the picture in my hand. They were the same. The same person, one alive and smiling, the other dead, her face ripped apart.

"Artie?" Hillel plucked at my arm and, only half conscious I was doing it, I slipped the photograph into my pocket and got up from the floor.

In Hillel's outstretched palm was a red cloth flower, the kind you see all over Chinatown. "I also found this. Red's good luck with the Chinese." He shook his head. "Some luck!"

Hillel's a realist. In his line of work, you have to be, not to mention his religion that gets in people's faces and makes them hate. The certainty, I envied; I wondered if there was anything that could make him doubt.

Maybe he has the inside track spiritually, but I don't get the prayer stuff, or the accessories, the shawl, the box on the forehead, and I'd be dead before I'd walk around with a yarmulke all day. I'm not that kind of Jew. I'm not sure I'm any kind of Jew.

"Look, I have some money." Hillel put a neat fold of bills on the desk. "You could use the money. I need your help." The phone was still in his hand and he spoke into it. "Dead. I told you. Yes. Sure, I'm sure. Sure. There's tracks on her face. Her belly's ripped wide open."

"I can't take your money," I said. Then I heard the sirens in the distance. The cops were on their way. "Hil, you'll be OK now. You will. I swear to God. But I can't do any more. If I get sucked into this kind of cesspool again, I'm going to fucking drown in it."

The snow fell, the wind tinkled on the window, the radio played more Sinatra. In the tangle of clothes on the floor next to the dead girl, I imagined I saw something almost alive, something I didn't want to name, hadn't wanted to think about from the second I arrived.

"You knew," Hillel said. "You knew right away when you came through that door, didn't you? Didn't you, Artie?" His voice rose. He was almost hysterical now.

"Yeah, I knew."

"She was pregnant, Artie. She was pregnant and they ripped up her face and cut her open. Then they killed her and the baby both."

★

A trio of diamond dealers in long black coats minced along 47th Street like old ladies afraid to fall on the ice and crack their bones. I had come out of Hillel's. Listening to the sirens, I sat in my car, waiting for the cops. A patrol car pulled up followed by a vintage silver Porsche. From it emerged a guy in a white jacket. He pushed his Raybans on top of his head and, without offering any to the cops standing around, took some cigarettes from his pocket and lit up. He gestured at Hillel's building, then turned to look in my direction. He wasn't looking at me, though. He was waiting for the TV van that, even while I was sitting there, came up 47th Street and stopped in front of Hillel's.

I'd seen the cop on TV. Chan? Chen? Something Chen? He was a big deal. When there was a case involving the Chinese, they called him in. Hillel would be OK now, I told myself. He'd be OK. I drove back to 10th Street and slipped into Lily's bed. Without waking up, she turned and draped her leg over me.

I lay awake and watched Lily. We'd been going out, on and off, for around a year and a half. There was someone else in her life, but he was mostly in England.

Asleep, all six feet of her, she resembled a gangly twelve-year-old. Lily's forty-six, maybe forty-seven. I think. She won't tell me. It's her Achilles heel, the age thing, not that I give a rat's ass how old she is. She's very smart. Nice. We get along great, the sex is great, we love the same music. There's never any hidden messages with her either, and she has great legs. Also, Lily was born in New York.

Like a special perfume, she wears the city in her skin, has its confidence, style, class. It's the air she breathes, and she reminds me of my dreams. When I met her, I felt I'd sailed into a safe harbor.

Outside the window, weird fat flakes of snow were failing very fast. I love New York when it's cold and sharp and the air has that awesome clarity, when you lie in bed and watch the day come up and do its tricks with light all over again.

Half asleep now, I drifted. Maybe it's the only Russian thing left in me, loving the winter. It's twenty-five, twenty-six years since I left Moscow, the asshole of world cities. Skating in Gorky Park is one of my good memories. That last winter, a daring park apparatchik put Domenico Meduno doing "Nel Blu del Pinto del Blu" on the sound system. We bribed him to put a Beatles number on and our parents caught a lot of shit for it, but my mother, who always laughed at the system, laughed even harder. A long time ago, I thought, trying to settle into the warm pocket of sheets next to Lily's back. But I was restless.

Lying there, I tried to reclaim the guy I'd been a couple of hours earlier. We'd been good, me and Lily, ever since I quit. Mellow is what I'd been feeling right up until Hillel called. I tried to get it back. I didn't want to tell Lily about the dead girl. My last case, the one in Brighton Beach, had scared the shit out of her, and I figured if I stayed off the job, if I finally quit, maybe we could have a life together. But maybe I was kidding myself.

"What's going on?" Lily opened her pale blue-gray

eyes, rubbed them, switched the TV on. "You OK? Artie?"

"Yeah. I'm fine."

"What happened?"

"Nothing much."

"Who was on the phone before?"

"Hillel Abramsky. He needed a favor."

"What kind of favor?" The voice grew tart. "Artie? What kind of favor?"

"Some trouble at his shop. I helped him out. I owed him."

"You owe too many people," she said, but she was smiling, sitting up, watching the weather report as intently as a gambler at the track now, watching his horse come in. "I think this is going to be the biggest blizzard in New York history, you know." She got up, grabbed her green silk pajama top from the floor and put it on.

"Come back to bed," I said, but Lily was already at the window.

"Snow." Gathering her hair into a pony tail and tying it with a rubber band she found in her pocket, she beamed. "Lots of snow. Lows, troughs, gale force winds, the whole awesome thing."

Her clear eyes liquid with delight, she blew me a kiss, then headed for the bathroom door, where she turned and grinned like a cat that's just spotted a huge dish of cream. "Like I said, impending disaster, toots." She meant the snow.

I was sweating bullets. By now I had realized what was driving me nuts. I knew her.

13

I knew the girl. I didn't know how I knew her or where, but what kept me awake, what made me sweat, was I knew the dead girl on Hillel Abramsky's floor.

2

The girl looks up at me hopefully from the photograph I've swiped from the scene at Hillel's. Half an hour after I left Lily's, I was drinking coffee in the front booth at Mike Rizzi's, the picture on the table next to me, trying to figure out how the hell I knew the girl in it.

At the counter, three taciturn customers knocked back their coffee like it was booze and, behind it, Mike fried eggs.

The photograph is crumpled and grimy, but the girl is fixed up like a million bucks. She's wearing the pink jacket with fur around the hood. She's posed next to that Cadillac, with its wire wheels and red leather interiors, and it confers some kind of status on her, you can see that in the sexy pose, one hand on her skinny hip, the other on the gold hood ornament in some imitation of possession. She has on too much make-up—she's maybe eighteen, nineteen, but she looks like a kid—and her head is tilted jauntily at the camera, the aspirant smile outlined in bright red lipstick.

"Artie? You want the eggs over easy? You want

15

anything on the bagel?" From behind his counter Mike was peering over at me.

Farm girls in the 1930s is what I was thinking of. In the Depression, girls went to Hollywood to make it in the movies. Had their photos taken in fancy clothes, with big cars, then sent them home to show they had it made in Tinseltown. Most of them ended up on dope or as whores, or dead, like this one, this Chinese girl in the picture in front of me. Who was she, this girl, this kid who is all make-up and longing?

Digging in my pocket, I pulled out the matches where I'd written her address, and I grabbed my jacket as the pulse in my forehead began to pound. Who was she? I looked out of the window. In the street, the snow gathered on the cars, the buildings, the sidewalk. Hurrying to work, people kept their heads down against the snow that fell now in a thick white sheet.

Through the snow, I could see my own building. It was opposite Mike's coffee shop. Home. I could crash, I could climb into bed and forget it, but adrenalin shot me out of the booth where I sat and I grabbed my coat.

"Artie? What about your breakfast? Where in the hell you going, man?" I heard Mike yell as my bagel flew from the toaster and he caught it. But I was already halfway out the door and into my car. Praying the sucker would hold out for one more day, I drove like fuck the few blocks to Chinatown.

Rats scuffled behind the door on the seventh floor of the building on Market Street. Something like rats, something that scuffled and chattered and scraped its claws along the floor. Taped to the door was a sign with Chinese characters; under it was a scrawl in English: Joy Fun Sewing Company, it said. I banged on the door. No one answered. In the dank hallway, the linoleum tiles were shredded and gray slush ran into puddles. I looked around. I banged some more and felt in my ski jacket for the gun; the little Seecamp was a gift from an old friend and I carried for it luck. "Police," I shouted and hoped to God I didn't run into any other cops.

Bolts turned. The door opened. A woman with a rough Asian face flew at me, screaming in Chinese. I shoved the picture of the dead girl under her nose and pushed my way in. The racket in the room was terrifying.

Most of it came from the sewing machines. Women, forty, fifty of them, were hunched over, pedaling like it was the Tour de France, like their lives depended on it. Lit from above by savage fluorescent lights that dangled from the ceiling, the room was about 1500 square feet. It was freezing. Drafts blew in under the big windows. A few decrepit space heaters gave off the stink of propane but hardly any heat. But it was the noise that got me, the rat chatter of the manual machines, the hiss of steam irons, the shouts of the pressers when they banged into metal rails where garments hung shrouded in plastic. From a boombox came the whine of "Yesterday" played on windchimes. Everywhere in the freezing shop, the women coughed.

On TV I had watched celebrities burst into tears over the sweatshops, but no one mentioned the noise could fry your inner ear so bad you couldn't stand up straight.

17

"Yes sir?"

The high-pitched voice belonged to a fat kid, a regular little Moby with a face like an undercooked dumpling. Zipping his pants up with one hand, a chocolate chip muffin in the other, he lumbered out from behind a curtain. He took it all in: me with the picture in my hand, the rough-faced woman staring at it. As soon as he appeared, she retreated.

"Is that woman your mother?"

"Yessir," he said.

"Is this her shop?"

"Yessir," he said again and ate the muffin.

I showed him the picture. "Do you know the person in this photograph?"

Prodding his teeth, he looked at it. "There is no such person here. Go away now. Cops already came."

Squatting, I looked the kid in the face. He was obviously the son and heir and he could speak English. As far as the outside world went, he ran the show. I looked at the lidless eyes embedded in his soft flesh. He was an insolent little prick and I said, "Think harder. Tell your mother to think harder."

Ignoring me, he extracted a monster-size Pay Day from his pocket and bit off a chunk through the wrapper. I snatched the candy bar away and threw it in a garbage can.

Someone turned off the music. Work stopped. The din died away. There was a communal intake of breath. Two visits by the cops the same day was enough to scare the shit out of all of them.

Crocodile tears dripped from the kid's face. The

18

mother reappeared and hammered on my arm and it took a while to peel her off. With protective fury, she clutched Porky and pulled him into a corner.

Two beats later, the women went back to work. Someone switched the music back on. Holding the photograph, I walked up and down the crowded aisle. Some of the sewing machines were the computerized Jap machines and they ran so fast the women who worked them, unable to stop for a second, were frozen into grotesque positions. Kids of nine or ten sat on mats on the floor snapping threads off garments. At the very back of the room the brick wall had been whitewashed and on it, someone had scrawled FIRE EXIT in red. There wasn't any door. The floors were filthy, the windows covered with scummy rags, the women packed into the room with hardly crawl space to stretch their legs. I could smell the stink of a toilet.

Against the wall, a girl in a red wool cap sat on a low stool sewing labels into jeans by hand. When I showed her the photograph, she looked at me and, right away, I knew she knew.

The labels read MADE IN THE USA and somehow the irony wasn't lost on her. She wore Coke-bottle glasses and, behind them, her dark eyes were knowing, alert, almost amused.

"Who was she?"

"Her name was Rose Yi. She's dead, is she?" The girl spoke good English.

"Yes. I'm sorry. What's your name?"

"Pansy. My name is Pansy Loh." She looked down at her work. "She was my friend . . ." She stopped suddenly. I felt someone behind us. "Go now," Pansy said urgently. "Please go."

It was the fat boy. He was watching. Listening.

"OK, Fatso, tell your mother, nothing here," I said. Then I beat it.

Desperate for a smoke, I climbed a short flight of stairs to the roof and went outside. It was a big building by Chinatown standards. It faced the on-ramp to the Manhattan Bridge and from where I stood, I could see the decayed ramparts of the bridge and hear the traffic that roared across it to Brooklyn. The snow was falling harder and people were going home early. Already, the city was closing down, and on the roof here, the black plastic garbage bags, the cardboard boxes, even the rusted pigeon coop were white with the stuff. I tried to light up, but the wind blew out the matches.

Chinatown was like a war zone. The snow falling, people scuttled in all directions, pulling plastic sheets over the produce that spilled onto the sidewalk. Split watermelons, the hot pink fruit showing between green rinds, looked surreal in the snow. There were guys selling bottled water, flashlights, and charcoal. In every grocery store, people shopped for the apocalypse.

In the twenty years since I'd been in New York, Chinatown had spread, a neighborhood on steroids. Back then it was a hermetic area, eight, ten square blocks with the ceremonial pagoda arch on Mott Street as its entry point. But Chinatown ballooned, pushing north to gobble up Little Italy where landlords complained about price gouging, then sold their bakeries and coffee houses and went, the oldsters anyhow, to live in Jersey. It bust its borders at Broadway, carried slivers off the financial district, rammed SoHo where at community meetings Chinese wholesalers and local artists screamed insults at each other. The poor bastards who work the First Precinct caught it in the ass, trying to help, but it was the 5th that ran the turf. Me, I hadn't paid much attention to it. Chinatown had been there. You shopped for groceries. You ate. Now, it was a city all by itself. "What street compares to Mott Street in July?" ran through my head, Ella singing, insistent as a jingle. What were the other lines?

"Fuck you!" a kid pushing crates of fruits screamed as I banged into his handtruck. I've always loved Chinatown for the food, the fireworks, the crowds. What was it Jimmy Breslin said? "Nature's finest site is a crowded city street." My motto, but I felt clumsy now, and big, like Gulliver, and I couldn't speak the language or read the angles. A fishtank in the window of a restaurant caught my eye. The fish, poor suckers, would be dinner later tonight. Like me, if I didn't stop messing around down here. One ex-cop. Dinner for two. Yum.

But the more I walked, the more I thought about the girl in the sweatshop. Pansy didn't seem surprised when she came out of her building for a break and discovered me loitering in the doorway. Although she walked by without saying anything, I had the feeling she was expecting me.

"Can I talk to you?"

"There's a park near Bayard Street." She hurried ahead of me until we got there. The park was deserted.

To get some shelter, we huddled underneath a kid's slide.

"I only have fifteen minutes for my break," she said. "What do you want?"

"Tell me about your friend, Rose."

"Do you know Detective Jeremy Chen?"

"No. Why?" It was the name of the cop I'd seen outside Hillel's earlier. Chen. Jeremy Chen.

"He came this morning. I don't trust him. If I talk to you, you must promise not to tell him anything."

"Sure."

From a large plastic bag Pansy took a photograph and handed it to me. It was a picture of herself. It was identical to the picture of her friend, Rose. Same pink jacket. Same white Caddy. "You can have it if you like," she said.

"Who took the pictures?"

"I don't know. A white man. Sunglasses. Hat. He took a lot of pictures. Made a fuss with the cameras. He always had several cameras. Fancy bags for the cameras, too. Snap snap. We called him Mr Snap. All the girls wanted pictures."

"What for?"

"To send home. To prove we have made it in America." There was sarcasm in her voice. "We call it the Golden Mountain."

For a few seconds we stood, watching the snow. Then Pansy took a thermos out of her bag along with a cup. "Would you like some tea?"

Moving to the swings, she sat down on one, poured the tea and drank some. The red hat concealed most of her oval face, but when she took off the thick glasses, I saw that some freak of nature had given her dark eyes a greenish cast. She couldn't have been more than twenty-two or three, but she had real guts, real moxie, talking to a cop down here. She figured I was a cop on duty. I didn't clarify. Her English was old-fashioned but it was good, and I said so.

A hard glint of amusement passed over her face. "We're not all rednecks and peasant villagers, you know," she said.

I said, "I'm sorry. Really. Where did Rose live?"

"Sometimes with me. She needed money. She worked nights in a restaurant," Pansy added. "On Canal Street."

"Shit. Shit."

"Excuse me?"

"Your friend—Rose—it's the dumpling place on Canal near Lafayette?"

Pansy looked wary. "You knew her?"

"Yeah," I said. "Yeah, I knew her."

Behind the counter at the take-out joint over on Canal Street, Rose had worked the late shift. It was a place where, after work, I had sometimes dropped by to eat. The dumplings were tasty. The place was open all night. No one bothered you.

She had been a plain, small girl with lonely eyes. She didn't speak much English. She hardly spoke at all. One night, she tried to make a joke with me, but she got tangled up in the language and hid her face in her hands. I didn't help her. I didn't make her feel better. I ate and paid and left and, now, she was dead. The naked girl on Hillel's floor. Christ, I thought.

"I'm glad if she had a friend," Pansy said and I kept my mouth shut. "Is there anything else you can tell me? How she died?" Pansy looked at me. "Please. I'd like to know."

"You knew Rose was pregnant?"

"I didn't know. Was it a girl?"

"Does it matter?"

"Not really." Pansy stamped her feet. The cold was savage. "I ought to go now."

"How can I find you when you're not at work?"

From her shopping bag, she produced a take-out menu, then handed it to me as stylishly as if it were an engraved calling card from Tiffany's. "The phone number is on it," she said. "You can leave me a message in the restaurant. The owner is a friend. I share a room in the apartment upstairs."

"Can I keep your picture?"

"Yes. I have no one to send it home to," she said without self-pity.

"Would you like something to eat?"

She brushed some snow off her hat. "Some chocolate would be nice," she said.

Opposite the park was a newsstand where I bought her a handful of candy bars. Pansy selected the Almond Joy, ate it quickly and put the others in her bag. "You won't tell Detective Chen you've seen me, will you? He wants too much."

"I told you. I don't know Chen. Too much what?" I asked, but she didn't answer. "There are other cops. Good cops."

"I'm an illegal."

"You trusted me."

"No," she said. "No, I don't. But you're all I've got." She folded the candy wrapper into tiny squares and put it into her bag. "Forgive me, that doesn't sound terribly nice. I am grateful."

She could have been at a tea party instead of on a corner in Chinatown where the snow fell on used needles and crowds fighting for space on the sidewalk. Pansy's elegant turn of phrase and her self-possession hooked me. I didn't know if she had me figured out, but I didn't care. I felt bad about Rose, but Rose was dead. Pansy was something else. With her alert eyes, the sense of humor, the survivor's tough charm, even the crafty perception of how to work me, I was hooked.

We stood on the crowded street, Chinatown pushing at us from all sides, the snow coming down, the wind burning her cheeks red, and I wondered what I could do for her. I hoped to God I was wrong, but I had the feeling that this was the first inning of an obsession and I was already up to my ass in it, floundering in it, like the city in the snow.

"I want to help," I said. "Tell me how I can help you."

"If you want to help me, find out who killed Rose." Pansy turned to go. "You see, if Rose is dead," she said briskly, "I'm next."

3

"I'm next." "I'm next." "I'm next." The subway clattered along the tracks. The train was packed. I hung onto a pole and closed my eyes. "I'm next." "I'm next."

I took the train because I didn't trust the piece of shit that passes as my car to make it more than a few blocks in the storm. I had to go. For days I'd been promising myself I'd visit the Taes. "Please come, Artie," Mrs Tae had said on the phone. "Please." Ricky Tae is my best friend and her son and he's been sick for a long time, because of me, in a way. Rick has a place in the same building as me down off Broadway. His parents own the restaurant on the ground floor. When he got sick, though, the Taes took him up to their house in Riverdale.

Before I went uptown, I had stopped by Eljay's place. L.J. Koplin is a guy I know who services camera buffs. I dropped off the two photographs. On the back of Rose's picture was a bunch of letters and numbers. There was nothing on the back of Pansy's. Eljay swore he'd see what he could make of them and call me, and then I got the train to Riverdale.

At the Taes' house near Wave Hill, the old trees were already heavy with snow; in the forty-mile wind, the branches wheezed eerily. By the time I got inside, my feet were soaked. I left my shoes in the hall and went into Ricky's room. It was dark. It was always dark, the shades down. The light hurt his eyes, Ricky always said.

"Hello, Artie."

In the corner, on a sofa, Rick was asleep, but out of the gloom came a voice that sent a shiver up and down my spine. It was a docile, girlish voice that said, "Hello, Artie." I felt a light dry hand brush my face.

"Dawn?"

"Hello, Artie," she said for the third time in the same pale whisper that was like a ghost talking. Ricky's sister, Dawn had come home from Hong Kong. I put my arms around her and she looked up and said plaintively, "Will he get well? Artie? Will Rick ever get well?"

I looked at Ricky. One leg hung heavily over the side of the sofa, as if he'd had a stroke. It had happened the October before last. I was in the middle of the Russian case in Brighton Beach and some hoods came after me. But Ricky was in my apartment and they whacked him instead. It should have been me. It was me that found him on the floor, twisted like a rag doll. We never caught the creeps who did it.

At St Vincent's, the medics said the best you could hope for was Rick would end up a vegetable. Persistent vegetative state, they called it. A bunch of celery, they

27

meant. A cucumber. A Sunny Von Bulow. His brain was all screwed up. I had to call the Taes and tell them their handsome, brilliant son was a vegetable at twenty-eight. If they got lucky.

Later, Hillel Abramsky started sitting with him. He went on talking to Rick until he came out of the coma. Then the depression claimed him and now he stayed in this darkened room, barely moving, a TV flickering in the corner. His misery infected everyone in the house: Mrs Tae never listened to the Italian operas she loved and Mr Tae locked himself in his study and played solitary chess against a machine. Dawn, who usually radiated an almost glittering excitement about life, was drawn, ashy and very thin. She clung to me and I could feel her sharp bones.

"Turn the fucking TV off," Ricky said angrily, opening his eyes. "The noise is driving me nuts."

I switched off the television and tried to talk to Ricky, but he turned his back to me. Dawn glanced at her brother and motioned me to the other side of the room where there were a couple of chairs. Tiredly, she sat on one of them. I sat down next to her.

"When did you get back?" I said because I couldn't think of anything else to say.

"A while ago," she said. "Pete had business in New York. He said I should come too."

"You didn't call me?"

"I didn't call because I didn't want you to see me like this." She constantly twisted the diamond rings Pete had given her when they got married. She had loved the big white stones, but now her fingers were thin and dry as twigs and the rings were too big. Dawn's long silky hair was unwashed. Her eyes were dull, the pupils dilated, the whites like rotten eggs. I knew that Dawn was on drugs.

The dark was oppressive. There was a floor lamp near me and I reached for the switch. Dawn pushed my hand away. "No," she said. "Don't."

"Come on, Dawn. Sweetheart? What's going on? Talk to me." I heard myself, garrulous, voluble, pretending nothing had changed.

"It's OK, Artie." She faked a smile. "Don't mind me, I'm just tired. We do a lot of traveling. Everyone's cutting deals before the Chinese really get their hooks into Hong Kong. July '97, a few months, hard to believe. The Chinese take over. After that, a year, two, then everything changes. Pete says it will be OK. Pete knows the Chinese. And we've both got American passports. We're OK." Like a hostage propped in front of the TV cameras, she seemed to be reading approved lines. "I'm only here for Ricky."

"Where's Pete?"

"I'm here. How are you, Artie?"

Pete Leung walked into the room and we shook hands. He's tall, rumpled and very rich. He was thirty-seven, a couple years younger than me. His shirt tails hung out of his corduroy pants, he wore wire-rimmed glasses and his hands were rough, stained with paint. Pete's a tinkerer. He takes things apart and puts them back together. I liked him a lot. You couldn't help it.

Pete left the door open. Light flooded into the room from the hall and, in it, Dawn looked trapped, like a deer in the headlights.

29

Just then, Rick looked up and he saw Dawn too. He tried to get up. I ran over to him and found some shoes under the sofa, but he couldn't keep them on. The shoes were too big. Rick's feet had shriveled up. They were gray and bony like the feet of old men at the beach.

"Help me," he said.

I held one arm, and Pete took the other. Rick took a few steps, wobbled, and fell. We heaved him up again. "Come on," I said. "Come on, Rick, you can fucking do this. You can. I swear to God."

"I can't," he said and then he crawled back onto his sofa.

I had to get away. I loved these people, they're as much family as I ever had since I got to New York, and I'd destroyed them. I needed air. I needed Lily very badly.

In the hall, where thick, soft Chinese carpets covered the waxed oak floors, I got my shoes and coat. Padding after me, Dawn raised her dark unhappy eyes. "Do you want to know how it is, Artie? Do you? Do you really want to know?" But a noise startled her and she flitted away again, down the hall to her bedroom. I heard her door close.

"I didn't mean to eavesdrop, but I don't know what to do any more." Pete looked exhausted and there were faint lines around his eyes. He took off his glasses and blinked. He had been born in Hong Kong to a very rich family, had gone to college in England and grad school in America and he was usually loose, easy, like the shirt hanging out of his pants. I wondered what it was like to have all Pete's millions and be as miserable as he looked

30

now. Bending down, he pulled on some green rubber boots.

"I've got to get out for a while. Fancy a few beers?"

"Yeah, sure, Pete. I could really use a beer."

The door to Mr Tae's study opened unexpectedly. Mr Tae put his head out. "You are leaving?" he said to me. "I have to go out myself. Let me give you a lift please," he said. It wasn't a question. It was a command.

Looking towards his father-in-law, then back at me, Pete Leung raised his eyebrows. "I'll see you then, Artie. Soon, I hope," he added and left the house, poor bastard, and I heard the rattle of his old VW Beetle and remembered how he loved that car.

The lights in the Taes' windows receded as Mr Tae's Mercedes pulled away. Mr Tae sat in front next to the driver—I recognized Winston who used to manage the restaurant. I was in back. There was dry classical music on the radio; Bach, I think.

"Do you mind?"

I said I didn't mind.

"You're a jazz fan, I remember that, Artie. Mr Stan Getz, is that right? Mr Tony Bennett. And Mr Art Tatum." Mr Tae was formal, as if conducting a conversation with a stranger.

I didn't know what to call him—I'd always called him Martin. But he was distant now, a stranger who tried to put me at ease with empty talk which made it worse. What did I expect? I'd fucked up his family.

Ricky's dad who told terrible jokes and got box seats for the Yankees had been replaced by a grave gray old

31

man with two sick kids. We chatted. I made noises about this and that, the weather mostly. Thought about Dawn, about Pansy. Outside the car, the snow falling was a peculiar bright white in the headlights. White as the dead girl, white as Dawn's face.

Fog rolled in as we headed south onto the West Side Highway. Fog ate up the river. The foghorns you couldn't see delivered their doleful toot and wind moaned as if for the chaos it would cause. The car was hot. I wanted to sleep. My lids sank onto my eyes.

The Bach ended. Mr Tae put on the radio. Some of the trains were already out, the tracks icing up as the temperature dropped; all three airports were shut. A white-out was forecast, freaky in early March; Manhattan would be cut off from the mainland.

Traffic clogged the highway in both directions. Sirens screamed, blue lights flashed through the snow and fog. The exit to the 79th Street Marina was blocked; a motorbike was flipped on its back like a massive bug. Around us, cars skidded and spun their wheels on the slick highway. Mr Tae never asked me where I was going. He never said what he wanted from me. Winston kept driving.

A flash of flame shot up near the Holland tunnel. Winston turned off the highway onto Canal Street and I saw three men standing over a fire in a garbage can. In the street, shadowy figures wrestled grocery bags home, and on West Broadway, a kid selling pink fur earmuffs shared the corner with a pair of shivering Senegalese who hawked fake gold watches out of a briefcase.

On Broadway, the car turned south and now I knew

where we were going. I guess I'd known for a while: we were going home.

The cast-iron building where I live is seven stories tall and a hundred years old. When Mr Tae bought it it was a wrecked commercial hulk. He opened the restaurant on the ground floor and converted the rest into apartments. The entryway for us residents is separate from the restaurant's entrance. Now, instinctively, I looked up at my own windows. I saw something move, but there was snow in my eyes and I figured it was only shadows up there, that or paranoia. It was fourteen, maybe fifteen hours since Hillel got me out of Lily's bed that morning. I was so tired, I was hallucinating.

"Please." Martin Tae put his hand on my arm and walked me into the restaurant. It had been closed for business since Rick got sick, but the door was unlocked and, from the back, a pink light glowed. Someone was waiting for us.

"Do you remember when Rick made us change the name to the Tiananmen Café, Artie? He said we should celebrate, commemorate. And we did. And then, my friend, the old PRC consul had to sneak in the back. His chauffeur had to park the Rolls in the alley. Remember?"

"I remember."

I remembered. For a lot of reasons, I remembered. I remembered how the Taes indulged their only son, Ricky, when he wanted to change the name of the restaurant. I remembered the celebrations. Mr Tae owns property all over town, but the restaurant was always the center of their family life. Dawn had had her wedding in the restaurant; we danced there together that night. Ricky got up on the bandstand and sang to her. "I Love You Just the Way You Are", he crooned. But now the Taes kept to the big house in Riverdale, Ricky lay there on a sofa in a dark room, and Dawn had come home from Hong Kong looking like death.

Mr Tae played me beautifully. As we walked to the back of the restaurant where I'd lost a million games of backgammon to him, he reminded me of all the good times. I'm a pushover for good times.

The light I'd seen came from the lamp on the last table in back. At it, a man waited, hands folded around a cup of tea, a cigarette gathering ash on a saucer.

"Artie, it's been a long time." Billy Tae rose to shake my hand. He embraced his brother and the two men whispered in Chinese. I was in a foreign country.

Billy Tae is Martin Tae's brother, Rick and Dawn's uncle; everyone calls him Uncle Billy. The family dandy, he wore his Irish tweed jacket over his shoulders and a silk ascot tucked into his shirt. Billy is a rich man with interests in shipping in Hong Kong, but he's a streetwise guy and he can always get a pair of the best seats for the Knicks.

I loved those games at the Garden with the Tae uncles: the hot dogs, the beer, the celebrities. "Woody Allen!" they'd whisper, pointing along celebrity row. "You saw?" They would nudge each other. "Whoopi! Spike!" They would slap their knees. "Harrison Ford!"

A plate of cookies in one hand, a bottle of Johnny

Walker Black in the other, Winston appeared and served us and returned to the kitchen.

"Will you help us?" Uncle Billy asked me.

"Sure," I said. "Yeah, of course I will. But with what? What can I help you with?"

"You've seen Dawn. We don't know what's wrong with her. You're a detective."

"I'm not a policeman any more," I said. I lit a cigarette. The door rattled. We all looked up, but it was only the wind. Billy poured a little Scotch in a glass and offered it to me. I took it.

Martin Tae said, "Our family is being destroyed," and I said again, "I'll do anything, but you got to help me here, OK?"

Uncle Billy smiled gently. "This is hard for us," he said, and for a minute we drank the Scotch and smoked, and I realized I had never thought of the Taes as foreign before. Mrs Tae's family had been in New York for generations. Martin Tae had been born in San Francisco; he had been an ace pilot in World War II. After I moved into the building, I'd spent a lot of time running up and down the back stairs that connect the lofts to the restaurant. The Taes became family. The building became my safety net, my nation state. It crumbled some when I found Ricky on my floor. The fucking barbarians had been at my gate. But they would never get inside. Never!

"Dawn is very ill," Martin Tae said bleakly. "Peter is unhappy. She doesn't talk to him. She doesn't talk to anyone, except her brother who can't help her. You saw his feet?"

35

"Do you think it's drugs?" I knew it was drugs, but I said it carefully; I was poking around a bad wound.

"I don't know, Artie. I just know we need you."

"What can I do?"

"I can't believe Dawn is on drugs but, yes, if she is, God help me." He began to weep.

Uncle Billy took up the slack. "We need to know what she's buying and who her contacts are. She leaves the house every day. We think she goes to Chinatown. I want to know if she's buying on the street. If she has to have it, I would rather get her good stuff. I don't want her dying from shit."

Uncle Billy glanced at his brother who nodded and I knew it had all been prearranged. "We want you to follow her. We want to hire you, Artie. Just keep an eye on her for a few days," Uncle Billy added. "Ricky would do it, should do it, but he can't."

It was the unspoken thing: Rick was sick, because of me.

Martin Tae gestured to his brother, who took a checkbook out of the tweed jacket. I pushed it away. "I'll do anything I can, but I don't get it. Why don't you just put her in a clinic?"

"She won't stay. Pete tried. She runs away. She's become a cunning girl." Martin Tae's eyes filled up again. "It's killing her mother. First Ricky, now Dawn."

"I'm sure you can use some money." Billy Tae echoed Hillel; everyone knew I was broke. "Also, there's a detective we know. He's very talented. His uncle is my friend. Perhaps he can help you. I hope you

36

don't mind, but we already asked him to give you a call."

"If you know a good cop, why don't you ask him for help?"

"He's not family. Not like you. There are things we don't take outside. You are family, Artie."

"Please take the money," Martin Tae said. If I was going to help anyone, I knew I had to take it. And I knew that I'd hate myself;

I got up. "I'll do whatever I can," I said, and we all shook hands. Then Billy Tae ripped the check from its holder; it made a brutal noise.

"What's his name, your cop?"

Uncle Billy tilted his head back and finished the Scotch in his glass. "Jeremy Chen. His name is Jeremy Chen."

After I left the brothers, before I went home, I walked over to the dumpling joint where Rose had worked—it was only a couple of blocks—and ordered a beer. I had been meaning to do it all day. Another girl had replaced Rose, another shy nameless girl, this one with a weary smile. I drank up quickly and left. I don't know why I went.

At home, I checked the locks on my door, poured the remains of some Merlot into a glass and flipped on the answering machine. The club, where I work some nights doing security, called to say it was closing early. Lily had gone to the movies with a friend and I could meet them if I wanted, at the Angelika, but I didn't want to see a movie or meet her friend. All I wanted was Lily. There was also a message from Eljay, my camera guy. He said he'd be in touch.

And there was Jeremy Chen. A summons, not a message. Meet me in the morning, it said. Breakfast. I had no intention of obeying some cop I never met. I swallowed the rest of the wine and looked out the window at the street.

Usually it was around this time of night that Ricky would stop in, and we'd drink some beer and gossip. His own apartment was locked up. I hadn't been up there in months. All day people had been asking for help, needing help, wanting things—Hillel, Pansy, now the Taes.

Across the narrow street, snow filled the curlicues and dusted the pediments of the cast-iron buildings. The fire escapes that criss-crossed them sagged under the quivering piles of white stuff. Snow was falling so fast the snowplows couldn't keep up. Below, a solitary man with a shaggy dog trudged through the drifts and Mike Rizzi put his head out of the coffee shop, then pulled down the metal gates. The green neon sign—The Athens Café, it read—flickered and went out, Mike got into his car to go home to his family. I was alone.

"Oh, cheer the fuck up," I said to myself. I turned on all the lights, looked around the loft that was all mine—white walls, big windows, wood floors. I put Fats Waller on the CD good and loud, threw off my clothes, took a long hot shower, put on clean sweats so old they were soft like cashmere, did six push-ups to prove to myself I could, and called Lily's machine so I could listen to her voice.

Upstairs, the guy who moves his furniture every few days was at work on his sofa and the hardwood floors creaked under him. Across the hall, the banker put on Woody Guthrie. Next door, the dachshunds yapped and the kids yelled. People were home, tucked in, safe against the weather. I was starving.

In the fridge I unearthed some hot salami, a jar of roasted red peppers and a chunk of real provolone from Joe's Dairy. I heated up some black bean soup, opened another bottle of Merlot and tossed a bottle of olive oil into the garbage, impelled by the weird stink it gave off. This was no virgin, as Ricky would have said. In the microwave I zapped a loaf of semolina bread. I scooped up some law school catalogues and the *Sunday Times* car section, sat on a stool at the counter that divides my kitchen from my living room, and ate. People could be dead and you could still be hungry.

I ate. I tried to imagine myself in a suit in an office, a picture of Lily on my desk, money in the bank, and a red Cadillac in the garage. Except for Lily and the car, the image was blurry. I changed the CD to Tony Bennett doing Rogers and Hart.

"Party time, Artie," someone shouted through my door. "On the roof."

I got dressed, grabbed my ski jacket, shoved open the back window and climbed out onto the fire escape.

The air was cold. Snow fell. Yawning to suck extra oxygen out of the thin air, I tripped over the pots of dead geraniums and climbed up to the roof.

Snow had gathered in knee-high drifts on the roof, on the water tank, on the shed where Mr Tae lets me keep my bike and pieces of a boat I bought one summer but never sailed.

In the downy snow, some of my neighbors had lashed a pair of canvas beach umbrellas to the shed and, underneath the yellow striped umbrellas, they sat, wrapped in blankets, playing poker with their gloves on. There was a yellow light fixed to the roof of the shed; in it, the faces were like Halloween pumpkins, round and flat and grinning.

From a portable radio, Springsteen sang "Born in the USA". A blue plastic pail was filled with snow and planted with bottles of beer and wine and vodka. Lois passed a jar of nuts. The door to the roof opened and Louise appeared. Head encased in a knitted hat with a pompom, she held a huge steaming box.

"Pizza," she called, triumphant.

"Beer, Artie?" It was Dave, an architect who lived on the second floor. "Rescue me from all these babes," he laughed.

"Where's Kathe?" I said.

"Still at the hospital." Dave's wife, Kathe, was a doctor; more than a few times, she had stitched me up in the middle of the night. "You in, Artie?" Dave said. "You want to play a couple hands?"

But the view in the other direction distracted me. Chinatown. That night, looking down from the roof, I saw it obscured by the storm, lost in snow, a village, a rural backwater, its lights almost invisible. It was an illusion. But it was there all right, spreading inexorably. It lapped at my feet. I had to go. That was what I told myself, but it was a fucking lie. I wanted to go.

Yesterday, I'd been a guy without much going on, now I was spinning a bunch of plates. I was wide awake, the adrenalin was flowing for the first time in a long time. It felt good.

"Save me some beer," I called to Dave. Then I scuttled back down the fire escape and through my loft, slamming windows. In the street, I jumped in my car. If it couldn't make it to Riverdale, it could get me to Pansy. To make sure she was OK. To make sure she wasn't next. To see her. I was a jerk to drive.

*

Halfway down a deserted street on the eastern fringe of Chinatown, my car skidded on the black ice that had formed under the fluffy deceptive snow and went out of control. I had to go with it or end up hamburger. For what seemed a lifetime, the car swerved in sickening, irrational spins, like a punch-drunk boxer, and then, finally, took a nose dive into a snow bank, pitched forward a few more inches and stopped dead.

Wind blew past the blank faces of the warehouses that lined the street, loading docks empty, metal shutters down. It snapped snow against my face like iced gunshot. The streetlights seemed to shiver, seemed alive as the snow and wind and mist whirled around them. There were no cabs, no traffic at all, only the eerie sound of the weather, like a white-noise machine, as New York slipped back a century, when the cast-iron buildings went up, the streets were piled with horseshit and gas light flickered. I looked for a cab.

Chinatown gave me the heebie jeebies, as my Aunt Birdie used to say. From nowhere, the thing came at me with the force of an ox.

At first, I thought I had slipped on something greasy under the snow. Then my legs turned into jello and folded up like a cardboard box. Jello. Boxes. My head hurt like a bruise as I crashed to the sidewalk. Fog draped over the buildings and mixed with snow. I was blinded. I licked my lips and tasted wet snow. Did I pass out? Was it my own head I heard bump down the sidewalk? Thump thump thump, I seemed to be listening to the sonic boom of my own heart like when your ears are stuffed, or maybe it was my skull, bumping on cement.

Somewhere, I heard someone giggle. I heard the cackle of derision. I was their joke, their prey. I was dead meat.

When I opened my eyes, I was in a freight elevator in one of the warehouses. In the dark, I made out that there were two of them, but they had on ski masks. Cold creepy fingers clutched at my neck and pressed on nerves I didn't know I had. Sweat dripped down my side like snakes. I heard the elevator doors snap shut, I heard the gears grind.

The elevator lurched and rose. Then it stopped. Panic drenched me. I was trapped and I couldn't get up. The floors were slimy from decayed vegetables. The gassy green smell made me want to puke.

One of them grabbed my arms from behind; the other one got me in a choke. He had muscles like an ox, like a bull. But there was no pain. I lost oxygen; he let up. I came to. He knew where to press. He came at me with moves that knocked the stuffing out, and I lay on the crates in the dark like a rag doll.

Somewhere a flashlight flickered. Light shone on a metal blade. It was a meat cleaver, the kind of blade gangs use to sever muscles in your arm, your back, so you can't work or feed yourself. You end up still alive and a complete cripple. He must have pulled off the mask because I got the impression of a face. A Chinese face, I thought, but the elevator creaked and then plummeted two floors. I was falling. Couldn't breathe.

Something whizzed so close to my head I could feel the molecules move. I was sucking air.

★

I'm in Moscow, twelve years old, stuck in the elevator of the Intourist Hotel on Gorky Street, it was then. It's winter. We had gone in to sample the exotic pleasures of the forbidden—foreign tourists, espresso coffee. A kid I know has an uncle who sells busts of Lenin to the tourists. The other kids dare me. Who can get to the top floor? Who dares?

I love a dare. It is the only thing that makes life OK, that and my mother who laughs at the system, and the scratchy copies of black market rock and roll records you can sometimes buy on the street outside GUM, the department store.

No one else is in that Moscow elevator. No one comes. I press the button. The elevator moves up. Then it sticks. I don't know what to do. If I press the alarm bell, I will be discovered and punished in ways that I can't imagine. So I sit on the floor. The light goes out. I sit on in the dark. Panic produces sweat, and although it's winter in Moscow, I'm drenched with it. Time passes. Eventually, someone reports there are problems with the elevator and I hear noises. Workmen are banging on the cables. They lower the elevator to the ground floor. They pry open the doors and find me.

A policeman, a gray cardigan under his greasy gray jacket, hauls me in, puts me in a cell for a whole afternoon. When my mother comes to get me, she isn't laughing.

Now, suddenly, in the freight elevator in Chinatown, the doors opened, shut, slammed. I waited. They were gone.

Scrabbling in the gloom, my hands felt the elevator panel and I hoisted myself up on it and shoved on the metal lever. The doors split open. I found a light switch.

My watch said ten-thirty. I had only been there five, six minutes. Legs shaking, I peered around the elevator, then felt along the wooden panel at the back until I hit something cold, something metallic. I yanked it out. When I got into the street I saw it was a five-sided spike. Four inches across its flat back, it had five vicious three-inch spikes on the other side, sharp as knives. It was what the goons threw past me in the dark.

They never said a word. Nada. Christ! No notice given, nothing asked. Was this what they called, what was it, expressive terrorism? A taunt? A threat?

Somehow, I got out into the street. I looked at the building and saw what had happened. The freight elevator was flush with the sidewalk. Produce could be wheeled in from the curb. The scumbags that hit me had dragged me in like a load of bok choy. When I looked down, I saw a red stain on the fresh snow. I had torn my hand on the spike. There was some Kleenex in my pocket and I wrapped the weapon as best I could.

My wallet was gone, so was my gun. I was pissed off at losing the Seecamp pistol—they go for four, five hundred bucks these days—but I was almost relieved. It was a mugging. An ordinary everyday New York City mugging. A couple of kids. An empty street. Opportunity knocked. Everything was gone, cash, license, credit cards. All they left me was the spike.

Think mugging. Think methamphetamines. China

White. Forget terrorists. Forget the dead girl and her friend, Pansy Loh, who talked English like Princess Di. All they wanted was my wallet or a few laughs. Then I realized they had my keys.

I had to get home; they had the keys, they had my address.

I could barely walk. There weren't any cabs, only a guy on skis who asked if I wanted a ride. A real comedian.

It seemed to take hours to walk a dozen blocks, but I made it. I buzzed Lois to bring my extra keys down. Miraculously, she was back in her place instead of on the roof.

"Get Kathe, too," I yelled into the intercom, and the two women came down and got me off the street into the building. From my apartment, I called a locksmith.

"Take off your pants," Kathe said. I lay face down on the floor. She prodded me gently, but I yelled with the pain.

"Who hit you?"

I rolled over and sat up. "Put something against the door," I said to Lois.

"It's locked."

"Just do it. Just do it. Do it. There's a gun in the top drawer of the desk. Just please do it, Lois, OK?"

Lois got the gun, put a chair in front of the door and sat on it.

"For Christ's sake, tell me, Artie," Kathe said.

"Muggers. Chinese goons, maybe."

"They do anything else to you?" she said.

"They choked me. I went out for a few seconds, I think."

"I don't know much about it, but it looks like some kind of martial arts thing. Amateurs. This stuff shouldn't leave any marks but there's already bruises on the backs of your legs. Even amateurs, you don't learn this shit at Harvard. You want me to make you an appointment with someone, a specialist?"

I didn't. I wanted painkillers. Kathe gave me some Percodan while I called Lily who was still out. I left a message: see you tomorrow. In my apartment, the women made nervous conversation and stopped me from drinking a bottle of Scotch with the pills, while I somehow canceled my credit cards.

Eventually a ratty-looking white guy with rasta hair showed up and charged me three hundred bucks to change the locks.

"Emergency overtime," he said. "It's snowing."

I was an accident of the freaky weather. It was just a couple of creeps cavorting in the snow. Muggers, I muttered, a couple of angry specimens with time to kill. I wanted to believe. How could there be a connection? Only paranoia could make me think I was a target.

"I'm next," Pansy said. "Dawn's in trouble," Mr Tae said. "Help me," said Hillel. Then someone threw a spike at my head.

Eighteen hours after Hillel calls me, I'm in something and I don't know what it is.

That night I was more numb than scared. The next morning I would be shit-scared, but that night, after it happened, after Lois and Kathe went home, I swallowed more painkillers, and before I passed out, I crawled to the phone and dialed Jeremy Chen.

5

"She didn't die from being cut," Jeremy Chen said. It was the next morning. We were in the restaurant at the Chinatown Holiday Inn. He examined his gold cigarette lighter and tossed me a menu. "You want any of this shit?" He leaned back, a sleek, good-looking guy, medium height, chunky, with tough thighs like a body builder. Tight black jeans. A black turtleneck, a fleece shirt. And silk thermals. In the cold, he always wore silk thermals, he told me. Tossed over the back of his chair was a white jacket. A Coco Katz, he said. It must have cost five hundred bucks. For a guy with his macho posturing, only Chen's mouth was wrong. It was a tight round mouth with plump lips, a mouth shaped like an asshole. Literally.

"Art, you listening? This girl did not buy it from the blade. She was fucking strangled first. Piano wire," said Chen. Then he waved at a waitress. "Where's my fucking coffee?"

"What are we talking about here?"

"You tell me." He held out a red and gold box of Dunhills.

49

"I thought we were talking about Dawn Tae. I thought that's why you called me."

"You called me. I left the message and you called," Chen said, as if the distinction mattered. The waitress brought coffee and toast and Chen buttered a piece.

The chairs were fake black lacquer, the napkins stiff pink linen, the plants green and dusted. Trapped by the storm that had dumped two feet of snow on the city overnight, disgruntled tourists drank orange juice and sulked. Three Chinese guys in Armani shouted into portable phones; the oldest wore his cashmere coat over his shoulders and smoked a stinky little cigar.

Chen put down his toast, glanced at the old man's coat and said appreciatively, "Nice. Vicuna."

"Whatever you say." My legs were killing me.

"Look, man," Chen said. "I can't fucking help you with Dawn Tae. I can't stalk her. Billy Tae knows my uncle. He thinks that's how it works, the old way, favors, associations. I don't have the time and if I did I wouldn't fucking do it. If the old boys think she has a problem with some kind of shit, let them put her into Betty Ford. Look, I was in school in England with Pete Leung for a while. At the end of the day, it's Pete's bloody business. Ask me, he could fucking slap her around a little."

Chen's accent was a mess, so was the lingo. He'd grown up in London, he told me, he worked there a while. He came to New York, became a citizen. He talked part New York, part Brit. The swearing got on my nerves. Some days, it's like the whole city has Tourette's syndrome, but Chen's mouth was world class. Shit-for-brains, he said, shit a brick, shit-scared, shithead,

50

shit and derision, whatever that meant, and all of it in the first few minutes after we met. Shit this, shitty that. Fuck fuck fuck. It didn't mean anything. I swore I'd clean up my own filthy mouth. Fat chance.

"So how come we're talking, if we're not talking about Dawn?"

"They told me to call you. I'm a good chap. I'm the fucking cop prince of Manhattan. Also, I knew your name."

"Yeah? How's that?"

"The Abramsky thing," he said. "There's a dead fucking girl. Chinese. When there's Chinese shit, they call me. I'm Chinese but I'm not Chinatown if you get the drift. I'm special squad. I'm not part of the shit that goes down here where no one trusts a cop and the cops gotta pay attention to all kinds of bullshit from the family associations. Abramsky got lucky, I was in town. I took his rolodex. You were in it. I had heard the name. Out of the blue the bleeding Taes ring me up. I think, fuck-a-duck, everywhere I go, it's bloody Artie Cohen."

"Small world," I said.

"I know a lot of people."

"So let's talk about the girl. Who was she?"

"Some fucking miserable illegal. There's loads of money in illegals down here, thirty, thirty-five grand per. You put three hundred in a boat, that's nine mill plus add-ons. For a single load. We're talking two billion a year. It's big. Bigger than anything around here. Bigger than dope. But you know all that."

I didn't answer.

"Where you been, Art?"

51

The check came and I reached for it, but Chen tossed a few bills on the table, changing the game so I owed him. He got out of his chair and looked at me like I didn't interest him that much; maybe I didn't.

Jerry Chen was slick. He pulled on the silky white parka, snapped the pockets, zipped the sleeves, Velcroed the front panel, slid the cigarettes and the lighter into his jeans, put on the shades, smoothed the high-priced hair and extracted a pair of cashew-colored suede gloves. "Let's take a walk," he said.

On Lafayette we set off towards Canal Street, Chen walking in the snow-covered streets like he owned them. Twenty-four hours after the snow started, the stuff was still falling from the sky.

"So who do you think let her into your pal's place?" Chen watched his reflection in the shop windows. I saw mine next to him. Chen was wired. I was the color of tripe. I needed sun.

"It was 47th Street. Could be it had to do with diamonds."

"Fuck that shit," he snorted. "This ain't *Breakfast at Tiffany's*, trust me, Art. I don't know why she was fucking dropped at your pal's. I don't know. These girls never fucking leave Chinatown. Was it some kind of dumping ground? Somebody used it to hide from the wife? From the cops? Who?"

"Where we going, Jerry?" I could see he hated it when I called him Jerry.

"Looking around." He strolled into a shop that sold ginseng and herbs. Chen prodded some old-fashioned scales, saw the balance was off, but he only shrugged.

52

"I'm not some beat cop," he mumbled to me. From behind the door to a back room came an incessant clicking. Click click click. It could drive you crazy. Chen said, "You hear it?", hammered on the door and shouted, "Police."

The door opened. Chen sauntered in. A man with a frightened face peered at him through rimless glasses and folded his arms anxiously. At a table, two other men played with the clicking tiles. A refrigerator stood in the corner, there was a chipped stove and Chen lifted the cover off a pot that sat on it and looked in. Flipping through the pages of a notebook, he tossed it back on the table, looked slowly around, said, "Just checking," and smiled; the power turned him on, he got off on his own performance.

I didn't tell Chen I had a picture of the dead girl, of Rose. Didn't show him the spike I had carefully bagged in plastic. We were still in the getting-to-know-you period. I didn't like what I was getting to know—he was too volatile, too angry. I wasn't ready to share.

"You get any of her prints off Hillel's place?"

Chen didn't bother answering.

"Why Abramsky?" I said. "Why his shop?"

"He's *your* friend, for fuck's sake. You tell me. The question is, who opened the fucking door? You think somebody who knows Abramsky knew the girl?"

"That's insane."

"Why's it insane? Jews don't fancy girls?"

All along the street, shopkeepers shoveled mountains of snow; the scrape of the shovels was grating. My head hurt. We passed a fish stall where I saw a couple of

Haitian women bargaining. In her arms, one of them held a large pink and silver fish like a baby. A fish to appease Gede, I figured, the god of misrule, god of good times. Smart.

Chen was still laughing at his own bad joke when a kid darted ahead of us and forced him to move to the right. Chen went for the kid, pulling him up by the collar, the two of them screaming. There's something chilling about the angry babble of hate in a language you don't understand. Then Chen smacked the kid hard and shoved him away, but not before I saw the reddish quiff of hair.

"Shitheel." Chen's mouth twitched. He dusted off his white jacket where the kid left sooty fingerprints. "Fujianese," he added.

"What's that?"

"You been on vacation the last fifteen years, Art? Most of the illegals coming in the last ten, fifteen years are Fujianese. Most of the smugglers, too. They call 'em snakeheads."

"Where's this place?"

"It's a shit-poor province opposite the Straits of Taiwan. The other Chinese hate 'em, they consider Fujian the armpit of China, a real redneck cracker kind of a place. Also, down here in Chinatown, the Fujianese want to grab some of the power away from the old guard. The Fujianese are pro-mainland. The old guys are Cantonese who still hate the commies. All the kidnappings, the extortion, the murder you been hearing about, it's all Fujianese. The kids are fucking feral, a lot of them."

"What did he say?"

Chen didn't answer. He was schmoozing a guy selling fresh lichees off a stall.

"You don't speak the language. You don't fucking speak it, do you, Jer?"

"Fuck's the difference? I speak some. Enough. I can get by when I have to. These people got four thousand dialects. Anyway, speaking that shit is pretty fucking FOS," he said. "From the other side, Art," he added. "I got a dead girl to deal with Art, OK, so you want to talk or you don't want to talk?"

At the corner was a bakery, the windows piled with buns covered in pink sprinkles. Chen sauntered inside and I followed. At a table in the window, he ordered coffee and some of the buns. They weighed a ton.

"The girl had a name," I said.

Chen feigned some interest. "You been doin' a little spot of investigation," he said sarcastically. "You been over to see some of Rosie's friends?"

We ate the buns and danced around each other on the issue of the sweatshop; I knew Chen had been there. He probably guessed I had, too, so I told him.

"Some dump, huh, Art? They all are. But business is good, you know? You remember that celeb chick who did the big boo hoo on TV over the fact her schmates were made in some shitty sweatshop? All the garmentos do it, every designer name you ever heard of, one way or the other. Piece goods. Labels. Knock offs." Leaning forward, Chen's voice was quiet and hard as steel. "The rag trade died in this city by the seventies, same time a lot of illegals start coming over, so someone smells the coffee. All these ills arriving. Spics. Slants. Pay 'em a buck an hour, pay 'em a dime an hour, they take what they can get. Boom time for the sweatshop business. Retailers buy from manufacturers, manufacturers sub-contract out with the shops, they pay slave wages, if they pay. The garmentos say, 'It's not my fault, darling. I don't hire them.' What the hell? I'm no bleeding bloody heart, am I? They do what they do."

He wiped pink sprinkles off his lip, swallowed the rest of his coffee and looked out at the snow. "Art, I got to rescue my car before any more of this shit piles up. You want to walk me?"

"Whose side are you on, Jerry?" I said.

"Mine," he said.

We walked. He kept the patter going, impressing on me his knowledge of sweatshops, gangs, tongs, internecine war, Chinese gang relations with Vietnamese, Jamaicans, even the Russians, God help me. In Jerry Chen's head, every immigrant that ever lived was a criminal or a victim. Except him.

Near headquarters where his car was parked Chen tossed a five to a kid who had been watching it, pushed some snow off the hood and opened the door. As far as I knew, you couldn't buy Jeremy Chen, but he liked it when people backed off; he liked the fear in their eyes. "Get in," he said. I got in. I had wondered how a cop got a Coco Katz jacket and a Porsche, but the car was on its last legs, it was practically held together with string. And style. I had to give him that. Chen had style. He passed me some cigarettes.

"So you want to tell me about the girl, Art? You thinking of doing that?"

"What girl?"

"You fucking well know which girl. Pansy, she calls herself."

"And if I did meet her?"

"Don't let her work you over, man. She's a tough cookie," Chen said. "And she's mine. I want her, Art. I got something coming up next Monday that could put away a few of the bad guys. I want her to testify. Tell her that for me, if you see her." He paused. "And you will see her, won't you? What is it with you? You wanna do her?"

"Leave her the fuck alone."

"Or?"

"I'll let you know, Jer." I opened the door.

"You don't know shit about Chinatown," he said. "We're top of the pops crimewise now that the Italians are toast. When we Chinkies only preyed on each other, no one gave a rat's ass. When we started selling smack outside Chinatown, people took a view. The City took a view." He paused, looked me up and down and said, "You got some taste, Art. Tell me what you think of the jacket." He stroked the white fabric of his own sleeve.

It seemed to matter a lot, so I said, "Nice. Yeah. Very nice."

"Yeah. Well, keep in touch. And remember, we're secretive bastards. No matter how many of us come on over from Hong Kong, Shanghai, Taipei—open banks, buy houses in Scarsdale, go to Princeton—we look different. You can't make us out, can you? We are the

57

yellow peril, and we are one out of every goddamn five people in New York City. Babe, we are the inscrutable East. You are going to need my help, Art."

Through the window, I looked out at the snowscape, pristine except for the clutter of human beings. I closed the car door. Chen was probably right. I wouldn't give him Pansy, though.

Taking the bag with the spike out of my pocket, I tossed it on the dashboard.

"What do you make of this?"

He picked up the bag. "Where'd you get it?"

"Some piece of crap tossed it at me."

Thoughtfully, Chen turned it over. He was impressed. "This is scary stuff. These pricks are pros. You can't buy a thing like this outside Hong Kong. You want me to check the prints? See if they match anything we found at Abramsky's? They throw a thing like this at your face, you can lose an eye."

"Yeah? Also, there's a warehouse." I told him the address. "You could check out the freight elevator."

Chen picked some imaginary lint off the impeccable jacket and said, "I'll do what I can."

"They took my wallet. I figured it was a mugging."

"Screw that," he said. "It wasn't a mugging. It was a message. A hit."

"I don't get it, Jerry. You run me a laundry list of every fucking thing, smugglers, diamonds, sweatshops, illegals, extortion, murder, hitmen, so which the fuck is it? Which?"

"All of them. Money is what we're talking. But this is bizarre."

"Why's that?"

"These scumbags don't usually go after cops. Not white guys like you. There's no fucking profit in it. Still, you never fucking know, there's always a first time. Could be they made an exception of you," he said, and I thought of the elevator that stank of green rot and it made my stomach turn.

"You're one of those guys who believe the city is a hundred per cent shithole, aren't you, Jer?" I said and Chen smiled.

"Yeah," he said. "Yeah. I believe it all, all the darkest fucking things you ever read about."

"That's fucking paranoid." I opened the car door again and made to get out.

"If you need me, Art, most nights I eat at Henry Liu's, OK? And like they say, if you ain't fucking paranoid, Art, you ain't paying attention."

6

"Someone's asking for you, Artie." Short and wiry, with sandy hair like Brillo, a crooked grin, and a fighter's shoulders, Mike Rizzi stood in the doorway of his coffee shop flagging me down.

Mike's place is on the ground floor of the building opposite mine. On my side of the street, most of the cast-iron buildings have been converted into apartments. A few of them, like mine, have great nineteenth-century period detail carved into the façade. On Mike's side, too, there are a couple of great buildings with columns and pediments. His side is still commercial, though the art dealers and film people have mostly elbowed out the tool and die shops.

On one side of Mike's is a tailor shop and next to it a wholesale fabric outlet. On the other side, there's a pretty ratty gym, then a drugstore and a parking lot. Above him is a sweatshop. I can look out of my window and see the gim-crack chimneys, and when it's hot, the stink of illegal cleaning fluid drives Mike crazy.

"Artie? I said someone's looking for you." Mike

jerked his head towards the coffee shop. "In there," he said.

"Yeah, who's that, Mike?" I said. "Let me in, I'm freezing."

Planted in the front booth of Mike's place was Sonny Lippert. As I entered the coffee shop, he saluted me with his cup. "Long time no see, Art, man."

My legs were killing me, I was preoccupied with the dead girl, the spike, with Pansy. What's more, Mike's kid, Justine, was perched on a stool at the counter eating a jelly donut. She grinned and waved. I blew her a kiss. What I didn't need right now was Sonny Lippert.

"Take a pew," he said. "I want to talk to you. I know you usually hang here, so I came over, just for you. Buy me some lunch?"

"I'm busy, Sonny."

"You're not too busy to do breakfast with Jerry Chen."

"How'd you know about that?" I sat down opposite him and while Mike brought coffee for me and seltzer for Sonny, Sonny let me dangle in the silence of the empty coffee shop.

"You look good, Sonny," I tried to make amends. "Have the BLT."

Past fifty-five, Sonny Lippert looks fifteen years younger, the tight curls still black, the skin smooth, the body maintained by a trainer who's at his office every day, the snazzy suits perfectly cut.

When I first got to New York, Lippert, who's a federal prosecutor with a fiefdom all his own, helped me get a job, then a Green Card. When I got sworn in as a citizen, he was there. I paid him back with help on several cases—his obsession was wiping out the Russian mob in Brighton Beach—and that was that. Recently, Sonny had been cross-designated from Brooklyn to Manhattan, to the Southern District. This means his office is on the edge of Chinatown, not far from where I live. Not far enough.

He's a real hot-shot with dozens of investigators who work for him and he oils his relationships with all the bureaus, but especially the police. Most times, it gets him what he needs.

"I'm sorry. I've got a few problems, Sonny."

He drank his seltzer. "You can drink that horse piss?" he said, pointing at the coffee, shutting his eyes as if the idea gave him pain. "What kind of problems, man? Look, it's me that owes you this time. I know about the girl at Abramsky's, I had to figure you'd take an interest, being Hillel's your friend. I'm your friend, man, and I don't want to babysit your sorry ass again, OK?"

"Don't patronize me, Sonny."

"Jerry Chen is very smart. He knows which side his bread is buttered on, so to speak. He keeps in touch. He's an obliging fellow. They think of me as one of them."

"The Chinese, you mean?"

"A cop, man." Sonny Lippert had been a cop a long time ago. He loves it. He walks the walk. Talks the talk. It makes his wife cringe with embarrassment, but he doesn't care.

I was never that kind of cop. I didn't go to other cops' houses much. People would say, "So what's it like being a cop?" I don't know.

"Artie? Man? You with me?"

"So you're a cop. So that means everyone I take a meeting with reports to you on it?"

"I don't know. Might only be Jerry Chen, babe." He looked out the window. "Don't get involved in this thing, Art, sweetheart, not without telling me."

"You're not interested in the Chinese, Sonny."

"Russians, Chinese, it's all the same. Cubans. Albanians. There's Vietnamese in East Berlin shooting AKs. There's East Germans swiping nukes from the Russkis. There's crazies in Hungary cutting up Arabs for body parts. The whole frigging commie bunch got let out of jail. And they're everywhere. They're here. They want a big piece of pie. They want the whole pie. You think Russians and Chinese don't get into bed together? They been doing it to each other in the ass since the 1950s. Before that. Where's your historical perspective, Art, babe? Wait until China really gets its hands on Hong Kong and the financial dominoes go down all in a row. Just wait for it."

"Thank you for the history lesson. You ever heard of a Mr Snap, Sonny?"

"What the fuck's a Mr Snap?"

"A guy that takes pictures of Chinese girls."

"For you, I'll ask around. You know I'm your friend, Art, and I want you to take care, OK? I already know that you got your head banged in a warehouse by some dirtbag. Next time they'll cut your head off. Chinatown might be around the corner, man, but it's not your turf. You need eyes there, an ear. You need a whole etiquette book. There are rules. Behaving like the schmendrick

63

you obviously are could end up them dissecting you. You fuck around, they'll carve you up like Peking duck."

"I like Peking duck."

"Very nice, Art. Very funny. Talk to me, man, I'll help you. Like we always help each other. Anyhow, I can get you something you want." Sonny stretched his legs. He wore beautiful brown boots instead of the usual tasseled loafers. Who was it said a man's vanity is invested in his clothes? Tolstoy? Dostoyevsky? No, it couldn't be, Dostoyevsky was always too hung up on Christ and sin to think about his shoes. I read all that stuff a long time ago. I forgot most of it.

"What is it I want, Sonny?"

"Your job back." He got up and put some money on the table. "I love you, Art. But you're a fake. You say to me, I hate the life, Sonny. I want a change. I call up this professor I know at Columbia, I say, Mrs H, I got this cop. He graduated college, he speaks languages. Smart. He should go to law school. But you didn't send the applications in, did you? So don't kid yourself, toots. You need the life, it's the air you breathe. That's why you're up to your ass in this Chinatown thing when you could have walked away."

Sonny put on his sheepskin coat and his leather gloves.

"Art, babe, if you are in it, watch your back," Sonny said as he got ready to leave. "Keep me posted how you go, OK, and follow the money."

"Where to, Sonny?"

"In the end? I figure, in the end, it's Hong Kong."

Hong Kong. What's he talking about? I thought. I waited while Sonny buttoned up. Hong Kong was a dot on the rim of China a zillion miles away, another planet from this frozen city and the miserable murder of a local girl. It was the snow making him nuts.

"Mikey? How many inches?"

"Sixty, Artie. More coming."

It was the snow. People were talking bullshit. Sonny was at the door and he said, "So did I tell you I got a part in the new Pacino movie? Lines also."

"Good for you, Sonny. I hope you win an Oscar."

Seeing Sonny leave, Justine jumped off the stool and pulled at my hand. She was twelve, very pretty and completely self-possessed, and she said, "Come outside," and pulled me into the street. She knew I'd do anything for her.

"Put on your jacket," Mike yelled.

"You any good at math, Artie?"

"I stink at math, you know that. What's going on?"

Opening her mouth, she collected snow on her pink tongue, stalling.

"What?"

"So, OK, like I don't want to make my pop nuts, you know, but I saw this thing on TV about a kid that was snatched from a bus stop."

The second day of the storm, the street was nearly empty. The few people who skidded by barely noticed us, a guy and a little girl, backs against the coffee-shop window, mouths open, eating snow.

"Artie?"

"Where did it happen that the kid got snatched?"

"Bed Stuy," she said.

"So, look, you don't live in Bed Stuy, do you? There's always stuff, you know that."

"I know."

"Also, you know I'm always there for you. You know anyone comes near you, they're toast. Right? And I'm right there. Across the street. Look. Your own personal bodyguard."

"Like Whitney Houston."

"Exactly. So, if you want, you could come over again soon. Watch some tapes with me and Lily. And I'll make pizza again. Home made," I said. "Come on, kiddo, it's cold."

Inside, Justine curled up in the booth and, in the warm air, fell asleep. I drank some coffee and thought about Sonny's visit. He was right. It wasn't my turf. I could get cut up. I looked at Justine. I was a lot more scared than I let on.

"So what's happening, Mikey?"

Mike looked anxious. I moved to the counter where he was pouring ketchup out of gallon jars into squeeze bottles. He works like a dog, he runs a one-man neighborhood watch, taking packages for everyone on the block, looking out for the kids, he lets me use the place as an office when I want. Mike was Ricky Tae's friend before I moved to the block. He's a good guy, but his wife is always on his back. Lina's always pushing him to open a fancy menswear shop in SoHo. Lina's a very pretty blonde, but she's ambitious and has vulpine eyes and long arms that seem ready to snatch you and hold you hostage.

An Italian guy, Mike Rizzi grew up over on Mulberry Street, but he's obsessed with Greece. Early on, he figured that the owner of a Manhattan coffee shop with a picture of the Aegean on the wall and a lifetime supply of cups with a classical-type frieze, Greece was his destiny. So on Mike's wall are pictures of Telly Savalas, Anthony Quinn as Zorba, even Mrs Papandreou, but this was for the customers, he claimed. "I was raised to be a classical scholar," he would say when he was plastered on ouzo.

"Spit it out, Mike. I have to go." I'm next, I'm next— I couldn't get it out of my head.

"Chink came by," he mumbled.

"What? Mike? Speak to me, man."

Mike poured some coffee. "Chinese guy, some kind of slant. Whaddya call 'em, Oriental guys down in Russia? Cheech 'n' Chongs?"

"Chechens, Mike." He knew, of course. Like half New York, Mike's an equal opportunity racist. Mostly he just vents, though, and he would put his hand in a lion's mouth to make you happy.

"So what did he want, this Chechen?"

"Chink, he was a Chink." Mike grew angry. "They get special treatment from the cops down here. Take the fucking vegetable wholesaler moved in round the corner, you know? He's Chinese. He dumps his stinking stuff on the sidewalk. Everybody from here up to SoHo screams. Nothing happens. Then I got to worry about which mob I could use to pick up the Chink vegetables. Jesus."

"Is there a reason you're telling me this?" I asked, but a couple of customers arrived, Mike got busy fixing food, and the phone rang.

"It's for you," he said. It was Lily. I said I was coming over, she said she was working. I said I was coming anyway and I hung up and got into my coat. Secretly, I was fucking pleased Sonny told some law professor I was hot stuff; I wanted to tell Lily. A lot of stuff had happened since the day before and I needed to see her real bad.

"Artie? Listen, I meant to tell you, there's been some lights on up in Rick's apartment a couple times. Probably just his mom cleaning up, or something. Right? Right, Artie?"

"Something like that, Mike," I said, but I should have paid more attention. I should have paid attention to Sonny and the noise of the spike when it whistled past my head, I should have listened to what Mike was telling me, but I didn't. I was thinking about Lily.

7

I first met Lily Hanes outside St Vincent's on a hot summer night when I was waiting for someone to die. It was almost two years ago. She had been a witness to the killing and we met up, her with the red hair that she constantly pushed out of her face and the long tanned legs. It took me some time to get her to go out with me, but since then there have been a lot of dinners. By our third date, I was already hooked. We were driving to Sag Harbor for the weekend and she said, "So, do you have a gun?" and I said, "Sure I have a gun, I'm a cop. You want to see it?"

In the long line of New York lefties Lily comes from, guns are considered the devil's work, but she took it gamely and held it between her thumb and her forefinger.

"Don't hold it like dirty Kleenex," I said and she laughed. It was hot out and, when we got to the American Hotel for dinner, Lily realized I only kept my jacket on because I didn't want to walk around in a place like that with a gun showing. She just leaned over and said, "I'll take it," and put the gun in her straw bag.

After I left Mike Rizzi's, I got a cab over to Gansevoort Street where Lily was working in a make-shift studio near the meat markets. Glasses on her nose, the red hair stuck behind her ears, she was typing stuff into a laptop like she was competing in the Olympics. She glanced up and blew me a kiss.

In her office, CNN was on a portable TV, the radio was playing and a guy I'd never met was leaning over her, gazing at the computer screen.

I like watching Lily work, and I leaned against the wall while a stream of people flowed in and out of her office, yakking, laughing, asking her questions. Currently she was helping set up a talk show for one of the cable channels. With luck, she said, she'd get to host it for a few months. It was what she did, and she was good, on screen and behind the cameras. She could write like a dream, but freelancing was pot luck. Before I met her, she'd been a correspondent for a network for a while, but she couldn't cut the corporate style. She was lousy at the politics, she admitted to me once. "I used to burst out laughing during the strategy sessions. I couldn't keep a straight face when they wanted to do hard news about the possibility of angels. So I became the in-house wiseacre."

In the end, she had quit because she got scared, first in East Berlin back before the Wall came down, then in Colombia where she just missed getting blown up. Enough, she had said and came home.

"You want to eat something?" I said. But Lily shook

her head, introduced me to the guy who leaned over her again and punched something into the computer, then disappeared.

"We're heading for a total white-out," Lily said. "We are trapped in some all-time awesome weather system, and there's maybe another storm coming in after it. Sixty inches! More!! All the weather guys say so, Al Roker, Storm Field. Storm says it is mighty big." She stretched her arms over her head. "You look a little wan, Artie, you OK? I missed you last night, doll."

"I'm fine," I said. "Honest. I just needed to see you." I wasn't going to let some two-bit hoods with a spike screw up my life. The way you got a regular life was that you just let stuff be.

"Lily!" A skittish demanding voice summoned her from the hall.

"Gotta go," she whispered. "Some of these guys you got to remind them to breathe. I'll see you later. Meet me over at my place if you want," she said and tossed me her keys.

"My cat is dead, OK? I got four more and they almost froze to death also, so gimme some space, Artie, OK. I'll do what I can for you." Eljay Koplin was next to nuts when I got up to his studio on Carmine Street. The place stank of cat, the shelves sagged under old camera stuff, but Eljay knew what he was doing. An orange cat, a nasty piece of work, slithered across my ankles.

"I got a dead girl," I said, but I knew, for Eljay, it didn't equal a single hair on a cat's ass.

"Like I said, Artie, I'll do what I can." He turned over

71

the picture of Pansy. "Not with this one. This one's a Polaroid. I can't do nothing with this one. This doesn't leave any tracks," he said and gave it back to me and turned to Rose's picture which interested him. He shoved his glasses up on his forehead and perused it like Kuntsler in court reading evidence. "This is something else."

"Why?"

"See the numbers on the back? Before this kind of system, if you had one print, it didn't mean shit. It was impossible to track. This leaves tracks. These numbers, see, it's a new system, Advanced Photographic System, they call it. APS. They all got it, Kodak, Fuji. It's got a bunch of crucial identifiers. Time and date. Conditions under which it got taken. A lab ID number that would allow you to track it back to the individual lab that did the processing. A number of the film cassette. You can program this thing to print out Happy Birthday, if you want, that kind of shit."

Bingo, I thought, and I said to Eljay, "Get me the lab."

"I'll do what I can. There's a million tons of shit falling from the sky out there, maybe you didn't notice, Artie. A lot of places are shut down."

I handed him the phone.

"There's another thing with this system." He waved the picture of Rose. "It allows you to take the same shot in three different formats."

"What formats?"

"Think of it as normal, widescreen or extra wide-screen. Look, you could have a picture of this girl with

72

the car normal size, the way it is. But if you set it for widescreen, you'd get a different version, more panoramic. You would cut off the top and bottom, though."

"But you could see something on the sides you didn't see in the first picture."

"Right on." Eljay picked up a cat and made purring noises in its ear.

"Get me the fucking lab, Eljay, OK? Just get on the phone and get me the lab. Now. Please."

The address Eljay got me was on Ludlow Street. It was a shabby four-storey building on a street that had been Jewish for most of the century but was Chinese now. On the ground floor was a souvenir shop, the window crammed with nylon Ninja outfits and Hong Kong girlie mags. And inside, filling up most of the cramped space, as out of place in the black hat and coat as a medieval holy man, was Hillel Abramsky.

His back was to me, but I could see his body shake with rage. He towered over the minuscule Chinese owner, who had a face hard and prickly as a lichee and was waving his hands. Even through the dirty glass window, you could feel these were a couple of men seized up with hate.

Without any warning, Hillel turned and strode out of the shop, the owner behind him, indifferent to the snow, fury driving him. Hillel moved fast, not seeing me, not seeing anyone, just running, running. A few hundred yards away, the street slick with ice, he crashed to the ground. The old man stood over him, yelling. I persuaded the old guy to beat it. Then I helped Hillel up.

Black coat wet, beard speckled with snow, he clutched a string shopping bag like a prop.

"You're a long way from home, Hil."

"I'm on my way to Orchard Street." Hurriedly, he looked around. "OK? Shopping. Some things for the children," he added, but he didn't look at me.

"Wet night."

"It's not night, not yet. Trust me, Artie, OK. I am here to do some shopping."

"I'll walk you," I said.

"No, that's OK. I know you're trying to help me get some answers about the dead girl and I been thinking that maybe I got you into something that it wasn't right to ask. I was going to call you." Hillel kept moving. I walked alongside him.

In some way I didn't understand, Hillel Abramsky was messed up in this whole thing. Was it that the Chinese had eaten up the neighborhood? That his uncle had to sell the shop on Canal Street? That some hood was shaking him down?

"Go home, Artie," he said. "Forget the whole thing. Forget I asked you, please. You don't owe me."

"I'm not sure I can do that, Hillel," I said, but he walked away from me. I followed him. I saw him turn into Essex Street, not Orchard like he said. What was there to take him to Essex Street? Abramsky was lying about something.

"The big man in the black coat, what did he want?" I said to the Chinese guy in the souvenir shop on Ludlow Street.

"The Jew?"

"Yeah."

"I don't know. He was like a crazy man. I saw him running in and out of buildings all along the street. He said, Did I sell cameras? Did I sell film? I tell him no. No camera. No film. I say, It's snowing, go home. Forget film."

"This number 218?"

"What if it is?"

"There's some kind of photo lab in this building?"

"I told you, like I told the Jew, no, no film, no camera, no lab, OK?" Like Hillel, the old man lied.

There was a lab in the building all right. It was on the second floor and it was shut up tight as a drum, tight as Jerry Chen's little mouth. I tried it. I banged on the door. No one came. I considered breaking in but it's not one of my skills and anyhow, I was out of the loop. I would catch major static if I broke down a door in the middle of Chinatown.

Outside I ran for a lone yellow cab that rattled down the street, but someone else got it and anyhow, something caught my eye. It was a shop window. The array of weapons took my breath away.

There were swords, broadswords, hooked sickle swords, swords in fancy cloisonné sheaths. There were spears, double headed, triple headed, Ninja spikes and a Ninja fan that could slice your head off with a snappy flick of the wrist like a girl cooling herself with a fancy paper fan. Grappling hooks were big, it appeared, so were blow guns and a thing called a golden melon hammer, not to mention the assortment of axes, all of them neatly labeled. What really had me glued to this window of horrors, though, was a rake with nine sharp teeth. It resembled a large-scale version of the multiple-blade spike that was maybe used to rip up Rose's face and intended for my head. Could Hillel Abramsky put a thing like that to a woman's face and rake away her skin? Christ, I thought.

Finally, the cold creeping through me, I backed off from the shop and got a cab to take me to the restaurant near the Seaport. Pansy was out. The owner was out and it was empty except for a part-time cook and two delivery guys. The guys sat at one of the three tables, complaining how the rich were the shittiest tippers in New York. There was no girl, they said. No girl named Pansy Loh, the guys said, but maybe they didn't under-stand me. Maybe they didn't. Or maybe everyone was telling lies.

I let myself into Lily's apartment. Someone was there ahead of me. Someone was in the apartment, padding across the living-room carpet towards me, and I felt for the gun, the old .32 I'd got out of my drawer the night before, and then a woman toweling her hair emerged and I felt like a jackass.

"Lily forgot to tell you I was here. Oh, God, I'm sorry. I'm Babe Vanelli." She held out her hand. "I live across the street and my hot water's on the fritz. Heat too."

I held up the bottle of wine I'd brought. "Lily's on her way. You want a drink?"

We were standing in the hall of Lily's apartment. To

the left was the kitchen with the swing doors, and Babe went to get some glasses while I went into the living room. Lily's living room is yellow, it's full of comfortable overstuffed furniture, the shelves are jammed with books, the walls with pictures and photographs. The cream linen shades were up that night so, through the windows, you could see the snow like lace curtains. On the upright piano was a glass vase full of yellow-and-red-striped tulips.

I put Sarah Vaughan on the CD player. Babe brought the glasses and curled up on the sofa. I opened the wine and sat in one of the armchairs. In my pocket I found a painkiller and swallowed it and the pain in my legs eased. The apartment was warm and bright and, for a while, Babe brushed her wet hair and we sipped our wine and listened to the music without talking at all.

"Better?" she said. "You arrived looking like a guy who just walked away from a plane crash."

"Much better."

Babe put her bare feet on the low glass coffee table; with the back of her hand, she wiped away the red stain the wine left on her upper lip.

I knew something about Babe. Beth Pressman Vanelli, known as Babe, sometimes Baby, was Lily's oldest friend. She and Babe grew up together in New York. After school, Babe, who married young, dumped Frankie Vanelli, as he styled himself, and headed west. She planned to be in movies. She wound up in make-up. When Lily worked a talk show, if Babe was free, she did the guests. We had never really met, though. Babe was always on the move.

"You do make-up, don't you? Lily says you're some kind of genius."

"Mostly I do movies now. For Lily, I'll do a talk show. She loves for me to work them over before she does an interview. I let them look down my shirt, you know? Then I wrap this gold towel around them and I whisper, 'Gold is for STARS.' They all fall for it. Put that out," she ordered as I lit up a cigarette. "It's bad for the skin, hon. You got nice skin, too. Tight. You could use some sleep, though."

"It's not always an option."

"In this town, hon, looking lousy is never an option."

Wet tendrils of hair curled over Babe's ears and, like so many women in New York, where there are more great women than anywhere else on earth, Babe could have been thirty-five or fifty. The three top buttons of her white shirt were undone and her skin was still damp. When she leaned forward to put her glass down, I could see she didn't wear a bra and the tits were spectacular: big, soft, the nipples hard. A smell of talcum powder and Chanel #5 came off her skin and the black jeans were so tight she must have put the powder on her thighs to get into them. I wanted to put my hands inside the tight black jeans and run them along those powdered thighs.

"Gimme some more of that wine." She held out her glass. "Hon, I'm fifty-three years old. And I'm pretty good at what I do. I do the gold towel thing, it works. You know what Richard Nixon once told me? He said it was thirty-five years since he had enjoyed conjugal relations with his late wife, Pat. 'Conjugal relations', that's what he called it. Lily says watching me make up some guy is like watching people have sex."

"I can believe it." The wine went down easy. In the kitchen I found another bottle and opened it. Flirting was Babe Vanelli's automatic mode and I was happy to fall in, drinking the wine, wiping out the worries, waiting for Lily.

"The cameras don't lie, you know? Trust what you see. People suck up to me all the time so's I'll make them look fabulous, but it's all there. Or not." She took the TV remote and switched it on. "Some weather. So," Babe said, kneeling up on the sofa so she could reach the bookshelves and change the CD to James Taylor. "So, you're Artie Cohen. Lily's Russian cop."

"Was. I was."

"Was a cop?"

"Was a cop. Was a Russian."

"I never heard such a New York accent in my life."

"I haven't been Russian since I was sixteen. I left. I did some time in Israel, then I came here."

"You were in jail in Israel? What'd you do, whack a rabbi?"

"I was in the army. After we left Moscow, we spent a few years in Israel."

"I'd've figured you for a New Yorker, born and bred. You sure don't look tired and huddled to me."

"I'm not."

"Women come on to you a lot because you're a cop?"

"Some." Too many, I thought. "How come I always go out with such wingnuts?" I once said to Rick. He said

I didn't notice the good ones. Until Svetlana, who was dead. And Lily.

"You tell them cop stories?"

"How'd you know?"

"You think they get it right on TV? I did make-up once for some TV cops," she said.

"Sure. It's just like TV."

"Don't smile when you say it. You like being a cop?"

"I did. Once."

"How did you start?"

"I thought it was glamorous," I said, but I thought Babe deserved better. "I was naïve. I thought I could maybe help people." I poured more wine. "Then I got a taste for blood."

"And?"

"And nothing." I didn't like talking about this stuff much so I pulled the snapshots out of my pocket. "What do you make of these?"

"Who are they?"

"It doesn't matter. You see anything?"

Like someone else would read palms, Baby read the faces. She held up Pansy's picture. "This one, I bet you, is a beauty behind those glasses. This one is sad"—she held Rose up to the light—"this is a girl with too much bad make-up that doesn't work. That's what's so sad."

"Spell it out for me."

"She's tried to make herself up to be pretty, she wants to look good. Women do it, hon, all day all the time, you know that, but this girl could make you cry she wants it so bad. Like her life depended on it."

Babe got up and handed me the pictures and I

followed her into the hall. Picking up a leather jacket from a chair, she put it on.

"Take care of yourself," I said. "There's a lot of scum out there."

"I always have this." Babe opened her bag and showed me the lipstick. She pulled the cap off the pink enamel tube, twisted it once and a knife popped out.

"Jesus. Where'd you get it?"

"Any ladies room in any club in town. Whatever you want. Lipsticks with knives. Mace in hairspray cans. Someone carts the stuff around town in a Bloomies shopping bag. So stay well, hon," she said. "Artie, hon, you don't know anyone has a place I can use for a couple days? My heat's completely fucked-up. I got a hot date coming in from the coast Saturday, Lily said maybe you'd know something."

"I'll make a couple of calls. I'll give you a ring."

"Hey, no worries," she said.

She reached up and caressed my face. "You're a very good-looking guy. I like blue eyes. You can't lie if you got blue eyes like yours." Babe kissed me lightly. "You want to go out with me sometimes?" She winked. "I'm kidding. Artie?"

"What?"

"Lily likes you a lot, you know. I've known her all our lives and she likes you a whole lot. More than you know."

"Yeah?"

"Don't fish. But you know what you should do, though?"

"What's that?"

"Give her a child." Babe was probably a little bit stewed from the wine. I was too. Lily had never mentioned a kid. Never. "I'm telling you," Babe said again, "what Lily really wants is a child."

8

"I'm very very glad you're here." Lily leaned against me and I forgot all about what Babe Vanelli said. I got a handful of her flesh; it was warm and soft against my fingers. "Maybe this is what married life is like. The guy waiting for you at home, the wine open." She took off the blue sweater and her white silk undershirt slipped off her shoulders.

Through the thin fabric, I could feel her breasts. The nipples were hard. I try to think of them as breasts. Steven, this guy I ride a bike with, tells me that all men are pigs, but how big a pig you are boils down to whether you think of them as tits or breasts, so I'm trying not to be a pig. I'm forty years old, I'm still trying to get the woman thing right. With Lily it was right.

It was after six when she got home and by the time we got to the bedroom, where we were now, she'd shed most of her clothes; most of mine, too.

I walked across the room to turn off the news.

"What's that on your legs?"

"What's what?"

"Your legs, my love. There's things on the back of your legs like blueberry pies."

Like an idiot, I bluffed. "I fucked up shooting some hoops the other day."

"Really?" Lily took a white terry-cloth robe and wrapped it around her. "When was that?" She tied the belt. "I think I want a drink," she said.

I put on the sweats I keep at Lily's place and went back into the living room where she was already pouring the Scotch. The lights were on and the yellow walls glowed. Avoiding the sofa where we could both sit, Lily sat down on the weathered leather chair she'd picked up in a junk store. "So," she said. "Hoops!"

So I told her. I gave her the picture of Rose and she put her glasses on and peered at it. "It's the saddest thing I've ever seen. All the aspiration, all the desperation. Who is she?"

"A dead girl. A dead girl who worked in a sweatshop and wanted her family to think she made it in America. But it's not my problem any more." I was lying and Lily knew it.

"Yes it is. Once you took that phone call yesterday morning you were in it. I'm not mad, Artie. It just scares me." But she was mad.

"I did a favor for a friend is all. I owed him."

"I see," she said in a voice that I hate a lot. I'm crazy about Lily, but there are times I get it wrong with her and I never know exactly why. The phone rang.

"Don't answer it," I said. "Let's go to bed instead."

Lily picked up the phone and listened for a second, her expression tightening. Then she slammed down the receiver. "What's going on, Artie? What is this?"

"What?"

"I could hear them breathing."

"It was a crank call. You're on TV. People know your face. You get crank calls. Maybe it was a wrong number."

"I don't want this again, Artie. You get that? Last time, I almost got cut up by a man with a knife who knew where I lived. You almost got killed. Ricky got whacked. I think you're already in this thing and you can't get out. Won't get out. You need it. It's your drug. You know something? Your legs look like shit, you probably haven't slept in a couple of days, but by God, Artie, you look more alive than you have for ages. Ages."

"Thanks."

"Don't mention it."

She wandered through the living room, straightening out books on the coffee table, fiddling with records on the shelves, adjusting flowers in jugs, her back to me.

Maybe it was the booze, the painkillers, the scars on Rose's face, the scumsuckers that jumped me, or Babe's talk of kids, I don't know. I should have kept my mouth shut, but I didn't. I swallowed some Scotch and said, "What is it with you? You only want to hear about the weather? You should watch that, you could end up on *Hard Copy* and call it journalism."

"You're not really going to law school, are you, Artie? Nothing is going to change, is it?" She pulled the Yellow Pages off a shelf. "So what about this?" she said. "Look. Private Investigators: Matrimonial, Armed

Escort, Asset Location. I sure wish you'd locate some assets for me. Look, Artie." She shoved the book under my nose. "Sherlock Hound. A private dick, isn't that what they call these guys? You could do that. Sherlock Hound! I love it."

She tossed the book on the sofa and banged open a window. Lily leaned out into the snow. I grabbed her hand but she pushed me away. I shuffled through her record albums.

"Where's that Tony Bennett album I gave you? The vinyl with Bill Evans."

Lily slammed the window shut and drained her glass.

"Where is it?"

"I'll get you another one," she said. Don't push me on this."

"I'm pushing."

Sucking an ice cube, she said, "OK, you asked. I lent it to someone."

"Who someone? It's Frye, isn't it? You gave my album to him."

When Phillip Frye went back to London last year, I thought it was pretty much over with him and Lily, but Frye keeps coming back like green peppers. Phil Frye is married, he always will be. But he calls her, she jumps. Frye's one of those do-gooders, always on some cause. Amnesty. Humana. Something I never heard of. He's crazy about the poor and the sick, preferably in faraway places, and from what I can tell he's a vain, sanctimonious guy. I think he lays a lot of guilt on Lily. Or maybe I'm just jealous.

She wears the diamond earrings and the cashmere and

she laughs about the family of old radicals she comes from, laughs pretty bitterly about it, but it goes deep. If a bum in the street asks Lily for money and she doesn't give, she feels lousy all day.

I poured myself more Scotch. "Why don't you just dump him?"

"I could have asked you the same question about Svetlana a while back," she said, but she put her arms around me and kissed me on the mouth, a big wet cartoon kiss. "This is stupid. Isn't it?"

"I guess." I didn't want to hear about Svetlana. Svetlana was dead.

"I'm sorry about the album, really. I am." She kissed me again and put on a CD. Bing Crosby sang "White Christmas". Lily put her arms around me. "You have to have Bing when it snows, don't you?"

"I don't get Bing Crosby."

"What's to get? You always say that. There's nothing to get. It's not Wittgenstein. It's not Umberto Eco. It's just goddamn Bing Crosby in an argyle sweater and a pipe singing 'White Christmas'. OK?"

When it's good, it's great; when it goes sour with me and Lily, it's like this. On the piano was a picture of Lily in an oval frame. I picked it up. In it, she was about two, hair on top of her head, wearing a tiny summer dress, carrying her teddy bear by its arms. The bear had no eyes. "My mother took them out so I wouldn't swallow them," she said once. "It's the only time I ever remember her worrying about me."

What Lily secretly yearns for, I sometimes think, is a regular guy, a doctor, a businessman, someone who will take her to the ballet and the opera—I hate them both. Instead, she's stuck with Phil Frye and a knucklehead like me.

My beeper went off. I ignored it. To hell with it. It could all wait. All the dead people, all the people I owed. I was scared and mad and I wanted her. I pulled her onto the floor.

The phone rang.

"Leave it."

"I have to."

"No."

"You're hurting me." She took her arm away and made a big show of examining it. "Christ, Artie, that really hurt." We both knew it didn't. She pushed her hair back, went to the kitchen and got the phone. I stood in the door.

"Hi, Phil," she said and let the door swing shut.

In the bedroom, I got dressed and put on my shoes— I had to hold onto Lily's desk to get them on, my legs hurt so bad. A folder lay open on the desk and, out of habit, I turned the pages.

"Precious to God," the brochure began and there were pictures of children and tales of woe. Children available: Ecuador, Korea, Romania, China. "Precious to God" is how the children were described. There were application forms for adoption in triplicate, filled out neatly in her handwriting, and Lily's mugshot, grim but game. The brochure in my hand, I barged back into the kitchen and waved it at her. It was a mistake.

"You're not serious, Lily, are you? 'Precious to God'?"

"Just go away, will you?" Lily covered the phone with her free hand and looked up with a hurt, angry expression. She pushed her hair away from her face anxiously. "Scram, Artie, OK? It's not a joke."

As I left, I heard her purr into the phone in the husky voice she sometimes used with me. "Hello, Phil?" she said. "I'm still here."

9

At the Red Swan, business was pretty good in spite of the snow. It had been snowing for thirty-six hours solid when I left Lily on the phone and went to Henry Liu's place down off Broadway. Phil Frye was a piece of crap. I wanted a drink, there was nothing happening anyhow because the snow jammed up everything and everyone.

Henry Liu's was a landmark. Even if, like me, you didn't normally have much business in Chinatown, you knew about Liu, who owned dozens of buildings along with the Red Swan. Liu, by reputation, was an old-time boss, the head of a big family association, a man who put his mark on Chinatown and everyone in it, including the police; rumor had it he had been the rabbi to at least half a dozen commanders in the 5th Precinct. I'd also heard that he had a snake tattooed around one wrist and wore a million-dollar platinum Patek Philippe on the other.

The ground floor of the three-storey food palace contained a fancy supermarket. A few people cruised the aisles, most of them rich babes with great tans, big furs and limos idling outside at the curb. There were lacquered ducks that resembled designer handbags and barrels of rare mushrooms that cost more than diamonds, and the women picked them over, rapacious looks on their faces, like they'd never had a decent meal. One babe, a full-length white fox coat over her shoulders, her slim arm wound with a gold Bulgari snake—I always read Lily's fashion magazines in the can—bought abalone at eight hundred bucks a pound. Her fingernails were black as dried blood.

Snappy hostesses in sharp black silk suits patrolled the restaurant upstairs, walkies in hand, high heels going tap tap on the marble floors and the see-through stairs where Liu had installed twinkling lights. The women guided guests up and down as if it were an ancient court in a walled city, this caste to that level, lesser mortals below, gods to Liu's private dining room. Like eunuchs at the palace, the muscle consisted of beardless young men who wore wire-rim glasses and Armani suits. I didn't know much about Henry Liu but, from the treatment I got, I figured, somehow, he knew about me.

"Have you eaten?" one of the hostesses inquired. "Would you care to dine? Drink?" She was solicitous, attentive, fawning, and so were the suits, as if Liu had been told I could be bent. In the second-floor restaurant, where a band played, I settled on a leather stool at the curving black glass bar, munched prawn crackers, sipped Scotch and watched the action.

A wedding snaked its way in and out of the tables, the older couples doing a dizzying two-step, posture perfect, feet moving in intricate patterns, like teams of figure skaters. The little kids bopped around, the teenagers formed a conga line then broke up and did the macarena. Waiters staggered under vast trays loaded with platters of food. The smells made me hungry and, before I even asked for a menu, a plate of lobster and rice was delivered to the bar, compliments of Henry Liu. Where was Mr Liu? I asked. Busy, an Armani told me politely. I finished the Scotch, ordered a beer and ate.

When I finished, I sat around a while. Jerry Chen arrived, which I half expected—he said he ate at Liu's most nights—and so did Pete Leung, which surprised me. Chen sat alone at a table, eating and reading *Vanity Fair*. Pete was escorted to a large table where he was surrounded by men in suits. But when he saw me, he beckoned me over. He got up and shook my hand and introduced me to the men, who also shook my hand.

Pete moved away from the table and lowered his voice. "I have to talk to these men for a few minutes, Artie. I try to do legit business down here. It's difficult. Hello, Jeremy." As soon as he saw Jerry Chen, his voice chilled right down.

Pete said, "Jeremy told you we knew each other?"

There was real antagonism between them, which was weird, considering the Taes asked me to get Chen in on the thing with Dawn. Pete was Dawn's husband after all. Maybe down here everyone knew everyone, but the tension between these two you could slice up for dinner.

"I was just fixing with Artie to have a meal," Pete said. He didn't invite Jerry Chen and Chen, looking angry, went back to his magazine.

"I'm sorry, Artie, I just couldn't stand him, not

tonight. All the swearing. The posturing. Is he gone? Can you see?" Pete craned his neck. "Look, I'm at my wits' end with Dawn. She goes out by herself. I'm scared all the time for her," he said. "Help me if you can," he added, which was tough for a guy like Pete. I said I'd try, and then he went back to the table of men.

Chen was waiting for me in the lobby.

"This meeting is accidental?"

"I eat at Henry's most nights, like I told you," Chen said. I let it ride.

"You want to talk about you and Pete Leung?"

"What should I fucking say about Pete Leung? Should I ask myself what the fuck he's doing here at Henry Liu's eating with a bunch of guys who support Taiwan, who hate the commie dicks on the mainland fifty years after they took over, before some of them were even born?"

"Why shouldn't he eat with them?"

"Because Pete is also mighty fucking chummy with the Fujianese who support those same commie dicks on the mainland. The same fucking Fujianese only recently got some clout down here in Chinatown and want to grab whatever turf they can away from the likes of Henry Liu, turf being power, money, influence with the City. You got all that? As in turf war."

"So maybe Pete's a peace ambassador."

"Pete cuts his deals with the reds. Pete's also got an American passport. Pete plays it both ways." Chen stopped for breath.

Me, I hadn't heard anyone call the commies reds for a real long time. "Sounds smart to me, Jer. Sounds like a guy who donates money to the Democrats and the Republicans."

I zipped up my jacket. Pete was a businessman. Jerry Chen was paranoid. "OK, so tell me, Jer. Every time you take a crap you call up Sonny Lippert?"

"I see. You're worried I'm in Sonny's pocket, is that it?" Chen laughed. "I tried you a couple times today, you didn't answer, I figured you don't love me. I figured I had fucking bad breath. Lippert is a useful man. Lippert is interested in anything that ups his profile. I know he uses me. He uses you. I use him. I like you, Artie, but like I think I said once already, I'm bored with the games. If you want to help out with Rose or any of this shit, and there's plenty of it, give me a call. OK? Just remember, I'm the good guy."

"So let's have a drink. Toast the good guys."

"I can't." He looked at his watch. "I have a date. But let me share this with you. You saw the way the dead girl's face looked raked? Like animals crawled over it? I guess you already figured out that the fuckwits that threw the spike at you used a weapon a lot like it on the girl. Well, I'm hoping we got a match with some partial prints that were found at Abramsky's place. And I'm thinking that the weapon they used on the girl is the exact same one they fucking tossed at your head in the fucking warehouse."

On my way home, I found myself behind a blind man. The man's seeing-eye dog pulled him along in the middle of the street like it was a ski run, the man laughing. The city floundered helpless, a big baby that flopped in the snowdrifts. The snow made a sponge for noise and there wasn't any traffic anyway, so the only sound you could hear was the man with the dog laughing and laughing as he flew up Walker Street. I followed him until I got to Mike's and went in for some smokes.

"You checked out Rick's place, like I said to?" Mike asked, tossing me some cigarettes.

"What are you talking about?"

"I told you earlier. You're running around in circles, Artie, you don't listen to what's going on. I told you. Recently I saw lights on in Ricky's apartment. I been meaning to check. Gimme the keys," Mike said. "I'm going up."

"You wanna play Kojak, I'll go with you. I have the keys."

Mike locked the coffee shop and I thought, what the hell, you didn't know. Someone mentions a building is vulnerable because the restaurant on the ground floor is not operating. People hear. Creeps hear.

I used to leave my door unlocked and it made Ricky laugh. "What's this, a macho cop thing?" he always said.

"Something else, Artie. The Chink kid that came by my place."

I laughed. "Your Chechen. Right."

"It's not the first time he's been here. I didn't tell you. I did some business with him before."

"What kind of business?"

"Remember when Rick was in the hospital and you and me and Hillel used to hang out?"

"Sure. Sure I remember."

"Hillel was getting a raw deal on supplies, so I helped him out, well, I was real sorry I gave him the deal because it went sour. The kid was their errand boy."

Christ, I thought; the kid with the quiff. "Toilet paper?" I said.

"Toilet paper, paper towels, paper cups. The kid was real anxious today, wired."

"It was a message?"

"It wasn't Pindar, the poet. One other thing."

"What, Mike?"

"He asked me about you," Mike said, and I felt like someone had grabbed my guts with a hook and yanked on it hard. "The kid asked about you, Artie. He knew your name."

Rick has the top floor of the building. The elevator opens into his apartment, and as I unlocked it, I banged on the door out of habit, like I always used to, to let Ricky know I was coming.

"Jesus, it's cold." Mike shivered.

It was cold. The windows were normally kept locked, but it was freezing and I noticed right away one of the window locks was horizontal. Someone had been here. A careless cleaning woman, I assumed, at first. The Palazetti furniture was covered with sheets. I checked the closets.

Like mine, Rick's living room is separated from the kitchen by a long low counter, only he put in a slab of dark green marble with white veins. "Beautiful stuff." Mike ran his hand idly along the counter, then picked up a plastic bag from the surface.

Alongside the bag were a few tools, including a flat knife like painters use. Mike turned it over. The apartment was quiet. The refrigerator shuddered. The old floorboards creaked under my feet. Then the phone rang and the answering machine picked it up. Ricky's voice, like a ghost's, played into the quiet loft.

Mike examined the plastic bag and the knife. "Someone's been working up here?"

"What?"

"This shit looks like plaster," he said. "I'm gonna check out the bedroom, and then let's get the fuck out. With Ricky away sick, this place gives me the creeps. I'll be back in a second." Mike made for the hall.

What repairs? What plaster? No one had been working up here.

"Mike?"

There was no answer. "Mike?" I played back the previous ten seconds while I scanned the apartment and I saw it. I hadn't seen it when Mike picked it up, but I saw it now: the red Chinese characters on the side of the plastic bag, the white powder inside it, the four long lines of the powder laid out carefully on the counter. The green marble with its white veins had acted as camouflage. I saw it now clear as day, clear as snow. I didn't have to taste it to know it was heroin.

"Mike, get out of there. Mike!"

"What? What? I got to check the bedroom," he said, reappearing. I wanted him out. Mike talks tough. But I didn't want another friend getting beat up because of me. I didn't want Justine to see her dad get whacked.

"Let's go. Now. Please."

"What's with you, Artie?"

"Just fucking listen to me," I said under my breath. "I think we should just leave. Come on. You get the elevator, I'll turn off the light and we'll just go, like we came up."

The elevator didn't move. Someone was holding it on another floor. Maybe someone was loading up gear for a ski trip. Maybe not.

"Stairs?" Mike said.

"No. Not from here."

"Move, fuck you," Mike screamed at the elevator. He was panicky.

I rammed open the window. "Come on." We climbed out onto the fire escape and I shut the window, but there was no way to lock it from outside.

Somehow, in the dark, the wind howling, we made it to the roof. A gust of wind came out of nowhere and picked up an umbrella from the party the night before, tossing it into the air like a spear. Between us, me and Mike, we yanked open the fire door and got down the stairs to the street.

"Jesus, man," Mike said. "What's going on here?"

"Someone's dealing in there. Someone was cutting stuff, bagging it. It wasn't plaster. It wasn't cement."

"Who?"

"Who knows? Anyone. One of the Taes' ex-waiters. Someone that came to clean Rick's place and made a copy of the key. Anyone. But that apartment is like a trap, back where the bedroom is. Look, if someone heard us coming and they hid back in the bedroom, they might have been feeling trapped. People who deal do not react well to feeling trapped. I'm not saying there was anyone there, I'm just saying it was a good idea to get the fuck out. Are you OK?"

"Yeah," Mike said. But I knew that it shook him up. When he got into his car he didn't invite me home for Lina's pot roast Saturday like he usually does, and I was betting he didn't want me around Justine right now. I was trouble.

In the wind, the building moaned. Behind apartment walls, dogs, housebound and restless, scuffled along the floors like rats, and the cat on the fourth floor screamed from boredom. In my apartment, I got a sweater and a bottle of Scotch and went back up to Ricky's to lock the window.

The plastic bag was still on the kitchen counter, so were the white lines of powder. I had a gun and I checked the bedroom, the bathroom, slamming doors hard, the noise intended to warn off any creeps. I could have called in some outside help, but with the snow everyone was working overtime. I didn't want to call the Taes if I didn't have to; they had enough grief.

I turned out the lights, pulled a sheet off a leather chair in the corner of the room, put the Scotch on the rug, the gun on my lap and sat down to wait in the dark. Whoever had been in the apartment earlier would be back to get the goods. I was sure of it.

Sitting in the dark, I thought about Pansy. If I didn't help her, she would be next. She would be dead like her friend Rose. "I'm next." Where was she, I wondered? Maybe she was already dead. Maybe there was a serial killer out there in the city who liked hitting Chinese girls. Maybe there was some gang thing in Chinatown going on that I could never penetrate, never understand. Maybe it was the kid who asked Mike about me. Maybe it was the guy who took the pictures. Mr Snap.

Whoever took the picture of her had killed Rose or knew who did. Mr Snap. Instinctively I knew it. I had to get into the lab on Ludlow Street, but there wasn't anything I could do, not at midnight in the middle of a blizzard. I thought about the freight elevator and I began to sweat. Without warning, my leg cramped.

In my socks, I got up, wiggled my foot, went to the window and opened it. Outside, a few night owls moved languidly, as if they were drugged. Stoned on snow. It was beautiful out, but dead.

Up here in Rick's apartment at the top of the building, you couldn't hear anything from the other lofts. None of the sounds of life—radiators, people, music, dogs, babies—nothing. I never noticed it before. Before, there had always been music playing, people yakking. Now, it was like a padded cell. I closed the window and sat down again. I was so tired.

It was like being alone on an empty liner in the middle of the ocean. I couldn't see anyone or hear anything. But I knew that, in spite of the storm, whoever had been in Ricky's apartment earlier that day would come back for the stuff. The white lines were laid out, the heroin was cut, the bag was full. Dread spilled over me because I knew. I knew that the bozos who attacked me in the elevator were coming here, into my building, onto my turf. Whoever had been here would be back tonight.

10

"Hello, Artie." When she saw me, she looked surprised, but not scared. Not really scared.

You enter an apartment, a man comes at you out of the dark with a gun, but even before you've really seen him, you're not frightened. Maybe it was the drugs she was doing. Maybe nothing bothered her, maybe she expected me. I wondered if, somehow, Dawn Tae had expected me.

A long sable coat clutched around her, she was quick as a cat as she backed up to the green marble counter. Before I could get to her, the plastic bag with the Chinese characters had disappeared into her handbag and so had the lines of powder.

With a faint smile, daring me, she set her bag on the counter, perched on one of the bar stools and let the fur coat slide halfway down her shoulders.

"I guess if I told you I came to get some things for Ricky, you wouldn't believe me. Would you, Artie?"

Dawn arched her back. She was thin and her face was as haggard as it had been the night before, but now she looked sexy. She wore a white silk shirt and a short leather skirt. There were diamonds in her ears and she fiddled with the long string of pearls around her neck.

"Can I have a cigarette?"

"Sure."

"Was it you here earlier, Dawn?"

"When?"

"An hour ago? Two? When I came up."

"No. Before that."

"Who left the window unlocked?"

"I don't know. Me, maybe."

"You've been here before? Other times?"

"Once. Twice. Oh, don't ask me. Please," she said. "Do you want to look in my bag, then, Artie? Go on. It's a nice bag. Have a look." She picked it up and held it out, testing me. Testing the friendship. I shook my head.

Dawn didn't run. She didn't say anything. She smiled at me, got off the stool, crossed the few feet between us and seemed to slide into my arms.

"Please," she begged. "Please. Take me away, Artie, OK? Just take me somewhere. You always took care of me. Only you, Artie. Be a friend, darling."

So I didn't ask and we left Rick's apartment and went down to mine. Dawn surveyed the loft.

"You kept it the same. I'm glad. I always loved it here."

I glanced out the window. A limo was at the curb.

"Yours?" I said.

Dawn looked out. "Yes. Do you want me to tell him to go away?"

103

"Let him stay. You'll need a ride home, my car's bust," I said, and she smiled because she knew I was kidding myself, knew she wasn't going anywhere that night. "She's become a cunning girl," Mr Tae had said.

Dawn sat on the edge of my sofa, took out a portable phone from her Prada bag and called home. "Fine," Dawn said. "I'm fine. Don't worry if I'm late. If I don't get home until tomorrow. I'm with a girlfriend," she cooed reassuringly into the cellphone—to her mother, to Pete? Dawn flipped her phone shut. "Do you think I can have some wine, Artie?"

"White?"

"You remember."

There was a pretty good bottle of Chablis in the fridge. I opened it and sat next to her.

"Hello, Artie, darling."

She drank steadily; we emptied the bottle, then, carefully, she put her glass on the floor.

"I'm grateful, Artie. I knew Pa would do something idiotic, like asking you to follow me. I knew, but what could I do? He has to show he's trying to help, you had to honor his request."

"I wasn't ever going to follow you, you know that," I said, but she put her hand over my mouth.

"So you did what he asked but you let me know. Thank you." She kissed my cheek.

I had promised Mr Tae I'd find out what was wrong with Dawn. I had taken his money. But I knew all along what was wrong. Dawn was taking drugs, smoking something, shooting up. Maybe, I should have asked.

The truth is, I liked her being with me in my place again, snow outside, the feeling there were only two of us, no one else, cruising the city in the building that was a ghost ship. I liked it a whole lot, but it was risky stuff. Dawn was Pete's wife, Martin Tae's daughter.

"So how are you?" I said.

"I'll tell you." She reached across me for the wine bottle and her sleeve grazed my arm.

"There's Scotch."

"Scotch would be lovely," she said. "You know, for months I'd wake up in my bed in Hong Kong and I'd think, soon this will be over and I can go home. Do you understand, Artie? And then I'd open my eyes and I'd think, this is my home. This is it."

I got the Scotch. She wandered around the room, her hand brushing old possessions of mine that she recognized, a chair, the stereo, some pictures she helped me buy when I had a little dough.

"I loved Hong Kong at first. Rich people making money, going to China, cutting deals. The house was beautiful. I didn't want to live with his family, though, so Pete bought me another house. I had a job. I was always good at money. There was his mother, she was very anxious for grandchildren, but Pete never really pushed. Maybe it was the miscarriage." She held onto the back of a chair. "My feet are wet, I think."

Dawn perched on the edge of a stool, her back to me. Almost primly, she took off her boots, then her pantyhose. When she moved, the coat fell off her shoulders again and the leather skirt rode up over her thighs. It was hard not to concentrate on the fact she had nothing on under the skirt. From her bag she took a little gold box and ate something out of it.

I grabbed the pill box. "Don't."

"It's only Valium," she said. "But I don't want to talk about me." Abruptly, she changed the subject. Tell me about you. Tell me a story."

"What kind of story?" I leaned my elbows on the counter and looked at her a few inches away seated on the stool, ankles crossed like a girl.

"Where you've been, what you're doing. Do you remember when you first bought this loft? Remember? Ricky fell for you first, then he discovered you liked girls. He introduced us. I fell for you. I wasn't even in grad school. I was just starting Yale. I came home and I thought you were the cutest guy I'd ever seen."

"Ten years ago. Ten?"

"Yes."

"You weren't bad yourself." I didn't know what else to say. This was a courting ritual and I didn't know the moves Dawn had in mind, so I leaned on my elbows, poured more Scotch into glasses, and waited.

"You were so up about everything. Like a kid let out of jail. It didn't matter—movies, music, riding your bike, sailing a boat, eating. And New York. Just being here seemed to charge you up like a lightbulb. You were so determined to be happy."

"I was happy."

"You were a real cop, I was impressed. Also, you had dimples. I thought that was very sexy."

"The dimples or the gun?"

"Both. And you were family. In a way, you

reinvented us as a family because you wanted one so much. We were yours, all of us, Rick, me, the parents, even Uncle Billy. You made us feel better about ourselves." Dawn crossed her legs. "God, I was crazy about you."

"Come on."

"I was, you see." She reached for my hand. "I really was."

"Why didn't you say something?"

"I was a kid. You weren't interested."

"That's not true. You never said."

"You always had two girls on the go, the ones I knew about, the rest of them. You could never make up your mind."

"And I was always broke."

"I didn't care about that."

"Why didn't you tell me?"

Lightly, in her bare feet, Dawn leaped off the kitchen stool, picked up her glass and, holding the coat that must have cost a hundred thou, went to the window. "I hate the snow. It's so lonely." She put her head back and swallowed the Scotch. "I don't want to talk any more, Artie, not now. I want to stay here and feel safe. You know what I'd really like?"

"Tell me, darling."

"Fun. I'd like to have some fun again. What scares me is I feel like an old lady and I'll never have any fun again."

I'm not sure what time it was when Dawn wandered towards the bedroom and I followed, Scotch in hand.

From the other room Stan Getz played "My Funny Valentine". I reached for the light.

"Don't." Dawn tossed her fur coat onto my bed. All she wore now was the leather skirt and silk shirt. "Perhaps I should take you back to Hong Kong," she added suddenly. "Come with me, Artie. I want to have some fun."

"Why go back if you hate it? New York is your home."

"I have things to finish there. While I can."

"You're going back soon. Aren't you?"

"Yes."

"What things?"

"If you came to Hong Kong, I could take care of you. I've got loads of money." The laugh, soaked in wine and Scotch, was husky. "I could keep you. As long as you want. I miss you, Artie. You always made me laugh."

We were standing next to the bed—there isn't much else in the room—and I could feel the desire as I put my arms around Dawn. "I don't want your money," I said, but it wasn't completely true.

The allure of dough was always part of Dawn's charm. She smelled of money—her parents' money, money she made trading commodities. Smelled of it like she smelled of perfume—Dawn was always drenched in Joy. And there were the clothes, the cars, the casual spending, the laughs. Dawn was the first American girl I fell for in a big way, and it was hard to separate her from the sheer pleasure the money made available. But she had married Peter Leung. Hong Kong was Dawn's big adventure. Also, she was crazy about Pete.

"Stop, stop. I can hear those ball bearings in your brain, Artie. Stop it now."

She unbuttoned my shirt and her hand was cold on my chest. Her pearls were warm from her skin.

This was Russian roulette, being with her. People always found out. The driver in the car outside, still waiting. There was Pete. And Lily. There was the frustration with Lily who I couldn't seem to make happy. I guess the way I feel for Lily, I wasn't supposed to want Dawn. Some shrink would probably say I was a psycho for wanting Dawn. I reached down and picked up my glass and finished the rest of the Scotch.

"I really was crazy about you back then," Dawn said again. The sense of missed opportunity smothered me and I pushed it away.

"If you won't come to Hong Kong, how about we hole up here for a while?"

Dawn took my arm. She pulled me onto the bed and I could feel the fur of her sable coat against my back. She wrapped herself around me.

"Make me feel better, Artie," she said softly so I could smell her voice. "Make me feel better like you used to when we sat out on the fire escape and you put your hand under my skirt. We never finished, did we?"

I didn't even try to move away. "It's so nice here," she said, and unbuttoned her shirt, slipped out of it, took off her bra, arched her back and pushed her leather skirt up high over her hips. She had nothing else on.

Dawn left before it was light. I hadn't slept much for two nights running and there was the booze and the painkillers. I got into bed meaning to sleep for a few hours. I slept all day while the blizzard switchbacked its way in and out of the city, dumped a few more inches of snow on it, let up, hesitated, and started again. When I woke up, it was almost dark.

I looked out of the window where night gathered over the street. Towers of snow trembled on my fire escape and icicles the size of cucumbers hung off the rusty railings.

When I swung my legs over the bed, I put on the TV. The schools had shut again. In parts of the city, there were power outages and telephone lines were down. When I tried to phone Dawn in Riverdale, I couldn't get through. A second storm was on its way up the coast from the Outer Banks, whatever the poor goddamn Outer Banks are, always getting socked in the face by some storm.

It was the third night of the blizzard. Crime was way off, some newsjerk announced. The crooks, not caring much for snow, stayed home and watched TV sets they had lifted off the back of a truck. In Bed Stuy, a tenement went up in flames because of faulty space heaters. Always a problem when the weather got cold, the landlord said, and there followed, on some dumb-ass talk show, a string of city officials who blamed each other and the landlord, a grisly Serb in a shiny suit. The mayor, with his bad hair and that rictus of a grin, popped up everywhere, shaking hands with the snow removal guys, congratulating himself on a great job, remembering, no doubt, how mayors before him lost their job over the lack of snow removal in the boroughs.

Still groggy, I got dressed, went out and wandered up towards SoHo. The city was suspended in a kind of surreal ballet: spontaneous parties spilled in and out of the bars; people brought their kids out of doors and showed them how to lie down in the fat new snow and make angel shapes. Underneath Broadway, a century-old water pipe had burst and flooded the street and where the water froze up, older kids twirled down the sidewalk on ice skates like something from a Dutch painting.

On Sullivan Street, on the steps of St Anthony's, the AA crowd was out, smoking cigarettes during a break. It was always a sharp crowd, the St Anthony's AA—models, actors, designers—I know people who joined up just to cruise the talent. Two doors down, Pino the butcher cut me some of his Newport steaks; across the street at Joe's Dairy, I stocked up on fresh mozzarella and provolone. Then I walked south to the Broome Street Bar where I ordered a bacon cheeseburger and a beer.

In my head, I reviewed the situation. A girl was dead on Abramsky's floor, her face raked with a spike that turns out similar to the one the creeps throw at my head in a freight elevator in Chinatown, maybe even the same spike. Some red-haired jerk who's pushing toilet paper shakes down Hillel Abramsky, drops by Mike Rizzi's coffee shop, and gets in Jerry Chen's face on a street in Chinatown. Chen, it turns out, knows Pete Leung and is also pally with Sonny Lippert, and Hillel Abramsky is running around Chinatown asking about cameras in a building where there's a lab that processed the picture of the dead girl. A lab that's shut up tight as a drum and, me, being out of the loop, I can't get a warrant. And who was Mr Snap?

What was Hillel's part in it all? Did Hillel kill her? Did Hillel get in over his head because the Chinese were eating up the family business?

I finished my burger and started home. Later I heard that that same night a couple of FBI sharpshooters went off their heads and sat on the sea wall in Battery Park shooting seagulls. Snow fever, we called it in Moscow. At home, I called Lily and left a message. I missed her. Lily could cure the fever. Then I called Jerry Chen.

Chen was slick and he was volatile, but I needed him. A sour woman answered the phone and said Jerry was out of town: Atlanta, she thought, or Toronto. He didn't keep her up to date on his whereabouts, she said bitterly, and I knew Chen was cheating on her; in this weather, no one left town.

Standing, phone in my hand, listening to Chen's bitter wife, I noticed something on my couch. A trace of white. I looked closer. Dawn had left her smell behind, and she had left this. I tried to scrape it off, but there wasn't enough. I tried to taste it but all I got was the flavor of old couch. What the hell was she doing? Where did she get her stuff? What was Dawn on?

11

"It can make you bleed from the ears, the stuff Dawn is using," Pete Leung said. Not that I asked him right out when I saw him at the club. I felt lousy enough, having climbed out of bed with his wife that morning without asking him what her favorite flavor of dope was. Pete didn't give any sign he knew about me and Dawn, but I didn't believe it. Not in my gut. People always know.

It was around seven when I got to the club, which is when Pete hopped off a souped-up mountain bike. Chance? Coincidence? My stomach churned.

"Good, don't you think?" Pete showed me the bike. It was fitted out with a contraption made of Velcro and nails. "I swiped the bike idea off a kid I met. It works brilliantly in this weather," Pete said, shucked his gloves and shook my hand.

There wasn't much traffic, but a couple of cabs rattled by, leaning on their horns, and a Range Rover with stereo speakers mounted on the front blasted out something by Tupac, who was dead now, and not missed, not by me, anyhow. "Fuck off back to New Jersey." The raucous voice came from the loft building next to the club. It was followed by the pop of an egg that spattered onto my jacket. Leung tried hard not to laugh.

"You've got some angry people up there," he said.

"Yeah. Poor bastards buy these lofts for half a mill, then this greaseball clubster opens up on the block, the drunks come, the junkies, when *New York Magazine* mentions real estate prices could tumble, they go berserk, so the clubster hires me to stand around a few nights a week and keep the peace, which is bullshit."

Pete looked up. "If it was me I'd want to kill someone. Can I buy you a drink, Artie? I need to talk. Can you spare me half an hour? I want to talk about Dawn."

Sly, as the doorman dubbed himself, held the moth-eaten ropes aside to let us pass. With his piggy face and a ring in his nose, he derived all his power from those ropes, like the immigration officer of some crappy country. I stuffed a five in his pocket and said I'd be inside.

We went in. I was hoping Lily would come by later, so even though I was edgy with Pete around, I figured it was better for Lily to find me inside with him than out in the street wiping egg off my face.

The club was a huge brutal cement space dotted with armchairs and leather sofas. Fake ancestral portraits adorned the walls and potted palms stood in brass tubs on frayed rugs. I wondered, like I always do, why anyone came to this place. It looked like shit. The music was canned crap, you couldn't dance, anyhow, but the place was packed every night, people trying to score or getting drunk or hoping they could eyeball Oliver Stone or Brad Pitt. It never happened. Mostly, it was kids in their twenties, micro-celebs, aspirant models, wannabes, the dregs of Euro-trash, though lately I was seeing a lot of Orios. Orio-trash, Jerry Chen had called them, which is what passed for wit with Jerry. Manila, Singapore, Hong Kong, Jakarta, they drank the most expensive malts. I don't know, could be I'm getting old.

Even in a seedy leather chair, Pete Leung looked like an aristocrat. His charm came from his enthusiasm. I think I had always been jealous all the years he and Dawn were dating.

He ordered Bud for both of us. "Thanks," he said when the waiter brought it. "Cheers, Artie," he added. "You saw her? Dawn?"

"Yes." I tried not to look furtive. "At her parents' house."

He swallowed some beer and took a cigarette from my pack and lit it, so I wouldn't see the pain, I guess. Like a lot of guys, he kept it in.

"I feel so ashamed. It's my fault and I don't know how to help her." He turned away, pretending to admire a couple of girls who blew him kisses. "You've known Dawn almost all her life, Artie. And you saw."

"When did it start?"

"I don't know. When we got married eighteen months ago, I felt as if we'd known each other for ever. We came from the same kind of family. We knew each other in grad school, we were friends, we were both crazy about movies, we even thought of starting a company together. Did you know that? Then we fell in

115

love, everyone was happy. The parents were happy. The gifts flowed."

Pete was rich, but Pete was unhappy. Currently, I was broke enough to work at the club. My car was in the shop and I found myself doing comparison shopping on paper clips, so to speak. In my dreams, the cash machine clanks and rolls, then fails to produce any cash for me at all.

"She loved her job, she loved Hong Kong. My mother's a bit nuts about the kid thing, but I said, look, Dawn's not a baby machine." His story matched Dawn's except for the miscarriage, but maybe he felt it was none of my business.

"I came home from a trip a while back—Dawn wouldn't come to the mainland, she said the Chinese were barbarians—and I knew right away she was using. The eyes, the highs, the sallow skin, the capricious behavior. There was a swagger about her when she was high. When she was low, she became crafty. I said, we'll go home to New York. I bought an apartment for us over on West 12th Street on the river. Dawn always liked being near the water. Now she stays in Riverdale and I stay downtown alone in that apartment and look at the water. You know how I pass the time?"

"How's that?"

Pete blinked. "I sit in the archives over on Varick Street. I work on the family. Mine. Dawn's. Things have gone so wrong. I keep thinking, maybe I'll find something in the past. Perhaps I'll find a clue. It's a pretty Chinese idea, I guess," he said with a wry smile and rubbed the bridge of his nose. "Hey, it keeps me busy."

"What's Dawn on?"

"Heroin is very easy to get in Hong Kong. It comes in through the Golden Triangle for the most part. It always was the most addicted city on earth, but it used to be poor people who used the stuff. Now it's the middle-class drug of choice. People are scared of what will happen next. Not only this July when the Chinese take Hong Kong back, but afterwards, in '98, '99. Everyone is jumpy. Heroin cools you down."

Around us people cruised the club, girls and boys looking for action at the bar, at the tables, but Pete never looked up. He looked at me with sad eyes and I really felt for him.

"Go on."

"So the Hong Kong demimonde looked around for something special. Rich kids. Our crowd, so to speak. For a while it was LSD tabs with pictures of Mao or Deng. Then cocaine became démodé. They moved on to heroin. But not the stuff secretaries were smoking. Someone heard there were these irradiated opium poppies—weird flowers, huge, some with six or eight flowers, some that grew upside down. There was a meltdown at one of the Chinese power plants; no one reported it, of course, but everyone knew. It was bigger than Chernobyl, they said. The poppies went into the drug trade. Into some of the morphine used at the hospitals. There were rumors. A myth grew up that you could get a fantastic charge. Ripped on Poppy, it became a legend. It made you exuberant, ecstatic, people called it a trip to paradise. Or it would make you bleed from the ears and eat a hole in your gut.

117

"Can I get another beer do you think?" he asked, and I waved my hand at a waiter. "One of our friends who smoked got bone cancer. Maybe it was accidental. One turned psychotic. People play Russian roulette with it. Which bag is hot? The myth got bigger."

"Can I have a martini?" a voice interrupted and I felt Lily's arms around my shoulders. Pete jumped out of his seat and shook her hand. A well-bred guy, I thought; better than me.

She took off her coat. She was wearing an old-fashioned ski suit an aunt had left her; it was one of those dark blue one-piece jobs Carole Lombard would have worn on the slopes with Gable in Sun Valley, and Lily looked terrific in it.

"I wasn't sure you'd come."

"I felt like getting out." She slid into a chair, then leaned over and kissed me and whispered into my ear. "I'm an asshole, sometimes. I'm sorry, Artie, really I am. I missed you."

Pushing her hair back, she smiled at Pete and he smiled back, but who wouldn't? The drinks came. For half an hour Lily kept up a comfortable stream of talk—she was a genius at making people feel good, and she understood instinctively that Pete was feeling lousy. And he relaxed. He was at ease in his skin and it made him sexy.

People arrived. The buzz grew. But Pete never shifted his eyes. All he saw was Lily. It was all I saw and for half an hour we joked and kidded around and drank martinis, but one of the waiters caught my glance and nodded towards the office. "Phone," he screamed over the racket of the club.

The club's office was a mess of party props, CD demos and samples of melon liqueurs, but I found the phone. It was Chen. When I got back to the table, Lily and Pete were laughing like kids. He excused himself and went to the bathroom, turning to call out to her, "Shall we have some more drinks, Lily? Will you order them?"

"Bombay, straight up, three olives?" She smiled invitingly. "Like mine?"

"Please, Lily. Yes. Just like yours."

"I have to go. I could give you a lift," I said to Lily, who was flushed from the gin.

"I think I'll stay a while," she said. "You don't mind, do you?"

"So what were you guys talking about?" I put on my jacket.

"Just talking."

"Yeah, what about?"

"You're jealous. You're really jealous, aren't you?" Lily put her arms around my neck; on her, even gin smelled good. "Don't be silly. It's nothing."

"OK, I'm jealous. So what were you talking about?"

"Babies," she said, and kissed me again as Pete reappeared. He walked me to the door and shook my hand, then held onto it like a drowning man. "I need you to tell me what you find out. I don't know how to save Dawn otherwise. Will you help me, Artie? I'll beg if I have to."

"You don't have to beg, Jesus, Pete. I'll help. You know that."

"Dawn is very mercurial. She disappears, she does odd things. I know my father-in-law asked you to check on

119

her, and I want to honor that, but it's hard. I guess you know that she sometimes uses her brother's loft without telling anyone. I guess you know that, Artie. Don't you?"

I thought about Dawn's limo driver the night before: was he Pete's man? Did the driver tell Pete Leung about his wife and me?

Pete opened the door for me: I asked him how he knew to find me at the club and he said, "You told me." But I didn't. Maybe Pete showed up to stick it to me, to let me know he was onto me and Dawn, or maybe he really was desperate like he said.

"The shit that Dawn uses. The heroin you were talking about. Does it have a name?"

Pulling off his glasses, Pete rubbed the back of one tan hand across his face. Then I saw his eyes unshielded by the glasses and I realized Pete knew exactly what I'd done with his wife. I don't know how, but my insides shriveled with knowing it, with guilt, and a faint whisper of fear. There were guys who would kill you for what I had done.

"Yes," he said quietly. "It has a name. They call it Hot Poppy. See you around, Artie."

12

He sat on the hood of the silver Porsche near the 23rd Street pier, a carton of coffee next to him. A cigarette hanging from his plump mouth, he played with the photographs like a deck of cards, shuffling them, squaring the pack, selecting one of the pictures and holding it up to the streetlight, then spinning it with his fingers, a magician at a children's party.

I'd been right about Jerry Chen. He never was out of town. I didn't know for sure until I got his call at the club and met him on 23rd Street. Another Chinese girl had turned up dead. An ice skater, on her way to the Skyrink over at the new sports complex on the pier, had tripped on something in the snow. It was a human arm. The arm was attached to a body.

"Another." I looked at the crowd that had gathered. "Dead?"

"Yeah."

"Claw marks? Like Rose?"

"Yeah." Chen tossed me a picture. That's her."

Fifty yards away, police tape cordoned off the area.

The yellow tape, the blue and white cars, the red lights and orange traffic cones were bright as kids' toys against the snow.

On the other side of the yellow tape, a couple of guys from the ME's office were arguing about the death, when, how, which angle, what temperature it was when she froze. When they had pulled her out of the frozen drifts, Chen told me, she was stiff, naked and white. No one seemed interested in the girl herself. As one of them said later, "She's already dead."

The white jacket was gone and Chen wore a dark blue coat. He was whistling, whistling and playing with the photographs when he saw me. He let a couple more pictures fly out of his hand. In a waist-high snowdrift, under a streetlight, two or three stuck face up. I didn't have to look to know they were pictures of girls, Chinese girls and a white Cadillac with wire wheels. I gathered them up.

Jerry reached over and took the pictures out of my hand. "Have you seen other pictures like this, Art?"

"And if I have? Let's say I have."

"What do I fucking know? Over the last year or so, these pictures have turned up. Pictures of Chinese girls that were dead. We even found one or two of girls who became dead soon afterwards."

"Who were they?"

"Girls who worked in sweatshops. Girls who worked in restaurants. There's also been a similar thing in Toronto." He watched as the body was zipped into a black bag and carted away. Then a TV crew arrived and Chen leaped off his car.

"Wait for me." Chen smoothed his hair. "If this thing leads where I think, the four bloody horsemen got a new addition."

"What thing? What?" But Chen was already in front of the TV camera. I walked over and watched the show.

Jerry Chen talked to a reporter and he was good, ignoring the camera but always aware it was on. He liked it. From what I'd seen of him on the box, it liked him back. Chen was cool, he was earnest enough and the hair wasn't blow dried. Jerry Chen came off ethnic but American and I noticed when the cameras went on, he dropped the British affectations and quit swearing.

Extortion. Illegals. Sweatshops. Exploitation. Chen talked frankly. He explained how good policing could help and how badly the city needed more cops. He did his turn, delivered his soundbites, smiled. Chen was a pro. There followed a round of handshakes with the reporter and crew. Chen gave the producer a friendly peck on the cheek and strolled back to his car.

"Right, Art. Let's talk. Get in."

I got in. "You ever heard of Hot Poppy?"

He revved the engine and pulled away. "Hot what?"

"Hot Poppy. Some kind of heroin that's coming out of China."

"I don't think so, Art." He laughed. "I heard of everything coming out of China, I'm the man to know on China, but I sure ain't fucking heard of some shit named Hot Poppy."

"So it's something new."

"Someone's handing you a line. There's a million names for all kinds of dope. Or it's old stuff in a new

123

package. If it fries your brain, who gives a shit what they call it?"

I kept my mouth shut and wondered how come Chen didn't know what Pete Leung knew.

"It looks like the weapon that destroyed Rose's face is almost a dead fucking cert to be the spike those goons threw at you in the elevator. I told you we thought there were some partial prints at Abramsky's that matched the spike?"

"Yeah?"

"Well there were also some prints at your pal's shop that matched some on a few of the pictures we found."

"The same as the spike?"

"No, different. Personally, I don't think it's Hillel, but they'll run all the tests. So you understand how the DNA thing works?"

"Some," I bluffed. "A little. Not really."

"Me neither," he said, and we laughed. For the first time, I liked Jerry Chen.

"Anyway we got some kind of match. We'll look for some fucking creep who gets his weapons in Hong Kong. The warehouse where they went for you, what sort of goods did you get the impression were stored there?"

"Produce. Vegetables. I smelled them."

"You won't be surprised to hear it was a front."

"For?"

"Paper goods. Toilet paper. Money."

"Money."

"Yeah, money. It's always money, And there's a thousand ways to launder it."

"I think one of them knew my name."

"I don't think so, Art. Unless maybe with all this fucking snow and not a lot of action, you stood out. You've been running around a lot. Like I said, they don't go for white cops a lot."

Possessed, like a crazy man with an evil wind on his back, Chen drove up the Westside Highway, then doubled back and drove downtown. The wind had cleared the sky and there were stars over the river. Between the new apartment buildings, we roared down South End Avenue, past the Holocaust Monument, back onto West Street and into Battery Park. In the snow, Clinton Castle looked like Dracula's Christmas card, and at the landing pier where the boats leave for the Statue of Liberty, Chen pulled up and cut the motor. He leaned back and looked out at the harbor and Ellis Island.

"Your people come over on a boat?"

"I took a plane."

"You feel American?"

"Yeah."

Chen raised his navy blue shoulders, his expression full of disdain and self-loathing. "I don't feel like any shit. So I bloody well don't feel China Chinese. So what?" Some kind of torment gnawed Chen's liver. He spat the words. "I hate all this shit, Art. I used to really fucking feel for the Irish on St Pat's Day, you know, Art? Everyone thinking the Irish are pukey fucking drunks or wobble-ass cops instead of Yeats or Roddy Doyle or something. You know what it feels like, if you're a slant, to be identified with pongs who kill girls? If you're a

125

slant, you're a money-grubbing dog who believes in lucky numbers."

"Take it easy, Jer," I said.

"You know what I fucking hate? I hate going to parties and hearing how everyone's adopting a Chinese baby because there's all these baby girls, because no one wants a baby girl in China. Funny, ha ha. Lot of smartasses want Chinese babies." Jerry laughed. "You know what I heard someone say at one of those dos on Central Park West, all these rich-ass movie people? I heard some woman say, 'Ask for the fat babies. They fatten the babies up for export.' You got kids, Art? Any little Cohen munchkins?"

"No. Why?"

"There's been some trouble in the schools around Bed Stuy. I'm not saying it's happening, but the fucks been asking where kids live, posing as members of the Board of Ed. If you know a kid, put them in the picture, OK?"

I thought of Justine. "Thanks for telling me. You got any?"

Jerry snorted. "My wife doesn't like kids. My wife doesn't like me. I think I'm drunk, Art."

"You want me to drive?"

"Fuck that shit," he said. "Listen to me, Art. I don't do lucky numbers. I don't keep fish tanks. I'm not a comic guy or a nerd. I'm married to an all-American girl who grew up in bloody Oklahoma City. I tell you about my wife? She didn't like London, we came here. I became an American. It's ten years already. She doesn't like New York. I drink too much. I got ulcers."

"There's something else. Isn't there?"

"Yeah. Yeah, I also happen to be in love with a regulation JAP. A Jewish princess, first division. I don't know which way to run. I lie to everyone. Fuck it." He took his Dunhills out of his pocket and pitched them through the window. "I hate these smokes," he said. "You got some Winstons?" Chen picked some cigarette ash off the coat.

"Vicuna?" I asked.

"Alpaca." Chen glanced at the harbor one more time, taking in the Statue of Liberty and the frozen scenery and said, "You didn't know we're just as fucked up as you Russians, right, Art?"

"I always figured you Chinese had class, Jer. Culture."

"Well there's high Chinks and low Chinks, and most of us are real low. We say, 'Oh, sir, I am an ant. I am nothing, don't know nothing about bullet hole in the wall of the store.' I hate the crooks and killers that get here by working the human rights angle, then victimize the whole bleeding community."

I shifted my aching legs. "Is there a point to this, Jer? Or is this some kind of immigrant pow-wow?"

"It's the same old crap. Some poor bastard steps out of line in New York, you lean on the family back home. Before, it was government fucks. Now it's criminal fucks. Make a mistake in New York City, your mommy in China pays. But the poor suckers keep on coming. The Golden Mountain. Promised land. Praise the Lord. Look at the pictures, the big white Cadillac, the smiling girls. Streets paved with gold. So it fucking goes." Chen got out of the car and pissed on the snow, then got back in. The cold seemed to have sobered him up some. He turned the key in the ignition.

"Let's go see my friend Henry Liu. He's always good for a laugh and maybe he knows something. I'm real fucking totalled. Pissed. Let's go get a drink."

On the way to Chinatown, he drawled, "So, Art, I am wondering if you've maybe seen a picture of the dead girl at Abramsky's. Rose, that is. Cause we didn't find one. I ask about the picture, Art, because I think someone is paying Mr Snap a whole lot of dough for the pictures. Someone, some hood, some bad fuckster is getting pictures so they can ID the girls that owe them. I think Mr Snap is even taking pictures to order. I think Mr Snap is either the killer or as good as and I know you know."

"Where did you get this Mr Snap thing?"

"Same as you," he said, the car weaving into Pearl Street, the slush spewing up onto the windows. "Same as you. From Pansy."

At seventy, Henry Liu was a natty dresser. He showed me his platinum watch; it had two faces, one that told the time in New York, the other in Hong Kong.

Liu watched us eat with patrician benevolence in a private dining room at the Red Swan. Chen sampled some crispy duck. "This is excellent, Henry," he said, flattering the old man, and added casually, as he reached for another portion, "Anything new, Henry?"

"This and that." Henry turned to me. "I tell you something. Me and Jeremy, good friends, do favors for each other. Lot of new illegals now, in spite of Congress hates immigrants. You think if Congress refuse driving license, it stops people coming?" He laughed raucously.

"All of them from where's the place, Jer?"

"Fuzhou."

Henry looked up. "Fuzhou. Canton. Even Hong Kong. People shit-scared of Chinese taking over. Hong Kong up the spout. Everything's gonna change. This year, next year. They ran away from commies one time already, like me. Like me, dive into Mirs Bay in 1949, swim with sharks, get to Hong Kong, cross over barbed wire." An old man with a real relish for life, he had honed and polished his story for almost fifty years.

"Supply and demand, Art," Jerry said. "A lot of people want to get the fuck out, a lot of people oblige with papers and transportation, for a price. What else d'you know, Henry? You know a guy that takes photographs of women, Henry?"

"Sure." Henry chuckled. "Plenty."

"A particular guy." Jerry patted his mouth with a napkin. "I'll have a little more of that garlic sauce if there is any."

"Maybe I know someone who talks to you, but he needs assurances. His lawyer say so."

"Where is he?"

"He's coming." Henry Liu took out a portable phone and flipped it open, spoke very briefly, flipped it shut, waved his arm to summon more food and, by the time a platter of lamb and scallions arrived, so did a skinny boy with a crewcut.

The kid who showed at Henry's was skinny and he looked frightened, but he was manipulative. He didn't speak except when ordered to speak and his mouth was turned down with the sullen expectation of punishment. With one foot he scratched the back of his other leg. The way he lifted his scrawny shoulders let you know he considered himself a victim, or wanted you to, a persecuted member of the disenfranchised. It was all horse shit. He was a hood.

Henry gestured to a chair. Even sitting, the boy stooped. Jerry Chen gave no sign of recognition, but I could have sworn it was the same kid I saw Chen slap around on the street Tuesday morning, maybe even the same kid Hillel described; the kid didn't have a quiff, but when I looked hard, the tips of the crewcut hair showed reddish dye.

Chen smiled charmingly at the kid and at Liu and said, "Henry, can you translate?"

"I try," Henry said, and spoke to the kid, who stared at his feet.

"Eat something," Jerry told the boy, doing the relevant mime. To Henry he said, "Ask him if he knows a man who takes pictures of Chinese girls. In a white Cadillac. Goes by the name Mr Snap."

Henry said to Chen, "He would like you can help him with driver's license if he help you."

"What's wrong with his license?"

"It got taken away."

Unperturbed by the preliminary bullshit, Jerry Chen took out a business card and scribbled on the back. "Tell him this will help. If he gets picked up, tell the patrolman to give me a call. OK? Now."

"Maybe he seen this photographer."

"How tall is he?"

"Like your friend." Henry pointed to me. "Very tall."

"How fat?"

"Fat," Henry reported. "Fat like two of you, Jeremy."

Chen led the kid patiently by the nose, took him around the territory to streets, apartments, even area codes I never thought of. I was rusty. Chen cajoled, smiled, patted the kid's knee, told him to eat. He was very good, a seducer, a detective of real talent. I had almost forgotten how slow it could be, like dragging your body through a swimming pool knee deep in molasses, all the digging around for evidence that could take you into a dozen blind alleys, the well-intentioned citizens who gave you the wrong information, the informants, like this jackass, who lied. Jerry never lost it with the kid. A couple of times, Jerry adjusted his belt as if he'd eaten too much, but it was so the kid would see his gun. It was an old trick.

"What else?"

The boy mumbled something to Henry.

"What's he speaking?" I said.

"This and that. I speak Cantonese, Mandarin. This boy is Fujianese. I don't like them, but I do business with them. You surprised, detective? Business is business. He say someone planning a big snatch on ship coming with new illegals."

"They take them straight off the ship if they can," Chen explained. "They figure if someone spends thirty grand plus to get over from China, they're gonna spend an extra ten to stay alive. Illegals spend six months on a ship to get over from China, creeps kidnap them right off

131

the ship. They take girls a lot of the time. It's easier. No one gives a shit. There's always more. Even if some fuckwit professor at NYU tells us, no more crime in Chinatown. Ha ha."

"There is someone who can maybe help you, he says," Henry reported, relaying a version of what the kid said.

"Is that the one they call Chicken Chicken?" Jerry said.

"No," said Henry. "Chicken Legs."

"Not Chicken Lips?"

"Chicken Legs," Henry insisted. To me he added, "You see Cantonese, Mandarin, Fujianese, all different. All different names. Sometimes we use nicknames that sound like name."

Under my breath, I muttered to Jerry, "This is where we enter the twilight zone."

Chen nodded. "This kid doesn't know shit."

"There's a whorehouse," Henry said. "The woman drives a white Caddy sometimes."

Jerry Chen sat up. His body tensed. "Where? Where? Where the fuck is this whorehouse?"

The boy shrugged.

"Tell me where it fucking is or I'll hurt you," said Chen.

The boy lifted his head half an inch in Henry's direction and said, "Ludlow Street."

Twenty minutes later, me and Jerry Chen, both half crocked now, were on the second floor of the shitty brownstone on Ludlow Street trying to pick a lock. The hall was covered with linoleum. The light was broken. From one apartment, I could hear a lot of snores. Someone cried. Someone puked their guts out.

"Why do I get the feeling you've been here before?" Jerry asked.

It was the building where I'd seen Hillel. The building with the photo lab. The gates were down on the souvenir shop, but we managed to jimmy the front door and now, we were outside the lab on the second floor trying to break in the door.

"I don't know anything about a whorehouse, Jer."

"It's not what I fucking asked. You want to tell me what we're looking for in this dump, if it's not for the whorehouse?" Jerry shoved at the door. The frosted glass pane rattled.

"Trust me. Let's just figure this is a little light burglary, official-style, OK? You're an official-style guy."

In his coat pocket, Chen found a bunch of locksmith's tools and messed with the lock some more. Without any warning the door to an apartment opened and a man bolted into the hall. He was in pajamas. He shouted at us. Chen chased him back through his open door. I followed.

The one-room apartment was about ten by twelve. In three rows of triple-decker bunk beds, eight men were asleep. I couldn't see much, but from the dark recesses came the snores and splutters, the cries and wheezes. The place was damp and fetid. Our guy stood near the doorway and stared hard at us. He got a good look, then crept back into his bunk. We backed out into the hall and went back to the photo lab.

"For Chrissake, Jerry, let me do it." I snatched the keys out of his hand.

"Fucking fine with me." He began to laugh. "You think this is how the bad guys do it? Try a credit card," he said and we cracked up, the two of us, drunk as skunks, trying to pick a lock in the middle of the night.

The lab was a mess. As soon as Jerry switched on a light I saw someone besides us had been nosing around. Boxes of photographs had been turned upside down. Chen lifted some of them off the floor and dumped them onto the sales counter.

"Fucking hell," he said. "How'd you find out about this dump?"

Rose's picture was in my pocket. I showed him the numbers printed on the back. I told him about Eljay.

"It's one of the advanced photo systems. I've got one of the same fucking cameras. Mr Snap is a state-of-the-art guy. He's using one of these." Chen pulled a small stainless steel camera out of his pocket. It was the size of a pack of cigarettes. Examining Rose's picture, he said, "The pictures we picked up before were always Polaroids. No way to trace them. This time the son of a bitch left us what we need on print. Right on the goddamn print."

"What was that?"

"What was what?"

I said, "In the hall. Shut up for a minute."

"Maybe it's the whores, Art." Already Chen was turning the boxes upside down, sales slips, prints, cassettes of film spilling onto the counter. "Look for anything with numbers that match the numbers on the

134

girl's picture. Anything. Sales slip. Other prints. You understand computer stuff?"

"About like DNA." I was looking through the shelves behind the counter now. There were piles of stuff—pictures, photo albums. Some of it was still on the shelves, some had been tossed on the floor. My guess was someone else wanted what we wanted. Then I heard Jerry Chen explode.

"Shit," he yelled. "Shit shit shit."

"What?" I got up from behind the counter. Jerry had his hands full of glossy prints.

"First, I thought to myself, why would anyone risk leaving evidence on the prints? Now I get it. It's because you can stick these pictures on a computer, you can send them by e-mail. Everything you can do with a big digital camera, you can do with this baby."

"So?"

"For years the snakeheads—the smugglers—had to circulate lists of names, the illegals that owed money. Now they can ID them with pictures. I bet they use it to lean on the families back home too. Extort them. Squeeze them."

"How do they earn that kind of dough? You said, what? Thirty, thirty-five grand." I pulled a box of sales slips off a shelf and sat on the floor and looked through them.

"You saw the way they live, across the hall? The poor fuckers live like that. They work six, seven days, two, three jobs. They don't spend. They can earn a thousand bucks a week."

On his knees now, Jerry scrabbled among envelopes

135

of photographs. Then he whistled. One after the other, he opened them, held them upside down and let the pictures fall onto the floor, a stream of glossies, a torrent of tits. He spread them around, turning them face up, one at a time, like a man obsessed with a game of solitaire.

"Jesus fucking Christ." Chen grabbed at my sleeve. "Look!"

Most of the women in the pictures were naked. Most of them were spread shots. The women simpered and smoldered and struck poses, every lewd pose you could think of, girls alone, girls on girls, with boys, and all of them Chinese.

"You think some of the girls that got snapped with the white Caddy also posed for a little light porn? Is that what we're talking?"

Chen scooped them up and got up off the floor. "I don't know. I'm going to find out, though. You know what I think? I don't think there is any whorehouse. I think this is it. It's the fucking pictures, man. I think we found our whores."

It was getting to be a long night and it got longer. I never went back to the club, never called. I knew I'd be out of a job, but I had to keep going. Something was fermenting, brewing, boiling up, something was going to happen before this night was over, I felt it in my bones. We left Ludlow Street. For a while, we cruised the downtown bars—Mercury, Match, Pravda, Bowery—Chen looking more and more hangdog at every stop. The photographs were in his pocket but he wasn't in any hurry to do a follow up. Instead, he drove around, slumped low in his seat, mired in some kind of obsession that made me keep my mouth shut and play his game. In front of the Odeon on West Broadway, he jammed the brakes on and slapped a police card on the dashboard. We got out.

"You're not gonna lock your car?"

He laughed. "What for? Anyone steals it, I'll just shoot them."

And then Chen's face lighted up like a kid in a candy store. "She's here, Art." He was excited. "She's here."

At a round table, a thin black style-guru who even I'd heard of was sitting with a no-tit English model. They were eating steak and mashed potatoes, and, between them, Coco Katz, the designer, held court.

Skinny, imperious and tall, Coco Katz looked up and Chen practically drooled over her. Eyes hopeful, smoothing his hair over and over, Jerry waited.

"I like your clothes," I said to Coco.

She looked me over briefly like I was bubble-wrap. "Do you?" she said. She turned to Chen. "Let's get out of here, Jeremy."

"She lost a big order, she's upset," Jerry said, as I made for the door. "You know."

"Sure, Jer. I know," I said.

He watched Katz get her coat on. "So, Art, you'll give Pansy my regards when you see her."

"Leave it alone."

"I can't do that," he said. "It's for her own good. I told her that."

He followed his girlfriend out the door. I went out

after them and stood a few feet from Jerry and Coco Katz as they waited for her limo.

"You gonna tell her, Art? You'll tell Pansy, won't you?"

"Your friend, Jerry, she uses the sweatshops? She uses them to make her fancy outfits, huh?"

"Fuck you. Just tell her. Tell her she has to talk to me. Tell Pansy Loh, if she isn't already dead." Jerry took a picture out of his pocket and flipped it to me.

"You found that at the lab?"

"Nope. This one I already had. This one I been fucking saving to give you, Art."

It was another picture of Pansy.

13

Queens, as a borough, is a lot like hell: it bleeds at the edges and becomes Long Island, but, after I left Chen in front of the Odeon, I went to Queens because of the sales slip I found in the lab on Ludlow Street. The numbers of the slip matched the numbers encoded on the back of Rose's photograph. There was an address in Flushing. It wasn't much. But I didn't have much. Also, I'd called Lily three times; she must be out with Leung. What were they talking about? Babies?

Like everywhere else, the streets in Flushing were dead. White and dead. Small neat houses, strip malls, all of them hunkered down, inanimate, frozen.

I stood in the middle of the suburban street and looked around. Where was I? I got out the map of the city which I always carry—a lot of times it's better than a gun—and tried to figure out where in the hell I was.

When I did, I walked a couple blocks and found the address. It was a vacant lot. A vacant lot full of broken bottles and piles of dirty snow. A brick wall ran along the back of the lot and I went to see what was on the other side when the thing fell on me. It grabbed my hair and clawed the dry cold skin on my face, but the adrenalin shot into my system and even my legs pumped as I threw it off, whatever it was. Without looking back, I ran like a bat out of hell. After a block I stopped and put my hands on my knees and tried to get my breath. I looked back. The street was empty and I realized what had jumped me in the vacant lot was a huge, fat, feral cat. The skin on my face was lacerated; the thing had missed my eye, but when I put my hand on my cheek it came away wet with blood.

Shivering on the corner in Flushing, I tried to orient myself and get to a subway. I was wondering if New York cats were ever rabid, when a gypsy cab stopped for the light and I leaped into the street and banged on the door.

"Going home, bub," said the driver.

"Where's home?" I said. He said Brooklyn and I got in. For thirty bucks, he dropped me off near the bridge; the bastard wouldn't even cross the bridge to Manhattan, so I set off, hands jammed in my pockets, face burned raw with scratches and fatigue.

I didn't know what to make of Jerry Chen. He blew hot and cold. He was a smart cop but a tortured angry man, and he was in thrall to Coco Katz. I pitied him for that; it happens to all of us, one time or another.

A wind tugged a cloud cover back over the sky, and the arches of the Brooklyn Bridge soared against the whitening sky. On the wooden walkway of the bridge, a man passed, a miner's light fixed to his forehead. By the time I got to the other side, I was half frozen.

"Hey, pal, you need a lift?" The driver looked down from the cab of the garbage truck that resembled a tank in the dark. "Come on. We'll take you home." He stretched out an arm and pulled me up.

I let him and his partner know I'd been a cop and they shared some lukewarm beer and took me home, tooting out the garbage-truck fugue. Listening to the wise-ass on the radio, we had a few yuks. More snow was coming. Lotta overtime, said the garbage men, and passed me a bag of pretzels.

From the imperial heights of the garbage truck, I looked back and saw City Hall and the courts and the building where Sonny Lippert works. The truck skirted Chinatown and then I was home.

Upstairs, I stood in front of the window while the truck ate some garbage. I waved at the guy who gave me a ride.

The three windows on the street are eight feet high; I felt like a man in a fishbowl and it wasn't the first time I'd had the sensation. For years I thought about getting some shades, but the windows are big and the shades are expensive and besides, I love the south light, especially in the winter.

Next summer, I always say to myself. I'll get some blinds when summer hits; but I never do. It's like airport security. I only think about the bad stuff after a crash.

Exhausted, I took a shower, stuck some bandaids on the cuts on my face and climbed into bed.

But I was hungry. I rummaged in the fridge. Somewhere, a clock I couldn't find was ticking. It was driving me nuts. I called for take-out and I didn't even consider the irony of it until I buzzed the delivery guy in, looked through the peephole on my door and saw the boy carrying the brown bag with my ginger chicken in it had a big red quiff. He raised his arm, winding up like a pitcher, and, in his hand, I saw the five-pronged spike.

I woke up. I had been dreaming.

The clock kept on ticking like an alarm clock you can't find in the middle of the night. You run around, you look under the bed, dive in the dirty clothes. I stared at the ceiling. It was after four a.m. I was wide awake. The blankets were a mess.

"I don't want trouble with the Chinese," I heard Hillel Abramsky say. It was what he said Monday morning when he called me, when he found Rose dead on his floor. Hillel said the family sold the shop in Flushing because the Chinese came in. The Flushing shop.

I got out of bed again, pulled on some jeans, got a beer, slammed on more heat. I ransacked the bottom drawer of my desk for old address books. Yes! I thought. Yes. The address on the sales slip, the address of the vacant lot was the same as the defunct Abramsky shop. A shop where Hillel's brother, Sherman, once worked. A shop where Sherm stole and Hillel fired him.

Sherman Abramsky. When Sherm was supplying hookers to a Hasidic brothel in Brighton Beach, Hillel had called me. I had only met him a couple of times, but it was plenty. Sherm the Sperm, they used to call him. Hard to believe him and Hil are brothers. But Sherm was a dirtbag, not a killer. He was also in Israel, last I heard, last time Hillel mentioned it. Fixing up his life, that's what Hillel had said.

I called an old number I had for Sherm on Essex Street. No one answered. I called Hillel's house. A machine picked up. Ash growing on my cigarette, I sent a fax to Haifa to a guy I went to college with who's a cop now. Then I called him at home.

"Adam's on his way to work," his wife said in Hebrew. I left a message. Then I waited and I must have dozed in the chair. I had dreams where Lily posed with a white Cadillac like the dead women. Like them, she wore a pink jacket; unlike them, she held a Chinese baby that was fat like a sumo wrestler and cried relentlessly. I took the baby to comfort it, but I didn't hold it right and it slipped out of my hand and cracked its head open on the floor.

I got back into bed and, in the groggy period before I slept, an Abramsky family wedding came into focus. Sherm had left the hall, then come back, zipping his fly, so's everyone would think he'd been upstairs with some woman. Then he started taking pictures. Hillel says, "No, no, you can't take pictures here. I don't want pictures you take of my family lying around," he says, like Sherm would steal their souls.

I don't know what time it was, but the fucking clock was ringing again. I threw the covers off and groped on the night table, knocked my gun onto the floor, crawled under the bed where all I found were a couple of rubber bands Lily uses to keep her hair out of her eyes. I couldn't breathe. I was losing my fucking mind. But it wasn't a clock that was ringing at all. It was the phone. Expecting Adam's call from Haifa, I fell on it.

"This is Pansy."

"Where are you?"

"On the corner," she said. "Canal near Mott. There's a telephone booth."

"Do you want to come to my place?"

"No."

"I'll be there."

It was dumb, what I did. I got on my boots and some ski stuff and I ran.

When I got to Canal Street, Pansy was leaning against the payphone, plastic shopping bag over her arm. She was wearing the red hat, two down vests, sweatpants and purple high tops.

"I've been looking for you."

"I want you to stop. Stop leaving messages for me," she said. "Please."

"Is someone bothering you?"

She glanced up and down the street and hesitated and bit her fingernail.

"Shall I show you something? Do you want to see?"

"Show me."

We crossed Canal Street. A few trucks rumbled towards the bridge. Some of the ice had melted under the heat of traffic and in the gutters were rivers of slush. The frozen ooze poured over Pansy's thin canvas sneakers as she turned into Eldridge Street. A ball of crumpled newspaper tumbled along the curb in the breeze, but nothing else moved.

Pansy walked into the middle of the street and looked at an empty parking lot. "This is where they unloaded us," she said.

"Unloaded who?"

"Are you cold?" she stalled. I shook my head and she started to talk. "I was lucky. There was a boat that was only ninety per cent full. That's how they do it: 'Let's put a few more on,' they say. They count the bodies. So many bodies, so many dollars. I received a stolen passport with my picture and name already in it. We traveled to Thailand first. Something was wrong with the ship, and a few of us were put on an airplane to Canada. Winnipeg, Canada. On the plane we flushed our papers down the toilet, so that we could claim asylum if we got lucky. The Indians took us over the border."

"Indians?"

"The reservations straddle the border. The Indians make their own laws. They're very poor. Then we got in the fruit truck." She walked towards the parking lot. She remembered.

"It was summer and you could smell the spoiled fruit. The truck pulled up before dawn. They said, 'You over there, you on this side.' There were three men who had quite a lot of guns. Several more arrived soon after in a large black car. It was very hot."

Walking slowly around the lot, Pansy conjured up the summer morning, humidity like primal ooze, a squad of men in Raybans with guns. The fruit trucks. The women climbing out of them, arriving in New York weeks, maybe months after they left China, faces glazed with incomprehension and fear. They climbed out of the stinking fruit trucks with only a small bag and a little silk pouch that contained a souvenir from home. A hundred women were divided into lines by men with guns and lists of names.

" 'You over there,' they would say," Pansy recalled. " 'You there.' It depended on who had paid the smugglers in full and could be delivered to relatives or friends, who had a deal with another smuggling gang and would be bussed to Brooklyn or Flushing. Others with no connections. Like me," she said. "A phone was passed. For fifty dollars, you could buy two telephone calls, one home, one to a friend or relative here. I didn't need the phone. I have no family." She paused. "Did you know you can order illegals? Two dishwashers, one cook."

Looking around the empty street, I imagined them: the women separated into groups, some with jobs and relatives, some not so lucky. I shivered, but not from the cold this time. Pansy laughed a short mirthless chuckle. "I owed a lot of money. But I had met a woman on the fruit truck who knew of a sewing shop that would take us. Someone else gave me the name of a man who owned a restaurant. He had a room above the restaurant. I rented a bed in it. He wasn't family, but he was a decent man. A friend. Better than family," she said bitterly and kept walking. "Is that enough or would you like to see more?"

Plastic sheeting covered part of the site where Pansy stopped abruptly. It was the poorest edge of Chinatown, near the projects and the South Street Viaduct, a sinister stretch of raw open ground. The building had been a warehouse or garage but it was derelict now, the scarred metal shutter covered in graffiti, the glass in the door at the side of the building was broken.

She pushed open the door.

The warehouse was empty, the concrete floor stained with damp. In a corner, Pansy found a construction worker's lamp on a long flex cord and turned it on.

In the back was a door that swung on a rusty hinge. I followed Pansy into a room where there was a cot, a table, two rickety chairs and a dead television set. A sink with rust stains stood under a small window. Yellow curtains sagged from a broken rod. The window was patched with duct tape and plastic.

Wiping the table with paper towels she took from her bag, Pansy sat down, put a thermos on the table, followed by two plastic cups, two teabags and some chocolate. "Please have something."

I unwrapped a Chunky and ate it and Pansy chuckled. "We steal it from the fat boy at work, you remember him? He's an evil child. He spies on us. Do you have a wife, detective?"

"No."

"A girlfriend?"

"Yes," I said.

"Does she have a name?"

"Her name is Lily."

"Is it her real name?" she asked, and I wondered if the chat was some kind of defense, a way of making the ugly hovel fit for human beings.

"Yeah, sure. Why?"

147

"Well, it's the name of a flower. Like me. Shall I tell you about this place?"

Pansy removed her wet purple sneakers. Wind rattled the plastic sheets outside into sails that crackled. Footsteps came, then went. Greedily, she ate more chocolate and looked up. "I am addicted." Touching her mouth daintily with a piece of rough paper towel, she began to talk again.

She was illegal, Pansy said. Her father was a Chinese-American who fought in Vietnam at the end of the war. Her mother was ethnic Chinese, her own parents from Fujian Province, and a Catholic. She had been a school-teacher in Saigon. It was a last fling before the helicopters lifted off the roof of the U.S. embassy. They were stranded: Pansy who was a baby, her mother, a son from the mother's previous marriage. Eventually they scraped up the money to buy a place on a boat and got to Hong Kong. Were put in a camp.

"You would not put pigs in these camps," Pansy said. "Nothing to do. Brutal guards. Hong Kong just over the barbed wire, but Hong Kong didn't want us. No one wanted us. The young boys in the camps became monsters. Some of the monsters are here."

"How do you know?"

"My brother was one of them."

"Where is he?"

"Dead, I hope. I haven't heard from Thomas for years. I hope he is dead." She crossed herself, and then leaped lightly from the chair and, in her wet green socks and the red hat, did an ecstatic little dance.

"May 1996," she said. "I helped to burn the camp.

148

We danced by the fire. You could see the light for miles and miles. Then we ran. I lost Mom. A few of us got away into the hills. Later, I heard she was dead."

Pansy had learned Cantonese in the camp and her English was good—her mother had taught her and it was her secret weapon. She hid in the hills, then ran again. She worked wherever she could. She scraped together enough money to bribe someone who could fix papers and the passage to America. To the Golden Mountain.

I showed her the red cloth flower Hillel found with Rose. She spread it on her hand.

"I've got one. Rose made them for us. She was a simple girl. She said it would be our lucky charm. She owed the smugglers even more than I owed them."

A thin morning light showed through the window and I could hear the trucks rumble past and I said for the second time, "What is this place?"

Pansy hesitated for a few seconds. In a low expressionless voice she said, "This is where they brought us."

"Brought who?"

"Rose and me. We were kidnapped together. They brought us here." Pansy clasped her hands around her cup. "They were waiting for me after work. They took Rose off the street on her way home. There was a man they took, as well."

"What happened to him?"

"They killed him. They made us watch. They strangled him with piano wire and dragged him away. Later I heard that they had tossed the body somewhere off the Long Island Expressway."

I held out a pack of cigarettes, but Pansy shook her

149

head and broke a chocolate bar in half. "That month, I didn't even owe, I was on time with my payments. But they have become impatient. They take you even if you do not owe them. They take you and squeeze you for more money. I thought it would never happen to me. I was too intelligent." She got up and stood at the window and I wanted to put my hand on her shoulder, but I didn't. I just didn't.

"How long did they hold you?"

She stared out at the building opposite. "A few days, I think. Rose was a silly girl. She was a good girl, but she wasn't pretty. She couldn't earn extra money like some girls. As a whore, you know? She worked all the time, but she could never keep up with her payments."

Quietly, Pansy emptied her thermos into the sink, screwed the cap on, put the chocolate wrappers in her bag and began pulling on the purple sneakers.

"They raped us." Her voice was barely audible. She tied her shoe laces very carefully, first into knots, then into bows. "They raped us over and over. They made us have sex with each other, Rose and me. They were animals and they drank whiskey and watched. They made bets on how long we could go on, and behind their masks, they laughed. They were cowards who wore ski masks. Do you want me to continue?" she asked formally.

"The men wore masks all the time?"

"Yes. But I felt they were young, boys, not men."

"Could you see the hair?"

"It was dyed. Henna. But so what? Many of them do this. Do you want to hear about the flashlights they put

150

in some of the women? Do you want to know how they cut off their fingers?"

"Tell me what you want to tell me."

"They called Rose's mother in her village."

"How? How did they call?"

"There are telephones everywhere now. The snake-heads have phones. They put Rose on with her mother and she cried. Then they grabbed the phone away and told her mother she had four hours to raise ten thousand dollars. Four hours. They hit Rose some more. I heard them in the next room. They hit her and she cried. Then they went away."

"Why?"

"Why? God knows why. It happens. They hear something. They get scared. The boss tells them to stop."

"What boss?"

"I don't know." For the first time she averted her eyes as if there was a lie embedded in what she said. "I don't know. I broke this window and dragged Rose out with me. After that, I rarely saw her. She went to work in a different shop. She called me and said she was all right, she had met a man. Then you told me she was dead. I tried to call her mother. I left a message. Rose gave me a few things to keep and I sent them to her mother, but her mother had gone. Maybe she is also dead."

"I'm sorry."

"Do you know that I am not sure if, until the day she died, if Rose ever had a day off, if she ever left Chinatown. She was always frightened. Always."

We left the warehouse and Pansy said, "I must go now."

"Why are you telling me all this?"

"Things are getting worse. More illegals. More kidnapping. More opportunity. When Hong Kong goes, or the year after it goes, it will be a field day. Smuggle, kidnap, extort, kill."

"How do you know so much?" I asked. Pansy didn't answer.

"I'll try to get you some papers. Some money."

I could see she didn't believe me. "Thank you," she said. "The money will be good."

"Does Jerry Chen know all this?"

"Some. He knew about me."

"How?"

"He knew because I told him." Pansy looked at me as if trying to divine something from my face.

"I'm not Jerry Chen."

"I went to him. I asked around. Chinatown, immigrants, news travels like wild fire, especially about the cops. Everyone gossips about the cops. Even about you," she said. " 'I'll take care of you,' he said. But he lied. No one took care of me. Or of Rose."

"Who took the pictures?"

"I told you I don't know. A large man. He never said his name."

"American?"

"Yes. He always wore sunglasses. He changed places. Someone always knew where to find him. We all wanted pictures. To send home, show we made it on the Golden Mountain. Then he started coming to us. He wanted pictures for himself, he said. But for what? Not for *Playboy* magazine, surely," she joked.

"Do you think he killed Rose?"

"Perhaps."

We stood together on the street and I said I thought she had guts, but it embarrassed her.

"Some of us are normal. Human, you know? Not all of us are pathetic girls with the names of flowers. You always think of us as girls, don't you? You don't even ask our real names."

"Is Pansy your real name?"

"My mother was a good Catholic. She attended a French convent in Saigon. I was baptized Marie Christine." She took a slip of paper from her pocket and wrote neatly on it.

"Try this address. It's a playground. You might find the white car in the photo. I have to go to work now."

"I'll walk with you."

"No thankyou." She pulled her hat down hard and glanced at the whitening sky. "I'm not frightened. There is nothing left they can do to me." She looked back at the warehouse and behind the glasses her eyes glittered the way they did when she told me she helped burn the camp down. "If they come near me again, I will kill them."

"Again?"

"It happens. They have no souls. While they were still beating Rose, one of the boys yanked her hair so hard it came out in his hand, and then he said to his friend, 'Why don't we just strangle the ugly one?'"

14

But Rose had been outside Chinatown before she died, it turned out. I found the evidence in the white Caddy the morning I left Pansy at the warehouse. I headed towards the river, her words echoing in my ear. "Why don't we strangle the ugly one?" Pansy wasn't ugly. Did that make her safe? If being pretty somehow protected you, why did she hide her looks? Who was she behind the glasses?

The white Cadillac was parked, like Pansy said it would be, behind the backboard of a handball court in one of the rag-tag parks near the projects along the East River. The car was stranded in frozen snow, the bodywork streaked with grime. Someone had dumped it in a big hurry.

I'm lousy at picking locks. Breaking into cars is something else. The way I carry a gun, I carry a couple of car remotes. It took me about thirty seconds to tune one of them to the right frequency for the Caddy. I was in.

One whiff of the interior had me reeling. Someone

had been sick as a cat inside the car. On the red leather seat was an empty pizza box, a pile of girlie magazines, the pink jacket with fur around the hood and a shoebox. Holding my nose, I grabbed the box and slammed the door. In the street, I butted heads with a delivery guy on a bike. An order of sesame noodles flew up in the air and fell on him. I didn't care. I had the car. The license. A box of goodies. Finally.

Even before I got home, I pulled a handful of cassettes of undeveloped film out of the shoebox. By the time I got to my place, the fax had spit some paper onto the floor. I threw off my jacket. The fax was from Haifa. Call me, Adam said. Call me ASAP. Kicking off my boots, I dialed Israel. Adam came on the line.

"Artie? We picked up some guy similar to the one you mentioned, but a different name. Maybe it's an alias. I'm looking to get you a picture of him. You got e-mail or what?"

"Fax me," I said. "What did you pick him up for?"

"We found out he was dealing in a little light porn. Not worth upsetting you Americans by holding a citizen. We put him on a plane and told him to scram for good."

"What kind of porn?"

"Girls. Young women. Mostly Oriental."

"Put a rush on this."

"We're overloaded here, but I'll do my best. You want me to look in on your mother, Artie?"

My mother's in a nursing home in Haifa, her mind claimed by Alzheimer's as if by some evil cult master. Every year, I make the trip. She doesn't know who I am.

"Artie?"

"Thanks, Adam. Yeah. Take her some candy, OK?"
I hung up and called Hillel. A machine answered.

"Hillel, please, pick up the fucking phone." By now
I was cheesed off. Hillel Abramsky had been evasive, he
had lied to me. "Pick it up."

"Yes?" Hillel sounded dog tired.

"You know this address in Flushing?"

"I know."

"What is it?"

"It's my uncle's old shop. The little shop he sold when
the Chinese took over the neighborhood. I have to get
off, Artie."

"Who else has keys to your place on 47th Street, Hil?
Don't fuck me over."

"No one. Like I told you, we got excellent security. I
keep a set at home, but only Judith knows where."

"Who else? If you won't tell me I'm coming out
there. Talk to me. You got me into this. You owe me
the truth."

There was a long silence.

"Don't ask me that, Artie," Hillel said and the phone
went dead.

The rest of the day, I worked the phone. There were
still a few friends out there I could call and I got someone
to try running the license plate on the Caddy. Eljay
Koplin came by and picked up the film cassettes and
swore he'd get the prints back that night.

I slept for a few hours, but the phone woke me and I
fell on it, figuring it was the picture Adam had promised.
The American who took porn pictures. I was wrong.

"You don't care, do you?" Dawn was so wired she could barely speak; she was needy, demanding, incoherent. Someone took the phone away from her and I heard her gasp.

"What should I do?" Pete came on the line, voice imploring me. "What do you think? What do you understand about all this, Artie? Tell me. Help me."

I said to keep her at home, if he could, and then I called Uncle Billy Tae and told him to get the locks on Ricky's apartment changed. Some break-ins in the building had been reported, vandalism due to the storm, I lied. Lying was second nature by now.

Billy didn't ask any questions. He said, "I'll do it right away," and I wondered if I had dropped Dawn Tae into worse shit, if I had forced her onto the street to buy what she needed. Hot Poppy was what she scored, snorted, smoked. Hot Poppy that could make you bleed from the ears, according to Pete.

That night, Eljay returned with some prints; most of them were of scenery. The tenth snap I looked at was of Rose.

It was identical to the picture I'd found on her body, except this one was a widescreen view. It showed Rose and the car, but included in the margins now was a piece of boardwalk, a scrap of ocean, a sign in Russian. I knew exactly where that boardwalk was, I knew better than I wanted to. Rose had been out of Chinatown before she died all right. She had been in Brighton Beach. And if he took this picture like he took the other one of her, I was betting she'd been there with Mr Snap.

★

Huge snowdrifts were piled along the side of the Belt and the river spat up gray chunks of ice as I drove out to Brighton Beach in Mike Rizzi's old station wagon. Lily was with me. She had called early that morning and said she wanted to talk. Wanted to see me. Now, the road was clear, the sun out, she drank coffee and ate a raisin bagel, passing me bite-sized chunks and declaring her delight at a brief jaunt out to the beach. "I love the beach in the winter," she said.

After the night with Pansy in the basement, after the vision of hell down there, I needed to be with Lily. With her, even Brighton Beach would be OK. The last few days it had hit home: it was better for me with Lily around. I was a jerk not to tell her why I was going to Brooklyn.

She didn't ask me why we were going even though she knows I hate Brighton Beach. For half an hour, while I drove the ten miles south from Manhattan, Lily and I laughed and drifted apart and it was my fucking fault because I didn't tell her.

Brighton Beach. The Atlantic Ocean and the board-walk, the main drag covered by the elevated train, the ugly side streets, and everything Russian—the chatter in the streets, the restaurants—Odessa, Café Arbat—the food shops, even the Hello Gorgeous Beauty Salon, all Russian. A few years back I spent a lot of time in Brighton Beach. It had raised the specter of a past I'd worked real hard to obliterate. I hated coming here. What's more, I'd helped put away a few of the creeps who terrorized the neighborhood. People knew my face. If Jerry Chen had been right that first morning on the street in Chinatown, if the Russians and Chinese were doing some business together, it could make a guy like me very paranoid.

But Lily was with me and the sun felt good. We strolled, I kept an eye out for the sign in the photograph of Rose. It was probably a wild-goose chase, but I had to do it.

On the beach where the ocean pounded the sand, scavenger birds who didn't make it south for the winter hunted for crumbs like homeless guys looking for soda cans to recycle. Two old men lumbered across the snow-drifts that clung to the sand and dove into the freezing water.

We stopped at a café near the boardwalk and sat in the window. From the other tables came the chatter of Russian. Outside, a few passers-by cruised the board-walk. I watched intently. I don't know what I expected to find. Did I expect to see Mr Snap wander by, a Chinese girl in tow?

Lily ate a bowl of borscht. Then she ordered cherry strudel.

"Do you want to tell me what we're doing here, Artie? It's the thing with Hillel, isn't it? It's the dead woman from Hillel's." Lily was no dope.

"You know me pretty well." I lit a cigarette. "You know I hate this place. You must have known. I thought you were feeling better. You turn everything into some kind of mortal combat. This is who I am, OK? What is it with you?"

"Aren't you going to ask about my hormones?"

"For God's sake, give me some credit. When do I

159

ever lay that kind of Mickey Mouse macho trip on you? When? I need you is all."

For a few seconds we were both silent, then Lily said softly, "Tell me how I can help you."

Lily helped. I showed her the photograph. We poked around Brighton Beach for a couple of hours, then she spotted the sign in the picture. The sign on the window was in Russian, but it had been partly rubbed out and replaced by a sign in Chinese. The woman inside didn't know about any photographer. I leaned on her. It was getting cold. The sun was going down. A pair of old men passed, heading for synagogue. Friday night. Friday night! It gave me an idea, or maybe I just wanted to get out of Brighton Beach.

"Let's go home."

"Artie?"

"What?"

"Can I stay over at your place tomorrow night?"

"Do you have to ask?"

The mugshot of Mr Snap was on my fax machine when I got home and I snatched it, took Lily home, and drove to the restaurant. All I needed was confirmation. All I needed was for Pansy to ID Mr Snap. My scalp tingled I was so close.

In the restaurant, one table was occupied by customers scarfing up their food. At another Pansy sat reading a book. I pushed the mugshot across the table. "Is it him?"

"It's him. He takes the photographs."

"Mr Snap?"

"Yes."

"Do you know his real name?"

"Did you find him?" She was agitated. "Do you know who he is?"

"I think so. Was he Rose's special friend?"

"I don't know. Rose never told me. Will you arrest him? Soon?"

"Yes. I swear to God. And if it's him, if he's Rose's killer, you'll be safe. He'll be off the streets."

Pansy removed her glasses and rubbed her eyes. I saw a mix of disbelief and hope in them. "Then hurry," she said urgently. "Hurry."

I was back in Mike's station wagon when the cell-phone rang. The guy I know at Motor Vehicles was on the line. "I got a registration for you on the white Caddy."

"Go on."

"Do you know a guy name of, uh, Abramsky?"

My stomach flipped over. "First name? Is there a first name?"

"Yeah. Hillel. Something like that. Hope that helps, pal."

Christ, I thought. Jesus fucking Christ. If the car was registered in Hillel's name, he knew. All along he knew. I spun the car towards Brooklyn. Hillel would be in synagogue on a Friday evening. Then I slammed on the brakes. I called Jerry Chen and told him where to meet me. I needed someone official. This time, I planned on doing more than breaking into a car.

"Personally, I think it's another fucking waste of time. Art, but I'm on your side so I'll be there for you. Too right! I mean it's my fucking case. Isn't it?"

★

The sun was almost gone. Most of the shops on 47th Street had already shut. Chen was waiting for me in front of Hillel Abramsky's building and we went up the stairs. I banged on the door. Chen pulled off the remains of the yellow police tape and shouldered the door. He didn't have to bother. All we found inside, in the dark, were two frightened men.

Back against the wall, Hillel was smoking a cigarette. Near him, cowering on the cot, was the man Pansy had identified as Mr Snap, Hillel's only brother, Sherm Abramsky. The floor was still stained with Rose's blood.

15

It wasn't Sherm or even the stained floor that shocked me most when I turned on the light in Hillel's office. It was Hilly himself. The black clothes were gone, so was the beard. He wore a flannel shirt and jeans. He dealt with his grief by throwing away religious habits he loved. I realized he was a young, handsome man, but his face looked naked. I always wondered if there was anything that could make Hillel give up his faith; his own brother had finally done it. I never saw a sadder face.

Chen put handcuffs on Sherm. Hillel stayed where he was, smoking.

"You called me in because you hoped I'd find someone else to pin the murder on, didn't you?"

"No. Not at first. Not Monday morning when I called you. Monday night I found this." He held out a camera. "That's why I was running around Chinatown. But I still hoped. Forgive me, Artie. Forgive me."

"You found the camera here?"

"No. In my house. He left this in my basement. He

left the camera, he left dirty pictures. For my kids to find. For my kids!"

While we talked, Chen kept Sherm at bay. I was beginning to acquire a little respect for Jerry Chen.

"A car he uses is registered in your name, Hillel. Did you know that?"

"I didn't, God help me. I swear."

"How'd you know he would be here, at your office?"

Hillel laughed despairingly. "I figured out he would come here to hide, it being Friday night and everything on 47th Street shut early. I got a call from a cop in Israel checking on Sherm, I knew you must be closing in. He assumed he was safe here. He depended on my faith for it." Hillel raised his hands in sorrow. "My good faith."

Jerry Chen pulled me aside. "It's getting late. I can give you ten, fifteen minutes, if you want. After that, he's mine. OK?"

"OK. And Jerry?"

"What?"

"Thanks."

"I'll keep an eye out in case we get any company." Jerry turned to Sherm. "I'll be listening, asshole, you understand? Then I'm taking you in." Chen pulled a chair into the hall. He left the door ajar. Hillel remained standing.

There was a stool and I put it near the cot so I could look Sherm in the face. He was a large flabby man with dark glasses and a Stetson on his head. I removed the glasses. His eyes welled up.

"How about a cigarette?" he sniveled.

"Then talk to me, putz. Talk to me."

"I didn't kill anyone. Artie, you got to believe me. For my brother's sake." He was shameless.

"Why didn't you kill Hillel while you were at it? Why didn't you put a gun in his mouth instead of killing him slowly, like this? And the car, Sherm. Even that."

He wiped his mouth with his hand. "It was a joke."

"Shut up. You want to talk. Tell me about Mr Snap. How he made a living. Who paid him to take pictures. This picture, for instance." I put the photograph of Rose and the white Caddy on the table. "Whose car is it? Who do you work for? What's in Brighton Beach?"

"It's my car."

I got up.

"Artie, don't go. Can you get me something to eat? Huh, Artie? I'm hungry, man."

"Talk. Then you eat."

"It's no big deal. I ran a little business. I offered a package deal. I could do some Polaroids. Plus a three-minute call home on the cellphone, if they wanted. For fifty bucks. I could also take portraits. I was good." He glanced over his shoulder at his brother. "You think I'm just a fat scumbag that can't do anything, don't you?"

To me he said, "Our father wouldn't let me be a photographer. It wasn't right, taking pictures of women, he said."

"You took some of these, too?" Jerry had given me the nudie shots from the lab. I tossed them on the cot next to Sherm.

"Some." He barely glanced at them. "I smell pizza." He looked at his hands, then at me. His eyes were round, damp and cunning.

Sherm was always crap. But until now I'd have cast him as black comedy instead of criminal, a pimp at worst. Now I saw there was also something inhuman about him. The animal desire to feed himself, the brutal disengagement with everything except his own appetites, the self-obsession, they made me believe he could have killed Rose. I looked at the stained floor. His eyes followed mine but his were blank as holes. No one human lived there.

"Tell me who really owns the white Cadillac."

"It's mine." The soft white face beckoned. I could happily sink my fist in it, I thought. I wouldn't even bruise my fingers.

"You never earned enough money to buy a car like that and you're too stupid to steal one."

"Gimme a smoke."

"I have other things to do. I'm sure Detective Chen will be happy to talk to you instead."

"Wait." The voice quavered.

"I'm waiting."

"OK, I knew the dead girl."

I sat down again. "What was her name?"

"She said her name was Rose. She was nice. I met a lot of nice girls."

"Whores?"

"Rose wasn't a whore. She wasn't pretty enough." For girls like Rose, ugly could be the same as dead.

"You took pity on her, is that it, Sherm? You helped her out."

"Yeah. She was my friend. She was nice. I showed her a good time."

"In Brighton Beach?"

"That's right. What's wrong with that? She liked the ocean."

I showed him Pansy's picture. "Was she nicer than this one?"

"They were friends, Rose and Pansy."

"Did Pansy know your name? Who you were?"

"No. I saw her once when I took her picture. She was very stuck up. Not like the others," Sherm went on. Hillel chainsmoked.

I leaned into Sherm's face. "Who owns the fucking car? Who set you up in business?"

"One of the Chinese guys. He said I could use it if I gave him a percentage from the pictures. Also he wanted copies. He got me a fancy new camera."

"What's his name?"

"I don't know. Everything was done by beeper or fax, except once in a while the errand boy came and got pictures from me."

"The errand boy who tried to shake down your brother? A guy with a line in toilet paper? A guy with red hair and a quiff? Or a crewcut?"

"I don't know. Both."

"Both. Jesus, Sherm. I'm getting tired of this shit."

"Maybe he changes his hair style."

"The girls came to you?"

"Sometimes. At first it was girls who wanted the pictures. To send home, you know? Then they started telling me to find this girl or that."

"They as in who? Give me names."

"I told you, some Chink guys. I don't got names."

"Which was Rose?"

"She was on a list. She owed money. It wasn't fun any more. They were always on me. More pictures. It wasn't fun after a while."

"By then you owed them money." It was a stab in the dark.

"Yeah. I borrowed."

"How did Rosie end up here in Hillel's office?"

"I don't know."

"Then I can assume you brought her here and whacked her yourself."

"That's not how it was."

Jerry Chen put his head through the door. "I got to take him in," he said. "I'm calling for back-up, Artie. It's time."

"Five minutes, Jerry. How the fuck was it, Sherm? How?"

Hillel walked towards his brother and stood over him. Voice cold as ice, he said, "Tell him what happened. Or I will tell our father."

Sherm seemed to shrivel. His face caved in. His voice dropped. "A while back, four months, or five, I don't remember, Rosie disappeared. Someone beat her up bad. I took care of her and . . . ."

"And? And fucking what, Sherm?"

"There wasn't a lot of nice places we could go, you know? I brought her here. Who would notice? I was Hillel's brother."

"You brought her here to play hide the salami, is that what you're telling me?"

"I didn't kill her, I told you. We came here. It was

Sunday night. We fooled around. I went to the toilet down the hall. Maybe I left the door to the office unlocked, I don't remember. On my way back in here, I heard their voices, they were already in here, in this office, you understand? Maybe they followed her, or me. I owed them. She owed them."

"Is there another way out of this building?"

Sherm nodded. "I got scared, Artie. I just got scared."

"So you left her alone with them and they ripped up her face, strangled her and stuck a knife in her gut. You ran and Rose died."

It didn't take Sherm long to figure it: better to admit he abandoned his girlfriend to some goons than he killed her himself.

"Yeah," he said. "That's how it was. Can I eat now?"

Without looking at his brother, Hillel crept out of the room.

"You knew your Rosie was pregnant."

He was silent.

"Do you think it was your kid? You'll never know if that was your baby all over this floor, will you?" I was ready to get the hell out. I had one more question. "How did you get your brother's keys?"

A smile flickered around Sherm's mouth. "Hillel gave them to me. My brother gave me his keys."

"I wish my brother was dead, you know. It would be better if my brother was dead like the girl he killed," Hillel said. "I don't know if he left her to die like he said or cut her up himself, but he killed her. Also the baby. Any distinction is splitting hairs."

We were at a pizza parlor near Hillel's. A cold pie sat on the table between us. A cup of black coffee was in front of Hillel, a beer bottle in his hand.

"Look, I have to ask. I didn't say anything to Chen before he took Sherm downtown, but I need to know."

"He told you I gave him the keys?"

"Yes."

"I gave him the keys." Hillel finished the beer, then leaned forward on the table and picked up the glass jar of red pepper flakes. He poured some in his palm and looked at them as if they were tea leaves and he could read them. Then he tasted his hand. "So many things I never tried," he said, and I thought he might be cracking up.

"I gave him the keys, Artie, because my little girl was sick. Sarah was sick and Judith had to go to her mother's because she also had the flu bad. I was home alone with the children. I left Sarah's medicine in the office. All the sickness, I was distracted. It was late. Sherm came by, he wanted a handout, as usual, so I said, 'Do something useful for a change.' I gave him the keys. He must have made copies somewhere, because it took him a while. The only time in my life." Hillel lit one cigarette with the butt of the other.

"Take it easy, Hil."

"In this way, with the keys, it was me also that killed her." He smashed his hand on his face. "I can never go home."

I took Hillel home with me. The tape on my answering machine had been consumed by Dawn's fury. She had discovered the locks on Ricky's apartment had

170

been changed. I jammed my finger on the stop button as the tape screeched to an end. She didn't leave a number. She wasn't in Riverdale. I didn't know where she was.

On the beanbag chair in the corner, Hillel sat, staring out the window at the dirty snow. I poured him a shot of Scotch and told him to call Judith. He wasn't ready, he said. I called her and said Hillel was with me.

He tossed the Scotch back, then held out the glass for more.

"Do you think your brother is a killer? That he was there when they did it? That he could stick a knife in that girl?"

"I don't know what he is. Yes, I believe it. My God, Artie. What kind of country are we living in?"

"America good," was the first thing Pansy's friend said when she introduced us in the kitchen of his restaurant. His name was Albert Huang, he said. Face dripping steam, he was standing over his stove. Deftly, he chopped vegetables and dropped them into the wok where they hissed. He was a handsome man, still young, but losing his hair. Wiping his hand on his apron, he held it out to me. "Everyone calls me Al," he said and pumped my hand.

"I've got him. We picked up Mr Snap."

Pansy smiled and went on washing glasses.

"You like Fujianese food?" Al asked. I nodded. "Please, go sit down."

Out front, I sat at a table. It was very late and, except for one delivery guy, the place was empty. Al appeared with two plates, followed by Pansy with two more.

There were spicy lobster chunks in their shell, squishy rice cakes, liver and two mussels, each one the size of an egg. Then Al produced beer, poured it into three plastic cups and raised one of them to me.

"Cops good here. Not corrupt. In China, cops corrupt. Everything corrupt. No work, either. If work in China, no one come." He sipped some beer and served me more lobster. Shyly, he showed me pictures of his kids.

Then Pansy got up. "I have to go to work now."

"At this hour?"

"I have another job also." She was evasive.

"Jerry Chen is going to lean on you to testify."

"Yes. I know that."

"I really want to help," I said.

Pansy took her down vest off the back of the chair and pulled it on. "I don't know how he keeps going." She indicated Al. "He's seen his community destroyed by kidnapping, murder, extortion, he hears how the Fujianese are all gangsters. But he works all day and night, he keeps his word, he watches over his children. He cooks, he smiles," she said.

"You know, I thought I was smarter. I thought I was different from the others. Better. I thought I could come to New York and earn some money and buy a Green Card. I would have a proper job. I was very arrogant." As she opened the door to go, she tilted her head sadly. "I thought I would become an American."

All the desire to be someone else, someone new, all the longing to dump a past and adopt New York. America good. The Golden Mountain. Suddenly I knew

172

why Pansy got under my skin: she reminded me of myself. She reminded me of myself twenty years earlier and dying to belong.

I should have been celebrating. I had a date with Lily for the next night. Jerry Chen had Sherm locked up. Pansy was safe.

Before I returned Mike's station wagon, I drove down to the river, parked near the Seaport and got out. I thought I'd grab a beer at a tavern on Water Street, but first I needed air and a smoke. I strolled to the river and lit up. It was cold and dark, but I didn't care. It was beautiful and I could breathe.

In that wintry setting, snow blanketing the old fish market, without a single car or human being anywhere around, the period buildings, the clipper ships looked eerily real. I took a last drag on my cigarette and made to toss it into the inky river when from the corner of my eye I saw the ashy tip of a cigar go red hot. Someone was just behind me, smoking, waiting, watching.

The muscles in my legs tensed. I wasn't sure how long I could stay this still. Finally, I threw my cigarette into the water and reached into my pocket.

"Don't do that," a muted voice said. "Leave your hands by your sides, please. Don't turn around. And listen to me."

"Where's your creeps tonight?"

"My monkeys?" He laughed. "I sent them home to bed."

"How many are there? Two, three? How many?"

"I don't know. It doesn't matter. You ask these boys

173

to show up, you tell them to blend in, they carry on like knucklehead extras from a cheap Kung Fu flick. What can you do?" The quality of the voice was pleasant, bland almost. California, I thought. Or Canada.

I started to turn my head, but I felt a hand on my arm. "Please. I really dislike violence. Just listen."

"Who are you?"

"It doesn't matter."

The wind came up. It whistled on the water. Across the East River, tucked under the Brooklyn Bridge, was the River Café. It was lit up like Christmas. People would be finishing dinner, ordering one last drink. It's Friday night, they'd laugh and order another nightcap to celebrate the end of the blizzard.

"Please, Artie Cohen, please mind your own business," the voice said. "We're not interested in you, we don't want you to be interested in us."

"Who is us? Who?"

"It's over. You've solved your case. Now leave it alone."

I was silent.

"Stay away from Chinatown. Stay away from the girls. For your own sake." The voice was unthreatening. Except that it knew my name.

"Or?"

"Oh, I'm sure you can imagine. Now, I'm going to leave. I'm going to leave and I'm going to suggest you do the same. Think of me as a friend."

"Is Jeremy Chen your friend, too?"

But no one answered.

16

After the guy spooked me on the pier I needed answers, and by Saturday morning I was pissed off with not getting them. I hunted down Sonny Lippert. I called his house. His wife Jennifer said she was going over to meet him at High Five, the discount clothing store near the Trade Center. I got there first and found him ferreting among the fine shirts that were always on sale. His arms heaped with goods, he saw me, waved and strolled towards the dressing room. I went after him, but Walter Cohen caught my arm.

"So Artie, sweetheart, last time, did I hit your taste level?" Walt said, grabbing me in a bear hug. He asked about Ricky who was his favorite customer because he looked good in everything.

Briefly, keeping an eye out for Sonny, I admired the tweedy black and white Hugo Boss jacket Walter held out. I put it on. The color of expensive ebony himself, he studied the effect of the jacket on me, like he was Leonardo studying perspective.

"Try on the pants. I'm sure I can do something with

the price," said Walt, who was a former point guard for the Utah Jazz. He had left New York, where he was born, for the west, then come back home to study opera at Juilliard. He's a basso profundo and he's good; already he has a following in the opera world. When he performs, groupies hang around outside the stage door.

I once asked Walter, who I've known for years, how he came to be Cohen, like me. "My great-grandaddy was a rabbi in Spanish Town, Jamaica," he said. "Me, I was raised Catholic. I like Jews, though," he added quickly because Walt's a diplomat. "I like 'em fine. They shop well. Very fine shoppers. You know who else is an excellent shopper? The Chinese. Very good. Thin. Rich."

"That suit is good on you, Artie. It's beautiful goods." Walt fondled the material. "This wool crepe, everyone's using it this season. Awesome. Giorgio. Donna Karan. Calvin, Coco Katz, everybody."

"I'll think about it, Walt," I said, and slammed into the dressing room where Sonny was admiring himself in the mirror.

"We got to talk, Sonny. Now."

"Relax, man. It's Saturday. You look like shit. Why don't you come on back to the office, Artie? I got something for you anyhow. I was going to call."

At the front of the store, Sonny handed Walt the shirts and broke into a toothy grin.

"Say hello to Jennifer." Lippert put his hand on his wife's arm.

I'd met her once or twice—me and Sonny didn't socialize—and she was an elegant woman with dark hair and pearl earrings and very fine legs. Sonny looked at her like he couldn't believe his luck.

"Jen? Honey?" She nodded and smiled, but she was caught up in a fistful of silk ties she had clutched in her hand like noodles.

"Let's talk about Jerry Chen," I said when we got to Sonny's office. It was a loose end. I planned to tie it up and forget it.

"Is this about that poor schmuck Sherm Abramsky?"

"You already heard about Sherm."

"Sure I heard about Sherm, man. You could have told me yourself, though."

"So forget that for now, OK? Just tell me what it is between you and Jerry Chen? What's going on?"

Sonny occupied himself with making coffee. He focused on the espresso machine that's brass and glass and has an eagle on the top, and while he measured and brewed the stuff, I looked at the scraps of colorless sky out the window. A second storm was blowing in that day; more snow was falling. I was sick to death of the snow now.

On Sonny's partner's desk were stacks of books. Dogeared books, paperbacks, books marked with slices of yellow legal paper. A history of China. Melville. Twain. Once, when he'd had a few, he said, "Did you know my father believed that ninety-seven per cent of all hardcover books in America are purchased by Jews?" It was the father who named him Leo, for Tolstoy. But his mother was past forty when she had him, he was her youngest, she dubbed him Sonny, and it stuck.

Sonny Lippert believed books contained information he could use if he read them right. Clues, evidence. For instance, if you wanted to understand Russian hoods, you read Dostoyevsky and Solzhenitsyn.

For a minute he seemed to drift into some dream world, eyes distant, a late, delicate child whose real world was in those books, who went out for sports only because it made him popular with other kids. He picked up a volume of Pushkin and turned it around like some delicacy he might savor eating slowly.

The coffee brewed, Sonny poured some for both of us, sampled it and put his cup down.

"Let's talk about Chen, Sonny."

His expression hardened up, the black eyes opened wide. "Jerry Chen uses me when he needs me, I told you. That's about it. He uses everyone. Sometimes I can use him. You talk to me, Artie. Tell me what you know," he added, then he shut up. He lay back in his leather swivel chair and kept his mouth shut.

I took him through it: Hillel's call, Rose, the attack in the warehouse, the spike, the creep who sold toilet paper to both Mike Rizzi and Hillel Abramsky, the same creep who turned up at Henry Liu's. I talked about the second dead woman, the one on 23rd Street. The gallery of whores in the photo lab. About Chen and Pansy. About the hoods who e-mailed photographs of illegals back to their village. I left out the Taes and Dawn, because that was private, and they weren't involved.

Sonny leaned forward. "It fits, doesn't it? I'm beginning to see how it fits, Art. Tell me something. What would you say connects all this stuff?"

"Illegal immigrants. A community of illegals trying to cut it, exploited by the smugglers, is that what we're talking, Sonny?"

"What else?"

"Tell me."

"Women. Female illegals. Girls and women for the sweatshops. Prostitutes. Bodies. Cheap labor for the rag trade means big bucks for the garmentos. Whores make life bearable for male illegals. Big bucks for fake papers mean huge profits for the gangs. With extortion for the icing, for the extras. Snakeheads, enforcers, errand boys, the debt collector at the top of the pyramid. An empire of trade in humans."

"And even the respectable get a piece of the pie. The more illegals come, the bigger the Fujianese community gets, the more they grab a piece of the political turf. Not bad for China either. The lines to home are always open."

"You're a smart guy, Art."

"And you want your taste. You want to collar as many as you can of the scum that exploit the whole situation."

"You been in the sweatshops?"

"Yeah."

"I want them. There's thousands of them. I hate what those pissant specimens do to women in those places." Angry now, Sonny got up and came around the other side of his desk. He leaned against the edge of it. I got up. He told me to sit down. "You didn't really believe that schmuck, Sherm, murdered these women, do you? You don't believe he carved the pregnant girl with some martial arts spike?"

"He's a lot more ruthless than he looks."

"My guess is someone used Sherm to take the pictures. He held out on them. He happened to be screwing a girl who owed them money. Very convenient. They went after her. But you did good, getting Sherm. Sherm the Sperm takes pictures of girls. Some of them get dead. I don't think it's the camera that's killing them, do you? I mean it's not stealing their souls, is it, Art?"

"So."

"So. Sherm's a front man. Sherm works for them. But who do the guys Sherm works for service? Where's the ladder go? How high?"

"How many murders have there been?"

He shrugged. "More than a few in the last year, two years. Do you want me to tell you about Detective Jeremy Chen now?"

"I'm tired of asking. Did you know he's having a thing with that designer? Coco Katz?"

Clasping his hands, Sonny cracked his knuckles. "I didn't know."

"Does she use the sweatshops?"

"Sure she does. They all do." He crumpled some paper in his fist, tossed it across the room into a wire basket and made the shot. "Jerry is a very ambitious guy. Very. He wants this case, he'll do what he has to. You have to believe that on this one, Chen came to me. Told me about you. Says to me, 'What's the deal with Cohen?' I say, 'He's my friend.'"

"Do you trust him?"

"For a lot of the brass, he's a kind of addiction. They

180

figure he'll fix stuff up in Chinatown because he's Chinese. Ethnic without an accent, you know what I mean, man? If you're really asking, I don't like him. I don't trust him. I think he's emotionally bent. He hates a lot. I also think the killer is still out there. More than one. They multiply like cockroaches and they'll last just as long," Sonny said. "This is corporate. The cockroaches got lists, they got phone numbers, beepers, e-mail, area codes. Electronic hoods. How can I beat them? Now they got pictures. It's not going to stop until we make a paper trail. Until we find the money. Until we figure out who the banker is, then, maybe we can nuke the cockroaches. Until then, we use Jerry Chen."

"Or he uses us."

"Yeah, that, too, Art. That's always possible."

Sonny finished talking and reached into his desk drawer. The manila envelope was eleven by fourteen. It was addressed to me.

"What's in it?"

"I don't know. I don't, man. It came through the Russian consulate. I was going to call you Monday. I really do have to go. But listen, remember, it's always about money. The killing will never stop until we find the money," he said. "I got to go meet Jen, Art. But use the office if you want. Finish the coffee, OK." Sonny opened the door. "You look perplexed, man. You didn't really think it was Sherm? You and I, Art, we both know Sherm Abramsky couldn't kill a lobster if it crawled onto the Passover table."

★

Inside the envelope that Sonny gave me was a brown cardboard folder, faded, the label neatly written in old-fashioned copperplate—writing I recognized. At Sonny's desk, I drank the coffee and looked through it. It had come from my Aunt Birdie in Moscow; I squinted in the wintry glare and my eyes watered.

The consulate had left me messages. I never called back. I don't want to hear from Russians. What did they have to tell me that I want to know?

Birdie was dead. My father was long gone, my mother was in the home in Israel.

Wrapped in tissue paper were some photographs of myself that I'd sent to Birdie, of my loft, of me clowning around with the Taes at a house in Sag Harbor. There was a picture of Svetlana I'd taken in the Russian countryside and beside her, her cousin Tolya Sverdloff who saved my life but couldn't save hers. I had met and almost married Svetlana the one time I went back to Moscow. Because of a job, because of me, she was dead.

I thought about Svetlana for a while. I put my hand near her face. Then I put the picture away.

There was something terribly final about the package. Birdie wasn't really an aunt but a distant relative who left Brooklyn for Moscow in what?—1930, '31—to support the Revolution, and never went home. When I was a kid in Moscow, she taught me English and about New York. She had been dead for more than a year, but this package was like a headstone. The end. It stuck in my chest like heartburn, and I missed her.

There was something else in the envelope, a stiff tan paper sleeve so old it crumbled in my hand. It contained a bank book. The Downtown Savings Bank, the faint logo said. Inside it, Birdie Golden had written her name. I thumbed through it carefully but the ancient paper left dust on my fingers.

When Birdie left home, Abe, her father, put money into the savings bank. She never withdrew a cent. Maybe she was saving for a rainy day. I knew better: she had been saving it for me. There was more than five thousand dollars in the account.

Goose pimples covered my arms. Five grand when you're broke is enough to make you feel pretty good, and I figured it had to be a sign of more good times coming. There was a branch of the bank around the corner from City Hall. I got on the phone; it was open Saturdays. I went home and picked up some papers and some ID and went to the bank.

The clerk at the bank said, "Nobody has touched this account for seventy years except for an annual deposit of ten dollars." Birdie had been meticulous. She had kept the account open, somehow putting in ten bucks every single year, though how she transferred the money from Moscow was a mystery. She had managed.

"Excuse me, sir," the clerk said and went away and returned with a supervisor who looked at me like I was a crook. I tossed him the notarized papers that proved, in two languages, that I was Birdie Golden's sole heir. The supervisor reconsidered and offered me a seat near a desk with a potted plant on it. Half an hour passed. Excited clerks scurried around. What's going on? I thought, and ate a stale candy cane out of a bowl on the desk. The supervisor returned and sat down and hit the keys of an adding machine.

He hit the adding machine a few more times, flicked his shirt collar under his jacket and tried not to touch the acne on his face. Then he talked rollovers, percentages, accrued interest. I tried to keep from getting excited.

"You have some ID, sir?"

I tossed it all on the desk, license, passport, ATM card.

Triumphantly, he pulled a long paper tape out of the adding machine and presented it to me. "It's quite a bit of money," he said excitedly.

"How much? How much?"

"Fifty-six thousand, two hundred and eighty-three dollars," he said. "And seventy-four cents. Would you like to roll it over, sir? Would you like us to open an account for you? We have excellent investment arrangements," he said and told me I was a valued customer. Very valuable. The bank would like to help me. What could they do to help me?

"One thing," I told him. "There's only one thing."

"Yessir, anything at all." He offered me more candy.

I took a candy cane, peeled the cellophane slowly, put it in my mouth, got up, shook his hand, yawned, and said, "I'll take the cash."

I was free!

Fifty-six big ones. And change. Even after they soak you for taxes, that's a pretty nice windfall.

I'm off the hook, I thought. I'm free. Free. People say money can't make you free: it's the other big lie.

For a minute, I didn't care about Chinatown or death or anything at all, only about the money. Who could I admit it to? Who could I tell I had suddenly become the guy I used to be, only better. Happy and rich. In my heart, I knew if I didn't watch it, I could easily end up one of those dorks who buys driftwood plaques that read: "Life is for the Living."

I took a cab to my own bank. I went to the teller and made a very large deposit. Then I went home. The first call I made was to the dickhead who owns the club in SoHo. I told him he could shove his job. He told me I was already fired, having failed to show up. I told him to go fuck himself. He replied in kind. Then I called my friend Rita at her flower store on Spring Street and sent Lily loads of yellow roses. I ordered a purple mountain bike for Justine. I was on a roll.

I put Tony Bennett singing Fred Astaire on the CD. I did a few dance steps myself and felt I was almost as good as Fred. Then I sat down at my desk and opened all the bills, even the ones I'd been scared to look at. Some were stuffed in the bottom of a drawer. Some had fallen behind the radiator. Crawling around on my hands and knees, digging into places I had pretty much forgotten, I got them out, opened them and paid them. All of them. Mortgage, electricity, telephone, credit cards, loans, to the last cent. I called the Salvation Army and offered them a tweed sofa-bed and two beanbag chairs. I ran downstairs and across the street.

"You want my car?" I knew Mike needed a second car bad.

"What do you mean, want it?"

"I want to give it to you. It's in the shop. It'll be OK in a few days. Do you want it?"

"Yeah. Sure."

I threw him the keys. "It's all yours." I swiped a cheese Danish from the cake stand, waved it at him and went out the door. I ate the pastry in the cab going uptown and gave the driver a twenty for a tip.

All my life I wanted to do what I did next. It was a red Cadillac. It had creamy leather seats. Pre-owned, they call it. Used, in other words. But this one was a honey; it didn't have much mileage. I'd seen it before and I had wanted it a lot. When I got to the dealership over on Eleventh Avenue, it was still there.

The dealer, who had seen me before, didn't pay much attention to me until I let him see a wedge of money as fat as his arm.

It had my name on it, this particular car, we agreed, oh, yessir, the salesman dripped sincerity. A slow season, what with the weather, the salesman told me. He could do me an excellent deal. Like I was some kind of high roller, I let the guy see the wad of dough again. He was awed. For cash he could do a very very nice deal, he said, and I could hear him thinking, Geez, in this weather, this is great. He gave me the keys so I could take the red Caddy for a spin.

Sure, I realized it was a Cadillac and so was the white car in Chinatown. But mine didn't have wire wheels or hood ornaments. Also, I didn't care. This much irony I could live with. This was the car I'd wanted for a long, long time. When I was a kid in Moscow, I once saw a red Cadillac in an American exhibition. At night, under the covers, I looked at it in the four-color catalogue. In Moscow, cars came in black. Sometimes gray. The red Caddy looked like America. One day, I thought. One day.

Shifting my thighs over the leather seats, I drove up the West Side Highway and back down. I watched the sun pop into the water, a gilded orange ball doing a flashy sunset, showering the frozen buildings with gold coins just for me.

The thing rode like a dream. I tested the surround-sound system with a couple of CDs I brought specially for this purpose, Gershwin playing his own stuff on the piano and a remastered version of Louis Armstrong doing "Potato Head Blues". The sound was magic, even a tune recorded in 1926 on mono sounded wonderful. I wished I could give Satchmo a ride. George, too. Back at the showroom, I bought the car. For cash.

I was driving the car, of course, when I pulled up outside Lily's that evening. She hates it if I'm early and she's getting dolled up, so I parked and waited, head against the leather headrest, eyes closed, music playing.

When I opened my eyes, I saw Pete Leung. I saw him saunter out of Lily's building. Her doorman, José, raised his hat to Pete which meant Pete had tipped him plenty. Saunter was what Pete did. No, it was a swagger. There was a swagger to his walk, a knowing familiarity, a sense he knew his way around the building and had been there before. He climbed into his battered VW that was parked at the curb. I don't think he saw me, but I saw him, saw him smile into his own rear-view mirror, a self-satisfied little smile. Could be that Pete Leung had other friends in Lily's building, I thought to myself, but I didn't believe it.

17

Baby Vanelli was dead.

The pink lipstick that doubled as a knife was under the rug the next morning when we found Babe Vanelli's body in Lily's apartment. The blade had some kind of dried mucus on it, along with hairs from the rug and dust from the floor. It must have rolled.

Babe was dead. Sherm was in jail, but the killing had not stopped. I recognized the scars on Babe's face; they looked like the tracks I'd seen on Rose. The monsters had been looking for me. Instead, they got Babe Vanelli.

The night before, after I saw Pete Leung leave Lily's building, the two of us went to Raoul's and ate bar steaks and drank a couple of bottles of Cabernet.

When I asked what she had wanted to talk about, Lily said, "Let's just have a nice time. Let's not talk tonight. I'm feeling good now." I didn't ask what Pete Leung was doing in her building. I should have asked, but I guess I didn't want to know.

Lily stayed at my place and Babe stayed at Lily's

because Babe had a big date Saturday and her heat was still on the fritz. In the morning, Babe was dead.

The hall table in Lily's apartment was turned over. A green pottery vase lay shattered on the floor, and the yellow roses I'd sent Lily were broken and scattered. The way Babe was lying on the hall floor, her arm stretched out, her fingers seemed to grasp for the shards of the green jug, and I thought I saw her short, sexy fingers twitch.

Kneeling on the rug that was soaked with water and Babe's blood, Lily tried to gather up the flowers. "Why?" She stared at the roses. "Why, Artie?" She sat down on the floor, some of the broken flowers in her hand, shoulders shaking.

It was a fight, said the cops who arrived. Someone attacked her. She fought back. After the cops, the MEs came, all of them crowding into Lily's apartment. Babe had probably been strangled.

Every time the door opened, I saw some of Lily's neighbors in the hall. Shuffling in their slippers, clutching bathrobes around them, they bent down to pick up the *Sunday Times* from their doormats and looked up quickly, frightened, furtive, eager to help, more eager to close their doors. Can we help, a few called out, then closed their doors again as fast as it was decent.

A cop from the Sixth that Lily knew came by to offer his assistance. He swore he'd keep me in touch with the case. I called Sonny Lippert at home and filled him in.

After everybody who needed to see the body had a turn, Babe Vanelli was zipped into a black bag and taken

190

away. By now, Lily was dry-eyed. She asked me to take her to Babe's parents on West End Avenue.

When we got there I said, "Should I come with you?"

Lily shook her head. "I should tell them myself. I should do that, don't you think so, Artie? You go find the piece of shit who did it, OK? You find him. I think I should go alone," she said, and I watched Lily get into the elevator and the doors close.

It didn't take long to put it together. The guy from the Sixth was as good as his word. Babe's date had not flown in from the coast the night before. Instead, she had phoned an actor named Dirk. She told him she was free. Dirk and Babe spent the evening together.

All this we learned from Dirk because Dirk called the cops as soon as he heard about Babe on the local news. His story checked out. I checked it. I promised Lily.

Dirk spent the evening with Babe at Lily's place and around one a.m. he got a cab and headed for his apartment on Hudson Street. Before he went upstairs, he ran into a friend in a deli on Sixth, talked to the deli man, bought bagels and the *Sunday Times*. José, Lily's doorman, is a fat fuck but an honest witness, if you give him some cash, and José said Babe had buzzed him to get Dirk a cab after midnight. José saw Dirk get into it. Dirk himself said Babe was pretty stoned when he left her. She might have opened the door, thinking he had left something behind or that he had come back for more, Dirk said. Not a sensitive man exactly, but he didn't kill her. The pieces all fit.

The time of death, after they got finished wrangling about angles and cuts and semen and blood, was put at roughly three in the morning. One of Lily's neighbors reported that, when she took her dogs out around six on Sunday morning, the basement door was unlocked. Except for tenants with a key, there's no access to and from the basement from the alley that runs alongside the building but, what with the lousy weather, people used it as a shortcut to the lobby. Someone forgot to lock up.

Later that day, a Chinese kid wandered into Beekman Hospital with a hole in his eye. Someone had stuck the kid in the eye with a weapon that turned out to be a lot like Babe's knife-in-a-lipstick. It didn't take long to make a preliminary match. Tissue on the knife appeared to be similar to the eye tissue. I called Eljay Koplin's brother, Dick, who's a brilliant eye doctor, and he asked me was there any vitreous material on the knife, any of the iris? "Ask," he said, then added it didn't really matter because it was the DNA that counted.

The pain was worse than the fear, which was why the kid showed up at the hospital. When I saw him, I hoped Baby had done it; I hoped, before she died, she stuck the knife in his eye as hard as hell. I hoped he suffered and would keep on suffering and, after that, we would fry him.

He lay on the bed connected by a bunch of tubes to various drips while Jerry and me, we stood and looked at the creature, this lousy specimen of a human, the eye and part of the head huge with bandages. This was the man who killed Babe and now he lay here, dope running into his veins to stave off the pain.

Chen looked at the plastic pouch that hung over his

head. "I'd like to pull the fucking drip," he said. "Let him feel the fucking pain." He peered into the bandaged face, then turned to me. "You think it's him, Art? You think it's the animal that fucked with you in the freight elevator? That killed Rose? A motherfucker with a five-sided spike he likes to throw around?"

Black and red stubble showed on one side of his head. If it was him, he moved fast. He was everywhere: the warehouse where I was attacked, the street where he went at Chen, Henry Liu's. Or maybe there were more of them, him, the other one, four, six, a hundred. Creatures who moved through the urban jungle, heads full of beeper numbers, area codes, the names of girls who owed money and could be kidnapped or extorted.

Sherm Abramsky was dragged in to look at him and he didn't hesitate. "One of the errand boys. He brought me lists of names. Of girls. Names. He was a gofer."

"You're sure? Even with the bandages?"

"Sure."

"The only one?"

"Recently," Sherm said. "Recently it was usually him."

If Sonny Lippert was right about Sherm—if Sherm had not killed Rose—then this was her killer.

"He's awake," Chen said.

Chen took over. In spite of it being Sunday, a translator was produced. The translator said the man's name was Wai Ng Cho, but he was known as Wayne. Wayne was Fujianese. He wouldn't talk.

Chen turned to Wayne. "We already got your pal, he already identified you. Make life easy on yourself."

The translator talked. Wayne replied briefly, then shifted his body, tried to move his bandaged head, emitted a moan of pain.

"He says, OK, he killed one woman. Rose. It was her name."

I thought to myself, how come he's so helpful all of a sudden?

"He says he did it because he was bored. He was bored with ugly women, so he killed Rose."

"He's covering for someone," Chen said, but I knew different. I knew it was him. I knew because no one had mentioned Rose's name except him. And no one said she was ugly. It was him. "Why don't we strangle the ugly one?" This was the monster who had kidnapped Pansy and Rose, who raped them and beat them in the dank garage. Then he killed Rose and the child she was carrying. Then Babe Vanelli. He had killed and killed and killed.

"Why the fuck's he so eager to volunteer he did in Rose?" Chen said.

"Did he kill the woman by the skating rink?" I asked the translator.

"He says no, perhaps someone else."

"Someone who?"

"He forgot the name."

"Who does he work for? Ask him."

"He won't say."

"Make him say!" I was screaming now.

"I want her to look at him," Chen said.

"Who?"

"You know who." He pushed me out of the room.

In the corridor, where I could hear the squish of rubber soles on the linoleum of the hospital floor, Chen offered me a cigarette.

"Leave her be, Jerry. Not in the hospital. I don't want her here. Wait until he's locked up, for Chrissake."

"Fuck you, Artie Cohen. Pansy knows stuff she doesn't tell us. I want her now. I want her here." He looked at his watch. "Vanelli was your friend, remember, Art. Remember. Get Pansy for me. She won't talk to me. You get her."

"What makes you think she wants to help us?"

"I don't know. She likes you. Maybe she wants to fuck you. Why do you think? She wants to help. Some of them actually want to help, you know. They got guts. Some are OK. Like you and me," he added. "Like you, anyway." He snickered and I could hear the gurgle of bile. "Did you know Pete Leung left town, by the way?"

"So."

"I just thought you'd like to know. I thought you might like to know his wife went with him. You think I don't know you spent the night with Pete's wife? Well, good for you, man. I never did like him either, but I bet he was pretty agitated. It's OK, Art, I kept my fucking mouth shut. So you'll get Pansy for me, won't you? I'm relying on you. If you don't fucking care about the others, do it for Vanelli, for Chrissake."

"If I do this, you let me talk to her. And you give her some actual promise of protection. You make good on it. If I decide."

Jerry said, "That's a deal."

It was Jerry Chen who put some doubts in my mind about the turd in the hospital with the hole in his eye. That he, the turd who called himself Wayne, had killed I could believe. That he was the errand boy for some enforcer was evident. I was sure he had done all the worst shit you ever thought of in your life. What I didn't believe was that it was Wayne who spooked me at the edge of the pier two nights before. I didn't believe it was him who asked for me by name at Mike Rizzi's or that he was trying to fuck with my head.

Of all the possibilities in this grisly business, only Jerry Chen was a real enigma. I looked at Chen in the hospital corridor. His back was to me, head thrown against the wall, eyes closed while he puffed a cigarette. This guy lived at the intersection of ambition and self-loathing, and he was obsessed with a woman who used him. I didn't know how, yet. Jerry Chen had something Coco wanted. Not just sex. Something else. I was betting there was money involved and lots of it. Only Chen was crafty enough to play mind games with me, and for what? To scare me off? To get me off the case? In some convoluted way, did he figure if I got scared enough by Chinatown, if he scared me enough, I'd get Pansy for him? And if she testified, would that be it? There would always be something he wanted, some bigger fish to fry, some bigger collar to make.

I looked at him in the glare of the hospital lights.

"Jerry?"

"Yeah?"

"Nothing."

*

196

The apartment on West End Avenue was dark and the Pressmans, Babe's parents, seemed to have inhabited it for a hundred years. Lily opened the door for me. I shook hands with Mr and Mrs Pressman, who were small and old and sat together, side by side, on a brown settee in the living room. On the floor next to them sat Babe's sister. She was smoking cigarettes and tearing up Kleenex.

After I ate a chopped liver sandwich and drank some Canadian Club, Lily took me into an empty bedroom. She looked out of the window.

"Suddenly, I hate the fucking snow." Lily sat on a narrow bed covered with a salmon-colored spread. She picked at the nubby fabric and examined the cotton threads she extracted from it.

"We got him," I said.

"Why, Artie? Why? Things like this don't happen. They don't happen."

"I don't know. I don't know why, but I'll find out, I promise. I'm sorry," I said. "I really liked Babe. She was something else."

Lily's face was wet. Taking her bag off the bed, she held it against her chest as if for comfort and rocked back and forth. "She's dead is all that matters anyway. She was my best friend for thirty years," she said.

"Talk to me."

"No. I don't want to talk about it any more."

"We need to talk. Your apartment's not safe. They might have been looking for you. Or me." I reached for her, but she drew back.

"No, Artie. This is not a replay of you and Ricky Tae.

197

This isn't yours. It's mine. I don't want to talk about it, Artie. I'm not blaming you. I just need to get on with things."

"Stay with me. Stay with me at my place."

"I have to tell you something. Close the door, OK?" she said and I closed it. "There's not a chance in hell they'll release the body, is there? There can't be a funeral tomorrow like the Pressmans want, can there? Even if they're religious and they need it, it won't happen, will it?"

"I don't think so."

"I talked to Babe's sister. She said Baby would want me to go on with things."

"I'm sure she would. I'm sure. What things?"

"I want a child, Artie. That's what I wanted to tell you. I'm not sentimental. I just know I missed some boat that I want to get on. I'm too old, but I don't care. It's something I have to do."

"I see."

"I'm going to adopt a child, Artie. I mean I'm adopting one. It's happening."

"Why didn't you tell me?"

"I did tell you. I tried. I tried, but you weren't listening."

"When?"

"Soon. I'm going away to get her. To China."

I looked at Lily and thought, what if I lose her again? What if I fucked up and she went away? Maybe this was what it was like to discover you were in love with someone and it was too late, that you left it too late.

"We could have a kid. We could. Two if you want.

198

Our own. I could go to law school, like we said." I cranked the enthusiasm up until I almost believed it was real.

Lily smiled. "Thanks, Artie. But it's not who you are and I don't want you to be what you're not. I like you too much. A cop is who you are. For you, it's the most interesting thing in the world. You don't want a child. It ties you down, you know. It's why I never did it. There was always a job, a story. You have to get up in the middle of the night. But thank you for asking."

I took a deep breath. "Is it Phil Frye?"

"Not really," she said. Lily walked across the room and leaned on a painted wooden dresser. The paint had worn thin. She was wearing a grey turtleneck and jeans. "This was Baby's room when we were in high school. She was a few years older. She taught me how to smoke. I came here to escape. Sneak cigarettes. Iron our hair."

"You said you were going to China."

"No age requirements. Or marriage." She grinned wryly. "Single women can adopt. All the babies are girls. I want a girl. I got lucky."

"Is it Pete Leung helping you?"

"Yes, he helped me."

"How come Pete knows so much about it?"

Lily turned to me. "I think he felt sorry for me. He has so much grief himself. He wants a child badly, and he's trapped with a crazy wife. I don't care how he helped me. He has contacts. He's from Hong Kong. I don't know and I don't care. This is a totally selfish thing for me. I don't claim to be rescuing an abandoned baby. I just want her, do you understand?" She was shaking.

"Did you know Pete's gone back?"

"I think he said he was going. What difference does it make? All that matters is that he helped me. I nearly got one child a few months ago. It didn't work out. Then you introduced me to Pete. A few days later, everything was arranged."

"I understand."

"Do you? Do you want to see her?"

"Yes. Show me."

Lily sat down on the bed again and I sat next to her. I put my arm around her and she took a photograph from her bag and gave it to me. In it was a pretty Chinese baby girl with a rosebud mouth, pug nose, and chubby cheeks.

"She's kind of fat, isn't she?" Lily laughed. "But she's mine, Artie. She's mine. Her name is Grace." Lily rubbed her eyes. "It's exactly like everyone tells you. The picture arrives. The letter says, 'This is your baby.' Half an hour later, I'm thinking: this is my baby. She's mine."

Pete Leung had helped her and I was a jerk. All he did was help Lily get a child; all I could see was he was taking her away from me. In a way, I guess it was true. But not the way I thought.

"Try to be happy for me." Lily leaned back on the bed. She closed her eyes. For a few minutes we lay against the pillows together.

"When do you go?"

Lily got up. Tomorrow," she said. "Do you think that's all right, Artie? About Babe, about me leaving like that? I need you to tell me it's OK."

"It's OK. Of course it's OK. Do you want me to come with you? To China. I could come. I have some money."

"That's nice, Artie. That's really nice. Thank you." She kissed my cheek. "The arrangements are all fixed. It's really nice, but it's too late."

18

"Christ. One of the lucky ones," Jerry Chen said when we got to Al's restaurant. "Jesus Christ."

In Al's restaurant, where the tables were empty this time on a Sunday night, Pansy looked first at Chen, then, accusingly, at me, but I barely noticed the contempt in her eyes: the glasses, the red hat, the down vest were all gone; in their place was a different woman.

In a black mini skirt and a cropped black sweater that left her midriff bare, she made her way slowly across the room. She wore high-heeled leather boots that reached up to her thighs. Her hair was loose on her shoulders and tendrils of it curled over her forehead. A thin red silk scarf was tied around her long neck. She was ravishing, all cheekbones and almond-shaped eyes and she knew how to walk, how to play to men, even a pair of assholes like Chen—she made it clear how much she loathed him—and me. She was a chameleon.

Lifting her slender arm, she fingered the small silver cross on a chain around her neck, then gestured at Chen. "What's he doing here?"

From behind the counter, Al watched nervously, face dripping with sweat and worry.

"It's all right," Pansy called to Al. "It's all right." To Chen she said, "What is it that you want?"

"Tuesday morning," he said. "The day after tomorrow. Nine a.m. I want you to come into my office. You've been there before. I want to take a statement from you. Then we can go to court." Pansy stayed silent. "Do you understand?" Chen said.

"She's not deaf."

Chen moved closer to her so she was backed against the wall. "Your friend, Rose, is dead. You could be next."

Taking out his cigarettes, he offered them to her, and surprisingly, she took one. He lit it. Pansy was a glamorous smoker. She could have been in a bar with her legs crossed and a cocktail in one hand.

Jerry switched into his seductive mode. He tried to beguile. "This is for you. I'm doing this for you and your friends, I'm tired of women dying."

The come-on didn't work, of course. Pansy smoked and, in the kitchen, vegetables hissed in Al's wok and a tap dripped. Soft and sweet as the best KGB man I ever saw, Chen did his act. Except the seduction didn't work. Pansy wouldn't talk.

"It's Pansy, is it?" he said, although he knew her name, of course. "Isn't your name Pansy?"

She stared at him. "You already know it's what I call myself."

"You have another name. Don't you?"

"Not for you."

Quietly, Chen threatened her. "If you don't want to play ball, then I'll find a way to make you do it."

"What do you want?"

"I told you. I want you to show up Tuesday. And I want you to look at some pictures."

Chen put a spread of mugshots on one of the tables. From the kitchen, Al watched. A clock ticked.

"Please," I said.

Pansy shuffled the pictures quickly, picked one out, reached in her bag for her glasses and held it close to her face.

"Him." She tossed Wayne's picture carelessly at the table. It fell on the floor. Pansy looked amused; it was what she wanted, Chen on his hands and knees for her. When he got up, I could see he wanted to slap her. Her self-possession and looks made it worse; she wasn't even someone he could pity.

"What happened to his eye?" she said.

"Someone stuck a knife in his eye."

"Good. What did he do?"

"We think he killed a woman. You're sure it's him? Even with the bandages?"

"Even behind the ski mask?" I said it softly so Chen wouldn't hear. "Pansy?"

"Yes. He was there. In the room where they held us, Rose and me. I know I said the men wore masks. It doesn't matter. I would never forget this man." From a hook on the wall, she took a man's tweed overcoat and put it over her shoulders. "I have to go. I have a job."

"We'll go in my car," I said.

"A fucking Cadillac." Chen was sardonic when he saw it at the curb. "Very nice, Art."

Pansy got in front beside me, leaving Chen to climb in the back. At Ludlow Street, she told me to stop and the three of us got out. Pansy crossed the street, picking her way over mounds of frozen filth. She glanced at the four-storey brownstone, then at me. "You've been in this building before." Instinctively, she knew.

"Yes. There's a photo lab."

She started down the stairs. "They keep the shutters down during the day." She tossed her head. "Not him. Send him away."

In the middle of the road, Chen hesitated. He had left the Porsche back at the restaurant. He would have to walk. Muscles twitched visibly in his face which was white and tight with unexpressed hate.

"This is where Sherman, the man we called Mr Snap, took some of his dirty pictures." We entered a vestibule with pink walls. "This is the whorehouse where I work. Have you been in this whorehouse?"

"Not inside. I couldn't find it."

"They shut down for a few days last week during the storm. Even whores had to stop work during the snow." I didn't believe her.

In the vestibule was a desk. Behind it was a woman of about fifty. She was reading a paperback and barely looked up. Beyond her was a room with a couple of manicurist's stations. It was only a front, but a couple of women sprawled behind the tables. Two men with bored faces and weapons barely concealed under their jackets played cards in the corner. The walls here were also pink. This was where the pictures we found in the lab upstairs had been taken.

"Mr Snap, he came mostly during the day. I only work at night. I didn't make the connection. I wanted you to know that."

Removing her coat, Pansy spoke briefly to the woman at the desk.

"Have you got some money?"

I took some twenties out of my wallet and held them out; Pansy took what she needed and handed it to the woman at the desk. "Come in back."

In a cubicle there was a bed and a chair and not much else.

"The man in the picture that you showed me at Al's before, I think he brought the lists to Mr Snap. I think he took away the photographs. The boss was somewhere else."

"You know the boss? Pansy?"

Sitting on the bed, she crossed her legs. "I'm not sure."

"Can we go somewhere else? To talk?"

"We are talking."

"What about them?" I nodded towards the front room.

"Do you think the bad guys expect a whore like me and a guy like you to be talking here? In English?"

The cubicle was warm and I took off my jacket. A gold box fell out of the pocket. Pansy bent to pick it up; she handed it to me.

"It's for you."

She ate the chocolate slowly this time, admired the Godiva box, thanked me, then looked at her watch.

"I'll pay for your time."

"I'm expensive," she said and I tried to smile. "It's not a joke. I am expensive. This is how I pay my debt. This is where I get the money to pay off my passage to America and the Golden Mountain. I can earn good money. Very good. It's easier for me than for the village girls. They are modest girls when they arrive. Most have barely known any men, but if they're lucky and they are pretty, they can work here. Or in a thousand others like it."

"Who are the men?"

"Working men. Illegals also, many of them. On their way to work or going home."

"Condoms?" I asked.

"No." She looked at her watch again. "I have a job in a few minutes."

I got up and put my jacket back on, but Pansy took my hand. "I'll testify if you want me to, Artie." It was the first time she had used my name. "If you say so, I will."

"It's up to you," I said. Testify if you want. If you can. I'll go with you. Why don't we talk about it tomorrow? Until then I'll keep Chen off your back."

"Tomorrow is Monday. I will be working tomorrow."

"Tomorrow night, if you want."

"Monday night I also work. Sewing. At the Joy Fun. Monday is a double shift. You can come there late if you like," Pansy said. "Is there anything else you need me for now?"

Chen was waiting. He must have picked up his car and come back in a hurry, because he was there and when he saw me he emerged from the Porsche, rushed at me and grabbed my arm hard.

"What did she say?"

"Nothing she didn't tell you." I pulled my arm away.

"You'll bring her to my office Tuesday."

"I'll let you know."

"You're making a mess of this, Art, you don't fucking know what you're doing."

There was a few inches of fresh snow on the street, but the second storm hadn't amounted to much.

"Just go away, Jerry, will you?"

"What's the matter with you, Art?" He opened the door of his car. "You think that I killed them all? You think that I'm Mr Big?"

"Are you?" I said. "Are you? Well, maybe you are."

"Remember it's not your case. It's not your turf."

I looked at him. "Yes it is," I said. "It's where I live."

19

The fire engines outside my window interrupted the Knicks game I was watching the next night. Lily had gone to China. I was home watching basketball, working on a beer. A local anchor came on the air. Pictures of Chinatown. A five-alarm fire. A building I knew. The building where Pansy worked at the Joy Fun Sewing Company. By the time I finished zipping up my jacket I was in my car.

When I got to Market Street, the fire was already raging. It ate at the seven-storey building voraciously. From inside the building, flames curled and licked and fed on oxygen as they spat out of the windows and melted lumps of old snow on the ledges and the fire escapes. The dusk sky was black with the smoke and you could feel the heat even though it was freezing cold out. The noise—fire engines, police sirens, traffic on the bridge overhead—was obscured by the howling of the fire itself eating the building from inside.

"Look!"

I was at the back of a crowd of spectators and I craned

my neck and looked up. Through the cover of black smoke, something fell to the ground. It was a young girl. She fell through the smoke, slid along the icy sidewalk like a fish in a factory chute, then cracked her skull on a fire hydrant.

The crowd drew back.

The whole street was barricaded. Blue and white police cars had begun to arrive. It was cold and wet. The red fire engines were parked everywhere, and I saw a couple of firemen heft coils of canvas hose that unraveled suddenly, slithering like snakes on the frozen street.

Around me the air buzzed with the noise of controlled pandemonium, the cackle of talk, the wail of sirens, the cries of relatives, reporters, fire chiefs. A TV reporter was muttering about the Chinatown tenements. Built in 1900, she said. A fire trap. The City ignored it.

More cops arrived. The EMS guys were attending to people who had managed to flee the building and were crouched on the curb, some with silver shock blankets around them, some bleeding. In increasing numbers, they were stretchered out or helped into ambulances. Another crew began unloading body bags from a truck.

Across the street, against the ramparts of the bridge, the gate to the small park had been unlocked. Bodies were carried there in the bags. The black bags began to pile up. The mayor was there in the baseball jacket he wears to official tragedies; he walked around looking gloomy.

"Monday I work a double shift," Pansy had said. Monday. It was a Monday.

From overhead came the noise of a helicopter. Its blades beat away some of the smoke.

"My God." A woman next to me in the crowd began to scream. Faces in the crowd were illuminated by the fire. "My God", she said it over and over like a mantra until dozens of heads tilted back. And now the whole crowd, onlookers, relatives, cops, all looked up at the horror that was suddenly visible.

In one window, five floors up, two young men smashed the glass. One pushed the other out and as he sailed downwards and died on the street, his friend jumped after him.

On a ledge a floor above the boys, a woman held a child in her arms. You could see her clearly in the light from the flames, the way she held him, kissed him and then, blinded by trails of smoke, tossed him out. No one caught him. Even six storeys down from the fire, you could feel the sheer panic, hear the screaming. The fire had already spread to other floors. It spread to the top floor. To Pansy's floor.

Seven storeys up, on her floor, a fire escape was packed with people and it began to sway, sagging under their weight. The people on it, girls and women, held onto each other and screamed and seemed to be roasting alive. The flames from behind them were so bright the figures were in silhouette. The black sky was tinged with a reddish color, and on the surrounding buildings the snow melted in the heat and water ran everywhere in trickles, streams, gushes. The huge ladders seemed to drift almost aimlessly through the red and black sky, the firemen dangling from their rungs as they tried to reach the fire escape. Still holding his ladder, one fireman put his foot on the railing. He tested it. He pulled back. Then it swayed again and the women on it appeared to freeze into a solid mass as the thing shuddered, the charred metal fell apart and the women—about a dozen of them—fell with it.

As it went, two of the women clawed wildly at a ledge above them, holding on, like toys, firemen still out of reach, flailing around on the ladders. But the flames curled out of the window behind the ledge and burned their fingers. The women let go of the ledge. What was left of the fire escape simply snapped off like a rusty icicle.

Where is she? I thought, but I already knew. I pushed against the crowd. The cops and medics forced me back, away from the sidewalk, away from the barricades. I saw Pansy's friend, Al, and I tried to get to him but he didn't see me.

I lurched across the street and leaned against a mail box. I was hallucinating. In the chaos I had seen the boy with the orange quiff. But Wayne was in the hospital with a hole in his eye. What was he doing, prowling the streets? There was a payphone a few yards away.

Stumbling, grit in my eyes from the smoke, I beeped Henry Liu because it was all I could think of, and I waited by the phone until he called me back.

"He didn't get out," Henry said. "He's still in the hospital."

"Then what's he doing on the street?"

Henry said, "Ever think of twins?"

That was why Wayne had covered up for his pal; the

other goon was his twin. The twin was still on the streets.

Three hours later, the fire was out.

"You want to go in with me, Artie?" said Sonny Lippert when the flames were out and the building flooded.

"Put these on," someone said.

In a narrow alley that led to the back of the building, we climbed into the suits; I could smell the rubberized garments and through them, the smoke. A trail of ashes led the way, the smell of charred material seeped in under the hoods. Charred flesh. No one said anything.

The fire chief went ahead of us, Sonny next to him, me behind. The stairs were burned out and we could only stare at the wreckage. There had been some workers in a machine shop. In it were twisted heaps of burned metal. On the floor were ashes, charred bone and a grinning skull. I'd seen pictures of the Gulf War, the skulls in the jeeps on the desert. Smiling skulls.

We made our way to the elevator shaft and looked up. It appeared that some workers had tried to shimmy down the cables, but had failed and were burned to death inside the shaft.

"Artie?" Sonny was shaking me. I was still looking at the elevator, but he grabbed my arm.

"I talked to one of the chiefs," Sonny shouted through his hood. "The doors of the sweatshop were locked from the outside. The fabric caught fast. All that was left was part of a brick wall," he said. It was the wall that had no door but where someone had scribbled FIRE

EXIT in red. The flames had traveled through miles of flimsy fabric, eating up the building, the workers, everything. Nothing could stop it. Nothing.

"It has to stop." Ripping off his hood, Sonny dragged me across the street. "It has to fucking stop. I'm going to tear out their hearts if they don't crack down on these buildings." We leaned against the old stone ramparts of the bridge next to the park where the body bags were piling up like black rubber logs, and he began to cry. His face was the color of dirty snow and he looked old. His body shook. Tears bled from his dark eyes.

"My grandmother burned to death in the Triangle Shirtwaist Factory fire," Sonny said, wiping his face. "Did I ever tell you that, Artie? 1911. A few blocks from here, did you know that? She burned alive. She came over on a boat from Russia and died in a building in New York City because no one gave a rat's ass, man. She was an immigrant, a piece of shit in the eyes of real Americans. My mother was there with her. She was eleven. Someone hauled her down in a basket, so she was on the sidewalk when her own mother fell out of the window in flames. She always remembered her mother's hair, how it held the fire. She ended up like that." He pointed to body bags. "Except they didn't have bags then. It was just bodies."

"Let's get out of here."

"No," he said.

"I need to find someone, Sonny."

Wiping his face again, Sonny looked at me. "You knew someone in the building? My God. I'll see what I

214

can do, man. Come on. You got a car? I'm too fucking mad to drive."

In my car, Sonny worked the phone the way only he could, pestering, cajoling, begging, ordering. He checked the ERs, he got through to the morgue, the MEs, the cops he knew at every precinct in the area. I called Al Huang at the restaurant where Pansy lived, but there was no answer. Al had been at the fire site wandering like a lost soul.

The whole of downtown was ablaze with blue lights and sirens. The radio said there were more than a hundred dead, there were burns like napalm burns, burns from a war zone and not enough units. By now, I knew and Sonny knew that Pansy was one of the smiling skulls in the sweatshop or a heap of ashes. Pansy the chameleon, serious in her red hat and glasses, seductive in the whore's costume, she had slipped into my life and taken over. As I drove down from Beekman over to Beth Israel so we could check the ERs, my face was wet.

I told Sonny about the errand boys who were probably twins. "We'll get them both. We'll fry them both. But I want the guys that call the shots." Sonny fiddled with the radio and for a minute we listened to the news, then he switched it off. "You want to try a couple more hospitals? Look for your friend, Pansy? I know some people. I got friends," he said, and I kept driving.

"I'm going to crucify them, you know. I'm going after all of them, you hear me? The creeps who smuggle the girls to New York, then extort them so they have to work double shifts in these hell-holes. I want the scum that contract with the sweatshops right up the line, the department stores, the fancy designers, I don't care who the fuck they are, if any of them are doing it, I want them. I want whoever makes dough off the insurance on these places. Also, the building inspectors who get paid to ignore violations. I want the whole fucking bunch." The rage imploded.

"I think we took our eye off the ball a long time ago. I think we ignored that all this stuff is connected, the illegals, the sweatshops, the extortion rings, the kidnapping. We ignored that the strings are pulled in China."

"Yeah?"

"My opinion? My opinion is a lot of the money, wherever the smuggling gets done, the money, which is what counts, is run through Hong Kong. I've been reading up, Art. Did you know that the richest people in Shanghai got rich printing bibles? Now the fucking snakeheads are selling a different kind of paradise. The Golden Mountain, man. They use the photographs for propaganda. Come to America. Get a Cadillac car." Sonny looked at me. "You know how, once in a while, we get a lead on one of the big boys? Let me tell you. Once in a while, someone in a Chinese village tells a local cop and he's got a conscience. He calls someone in Hong Kong, they get in touch with us. If we get very lucky, one of the bad guys lives in Hong Kong. Or he goes for a visit."

"What's wrong with picking them up in China?"

Sonny snorted. "We can't deport. You probably knew. Every illegal knows it, word travels, man, but so what? These people got a lifetime of fear about the authorities. The illegals know. The crooks know. But maybe you didn't know we also got no extradition with China. None, nada. Fucking nothing."

He pulled open the glove compartment. "You got any cigarettes?" he said and I tossed him my pack.

"No extradition."

"You got it. After Tiananmen, George Bush signed a nice little executive order outlawing deportation with Chinese. I have to worry about the civil liberties of a scumbag that makes the victim drink his own vomit just before the scum strangles him." In the dark of the car, I could see Sonny's profile. He was possessed. He had begun to ramble.

"Did you know, Artie, that cockroaches can survive a nuke attack? With Hong Kong, at least we got extradition treaties. Hong Kong is the only place we can do business. Not for long."

"You told me."

"It's going to get worse. Enforcer types just cottoned on to all the possibilities. Some miserable Fujianese spends thirty-five grand to get here's gonna spend ten more to stay alive. Most of them too scared to talk. These days, they take them right off the boat. Victimize them, terrorize the community. Kill 'em. It comes in all forms." Sonny, who had quit years ago, puffed on his cigarette and coughed while I looked for a parking space.

"It's going to get bigger. People running from the commie dicks that already ran from them before. They did it before, '48, '49, when they used to race the sharks over from China. They'll be doing it again when time runs out.

"July is coming. This July, China takes back Hong Kong. The nuke attack is coming, so to speak. Trust me. So it takes a few months until the Chinese settle in. A year. Two years. For us cops, there's no time left at all. There's a billion capitalists in China, man, and as many as possible gonna want in on Hong Kong. I don't think human rights is high on the charts. What is it Chairman fucking Deng said? 'Not to get rich is to be a dumb bear.' Man, they ain't no dumb bears in China. Hong Kong neither. People are going to die, Artie. A lot of people."

Sonny's phone rang just then and we both jumped. He flipped it on, listened, then covered the mouthpiece.

"I got something. I got something." Sonny listened to his cell-phone. "Let's go."

I drove to St Vincent's, and we ran into the hospital.

"Let's go, let's go," Sonny kept saying as we ran, running even while someone gave us sterile gowns and masks and took us to a temporary burns unit where we saw her, a creature in so much bandaging, so wrapped up, it was hard to tell. They gave me a second or two and I crouched as close as I could and whispered. "Pansy? Marie Christine?" I whispered, using her real name, but there was no sound and only a faint whimper of horrible pain before a doctor pulled me away.

"Was it her?"

"I don't know."

Outside the hospital we sat in the car and drank coffee we got in the cafeteria. "I'm sorry, man, I am truly sorry." He sipped the scalding brew out of the paper cup.

It slopped over the edge. He put it in the cup holder, then held his head between both of his hands like it would split open from the anger.

The tension subsided, the adrenalin dried up, we sat, two sorry guys in a car.

"Where's Chen?"

Chen wasn't at home, he didn't answer his beeper or the cell-phone. But my foot was already on the pedal.

"Where are we going?"

"To see Jerry Chen."

"You know where he is?"

"Yeah. Yeah, I know."

The building on Chambers Street was dark. The security guard was asleep. The elevator was waiting. We got in and it took us to the tenth floor where a sleek white door was set into an interior wall made of glass bricks. Through it came the sound of flashy Latin music and laughter. The door was ajar.

We went in. The corner room was large and white and the huge windows faced north and west, the direction of the fire. Through the windows I could see the red tinge in the thick black sky.

In the room were three women with pins in their mouths and needles in their hands. They were fitting a trio of ravishing models—two Asian, one white—into skin-tight satin jumpsuits the colors of fruit.

You could cut the air in Coco Katz's showroom it was so thick with blue smoke the color of French cigarettes. There was the sweet tang of dope, too, and on every surface were cans of Diet Coke and thickets of wine bottles, full, empty. Wearing only some satin bikinis and nothing on top, a fourth model—she was the color of coffee ice cream—lounged in a director's chair and ate chunks of iceberg lettuce off a head of the stuff she held in her hand. Katz herself was not visible, but there was a door to the right and I figured it for her private office.

"I look like a fucking pear! I hate it." A shrill voice came from behind a screen that stood near one of the windows. It was made of sheer fabric and behind it were figures that bent and moved in silhouette. The salsa blared into the night.

"You needed that change." Now I could hear a soothing male voice from behind the screen.

The pear woman replied, "Yeah, I was fucking bored, you know. I fucking hated those highlights. I was bored."

"What about the red tone?" the man said. "Did we hit the red tone right? Coco has fruit in mind. Fall fruit. Apples, pears. Try to imagine you're a pear or at least a fucking bunch of grapes. Purple grapes."

Behind the screen, the shadows jumped some more and bent over and screamed at each other.

"Hi." The lettuce-eating model looked at me.

"Hi. We're looking for Coco Katz. We're friends of hers."

Legs up to her neck, she got out of her chair, sashayed in my direction and leaned down so we were eye to eye. "Tread carefully, darling," she cooed. "Coco's in a bitch mood. The show's in a couple of days and the collection's a mess. Coco should stick to men's clothes.

220

She should stick to conventional. Now she thinks she can put us in this fruit shit like Isaac did with the bugs. She thinks she's Isaac. But she ain't. Hope you've got your bullet-proof vest, darling." She pointed at the door. "She's in there."

Chen was in Coco's office with her and we saw him first, saw his reflection in the mirror that lined Coco's wall, as he strutted and preened and appraised himself and the plaid suit he was wearing. A coffee table held the wreckage of a meal and a couple of empty Champagne bottles. Lying on the leather sofa was Coco Katz. She was watching Chen. He saw us and span round.

"Fuck off," Chen said.

"I think you ought to leave us," I said to Katz. She rose from her sofa, raised a single eyebrow and said, "Sure. I've got more to worry about than him," then strode away into the other room.

Sonny turned to Chen. "Tell me, detective. Did your friend Coco there lose any business in the fire? Did she cry over it? Did she have contracts with the Joy Fun Sewing Company?"

"Don't be a fucking ass," Chen said. He took off the jacket and held it in front of him. "This is high quality goods. This stuff gets made in Italy, not in a shithole on Market Street."

"All of it? You don't know that for sure, do you? Do you?"

Sonny was sarcastic. I saw he was also boiling. "I think that what Jerry's girlfriend had was insurance. I think she had a piece of the insurance action on the building on

Market Street, that was the game she played, her and a lot of other garmentos and some of their pals in Chinatown. The designers sub-contract with the sweatshops. They profit from the slave labor. The shops are fire traps. Anything goes wrong, the building goes up, maybe they lose some garments, but they win big with the insurance. Nice, huh? Nice. You win both ways. Did you help her get in on the deal, Jerry? Did you introduce her around? Henry Liu, maybe?"

"You don't know anything," Chen barked, the slick charm disappearing. "All you know is what you got from some two-bit claims adjuster. There is absolutely no fucking evidence you can fucking pin on me. None."

"I didn't mention any claims adjuster. You did." Sonny Lippert had done his homework. He looked at Chen. "You're an expensive guy, detective. You got an expensive car, pricy clothes. And I got someone who says she saw you at the building around the time the fire caught. Says you didn't exactly run for the fire department. Says you ran in the other direction."

"I didn't set the fucking fire," Chen said.

"But you didn't stop it, did you? Did you, Jerry?" I thought of Pansy. Of the other women. Of the body bags. I socked him. I couldn't help it. Sonny gave me a warning glance.

From the other room came more laughter; someone changed the music to reggae.

"What is this, Art? Sonny been schmoozing you, Art?" Chen said. "Sonny been going on about the Hong Kong connection? I'm the one that ought to go to Hong Kong."

"You're not going anywhere." Sonny was livid.

"If you get to Hong Kong, Art," said Chen, "why don't you look up my goody-two-shoes cousin, Ringo Chen? He's your sort of cop. Him and Sonny are tight. You want me to be sorry, guys. OK. I'm sorry. Mea culpa."

"Please, Jer. Spare me. What is it you want to tell me?"

"You're wasting your time trying to pin stuff on me and you know it. You know fucking well that it's me the brass trust when it comes to Chinatown. If the city fucking wants to make things better, they got to cut guys like me some slack. Chinese guys, you understand. Guys that can grasp the culture. When I deliver the errand boys, no one's gonna care about some claims adjuster, Sonny, and you know it. Yeah, I picked him up, OK? They were twins. It's why the one with the hole in his eye said he did it all, to protect his son-of-a-bitch brother. I made the collar. Nothing else matters. Right? But you can see me on TV."

We both knew he was right. But I had one more question.

"Sonny, ask Jerry here if he's been playing games. Ask him if he's got some jerk following me every time I take a walk, some dirtbag asking where my friends are living, shaking down my pals." I opened the door.

"Hey, Art." Chen called me back.

"What do you want?"

"She's alive."

"I don't believe you."

"Henry Liu found her. She's at Henry's. Marie Christine, isn't that her name?"

Pansy was waiting for me just inside the door of the Red Swan. Her hat in her hands, when she saw me, she pulled it on, opened the door and asked me for a cigarette. We went out into the street. Pansy headed north and I walked alongside her. For a while, she was silent. When we reached the park where we had first talked on the day Rose died and the blizzard started, Pansy stopped. She looked at the sky, then turned to me.

"I did it, you see," she said.

"Did what?"

She tossed her cigarette into the gutter. "The fire," she said very softly. "I started the fire."

20

"Tell me."

The snow had stopped completely. The park was empty. Pansy brushed off a bench and sat down. "May I have another cigarette please?" I gave her one and lit it.

"Last night after you left me at the whorehouse. It was Sunday last night?" She puffed delicately.

"Yes."

"It seems such a long time ago." In her pocket, she found some chocolate. Elbows on her knees, she held the cigarette in one hand and the chocolate in the other. "After Chen threatened me, after you left me in the whorehouse, I went out on a job, as a whore, you know? I don't know what happened. I don't know if someone knew I had spoken with you. If someone thought I might talk. One of the pimps perhaps. I don't know. But I was going out and they were waiting in the street."

"Again?"

"Yes. But different men from before, I think. Behind the building where we sew is a church. There's a smaller building in between, in a courtyard. They took me there last night. It was a room on the ground floor. They kept me all night and all day. I lost any sense of time. I could hear the noise of them hitting me as if it was happening to someone else, and I thought: I'd like to be dead. I prayed to die." She rolled up her sleeve to show me the bruises. "I didn't care any more. I can't ever make enough even as a whore to pay them. Even while they hit me, I thought about it. I was watching. I was outside myself. There was a space heater."

She paused and ate some more chocolate. "Excuse me," she said as she swallowed. "I had a silk scarf around my neck and I used it for a taper. I lit the curtains. If I could make enough fire, I thought someone might see it. But there was garbage under the window, a box of scraps or fabric, or a can of gasoline, I don't know. I saw the fire travel. The men who kidnapped me saw it and got scared. They ran away. I got out."

Delicately, she tossed the cigarette butt on the ground and crushed it with her foot. "The fire traveled into the factory building." She took a deep breath. "I tried to get in, but it was too late. The door to the sweatshop was locked. I ran."

"I thought you were inside. You told me you were doing both shifts."

"Yes. I should have been inside. I wish I had been." Getting up, Pansy looked in the direction of the fire again, then gazed around the desolate playground.

"The Golden Mountain. You saw my friend Al with his little restaurant where he works all day and all night. "America good, work here good." Everyone wants to come. They will keep coming. You do what you can."

She hesitated. "Do you remember when I told you if they got me again, I would kill someone?"

I thought of Sonny. "There are people who think this is all connected in Hong Kong."

"I don't know." Pansy took off the glasses and her eyes narrowed, as if she was in pain and didn't want me to know. "I'm sorry. My eyes bother me."

"What will you do now?"

"Work. Try to pay my debts. Testify, if you ask me. Pray. I'd like to leave here alone now. Unless you want to have me arrested," she said.

"No," I said. "I won't do that."

It was a week since Hillel called me, a week since I met Jerry Chen in Chinatown. Chen with his Porsche and his designer duds. Chen who went after the killers who extorted, kidnapped, butchered. But it was Jerry's insane, doggy devotion to Coco Katz that probably sucked him in. And the ambition. Maybe Chen thought he could play it both ways. And if he could solve the big cases and get rich, maybe all the self-loathing would stop.

I watched Pansy leave the park and walk away, her sneakers making prints in the last fine dusting of snow.

Someone was paying Jerry Chen. Someone in Chinatown who owned bad buildings and had good insurance. Someone uptown who contracted with the sweatshops. The smugglers fed them with illegals, fueling the garment business like a can of gasoline in an alley fed the fire.

My fix on this place had changed. For a week, I'd been scratching around this patch; I was still a tourist.

Chinatown was a walled city, even if the walls were invisible. It was hidden, not just under the snow and ice but in a deserted warehouse, a basement brothel, a room where people slept in stacks of three on eight-hour shifts.

On the surface, the place was the same aggressive sprawl of streets, sidewalks crammed, shops bulging with food. Guys like Al Huang worked eighteen-hour days, cooked, put food into take-out bags, sent their kids to school, tried to make a life.

Bursting now with international banks, shiny condos and high livers eating abalone at $800 a pound, the new Chinatown still made its deals in private rooms at Henry Liu's. Cantonese, Fujianese, halfway around the world from home, New York's Chinese fought out their ancient feuds and loyalties—to Hong Kong, the mainland, to Taiwan. The criminals moved as fast as they could dial a phone. Electronic hoods, they used photographs they got off digital cameras for extortion and sent them back to China by computer for propaganda. They referred to a job by its area code and their most potent weapons were the beeper on their belt and the cellphone in their pocket. Electronic thugs.

Billions changed hands. New York. The Golden Mountain. Hong Kong. What was it that Justine always said when she was little? "If we dig all the way down to the other side, will we come out in China?"

But this case was over. Sometimes I don't know if I should laugh or cry. There's always a two-bit slimebag like Sherm. Once in a while, there's a Pansy to break your heart. But not often.

Tossing my cigarette away, I left the park. Sherm

Abramsky's lawyer would fix him some kind of deal. The twin creeps, the errand boys who killed Rose and Babe Vanelli and probably the woman on 23rd Street, would maybe even fry, which would be sweet.

I was glad Pansy had escaped from the kidnappers. She had done it twice. Twice. A bell went off in my head.

Was she that smart? Or lucky? Who put up the initial money for her passage? How did she get here, to the Golden Mountain? Who would the snakeheads squeeze for money if she couldn't pay? "I have no family," she had said. "No one."

I was running. It was late. The streets were nearly deserted. I ran toward the site of the fire. On the other side of the street, under the bridge, I found her.

"Pansy?"

"Yes?" Her voice was cool.

"The first time they kidnapped you, when they took you and Rose, why didn't they come after you like they came after her? Why didn't they kill you?"

She stared at the smoldering wreckage across the street and said, "Perhaps I had some protection."

"What protection?"

"I told you I had a half-brother. Do you remember? I thought he was dead. Perhaps he is not dead. I think the man who gave the orders to the errand boys is my own brother."

Abruptly, her voice broke off. A man rose out of the shadows like the cat that had pounced on me in Queens. He threw himself on her. "Run," I yelled at her as I tackled him. "Run." But the last thing I heard that night was Pansy's voice and she seemed to say, "If you go to

China, Artie, look for the Eiffel Tower." So I knew I must have passed out. Either that, or I was dreaming.

The bruises healed. It took me a while to get my act together and I was shook up, but apart from a tooth that got knocked out I was OK. Three weeks after the fire, when I answered my door, Sonny Lippert was standing there, arms outstretched, a bottle of fine malt in his hands.

"How ya' doing, Art?"

"Have a drink, Sonny. Sit down and have a drink," I said, but he didn't take off his coat. I closed the door. Sonny sat on the edge of a chair.

"I need you Art. I want to put this case together, Art. I been working on it, and we can do it, the dead girls, Rose, your friend, Pansy, the photographs, Jerry Chen, if he's in it, if we can put it together, the deaths, the connections to China, side by side, maybe we can stop some of the dying. You with me, Artie?"

I opened the whisky. It was nice stuff.

"You ever talk to your friend Ricky's brother-in-law? You ever talk to Pete Leung about all this?" Sonny said. "He's good, Pete. He knows how money moves through Hong Kong. He helps us sometimes. He ever tell you anything interesting?"

"He told me something about a new-style heroin they call Hot Poppy. Mostly that."

Looking puzzled, Sonny said, "I don't know anything about that, kiddo. But there's rumors. There's someone who moves around a lot, smooth as silk sort of guy, between Hong Kong and New York. He pulls a lot of weight, a lot of strings, a money guy. We think he's the bank for the snake-heads."

"And?"

"I want you to go to Hong Kong."

"I don't think so, Sonny."

"What will it cost me?"

"I want you to fix things for her. For Pansy. If she makes it."

"She'll make it. The doctors told me she'll make it because of you, kiddo. What were you doing out there that night of the fire? John Wayne? John Woo?"

"Promise me."

"I swear on my grandmother," he said.

"A Green Card? All of it?"

"You're some manipulator, Art. Yeah, OK, whatever she needs, but I want you to go. I want you to find him."

"You're so sure it's a him?"

Sonny looked startled. "You got another idea?"

"How about you go to Hong Kong?"

"I'm fifty-seven years old, Art. I don't run so fast. I wouldn't have asked you, man, not to push you, but I got a medical thing. Don't ask. I got a case to make on the fire. The smugglers this end. Bastards. We could get some of these monsters, man, between us."

"Officially?"

"No. I could get you a ticket and some cash, but this is not department stuff. This is between us. Go find the guy who runs the bank for the snakeheads." Sonny Lippert pleaded. "Before anyone else dies, Art. Before anyone else burns to death. Find the man they call the Debt Collector."

PART TWO

Hong Kong

21

A wave of humid sensuous air that clung to my face like Saran Wrap to a boiled chicken hit me as soon as I got outside the terminal building in Hong Kong. After the frozen white and gray New York winter, Hong Kong drenched me with its heat and colors. And, pushing her damp red hair off her face and searching for me in the crowd of arriving passengers, Lily was waiting.

In the end, I went to Hong Kong for Lily. She had called me, crying, and Lily doesn't cry, not often. "Please, Artie, I need you. If there's any way you could come," she said. "Please." Sonny Lippert needed me there, and then Lily called, and I went.

"Enjoy the flight, Mr Cohen," the girl at the desk at JFK had said when she handed back my passport. Years ago, Sonny Lippert helped me fix my passport. Artemy Maximovich Ostalsky had disappeared completely. In my US passport, I am Artie Cohen, b. New York City. USA.

"Hi." Forehead damp with sweat, her clothes wrinkled, Lily held on to my arm.

"Hi," I said. I felt embarrassed. After the endless flight, I was also soaked in Scotch.

"Thanks for coming, Artie. Thank you. I called because I couldn't think of anyone else." I loaded my suitcase into the taxi she had waiting.

In the month Lily had been away from me, I had missed her. What got me most when I saw her wasn't the blotchy skin or the lank hair, the purple shadows under her eyes. What got to me when I met Lily at the airport was her silence, and the disjointed platitudes we exchanged.

"Everyone is Chinese," she said. "Isn't that weird?"

"Yes," I said, "just like in Chinatown. Look at the boys with the pony tails. Look at the old woman carting vegetables onto a plane," I said.

"How amazing," she said, and then we were in the taxi, driving through the sultry neon-lit night. Something was terribly wrong. There was bad stuff going on. I waited for her to tell me what it was.

At Lily's hotel she had fixed a room for me adjoining hers. "I can't sleep," she said. "I got you a room, Artie. Is that OK? Is it OK?" I had never seen Lily so unsure of herself and I put my arms around her and held her as best I could.

Even before I was unpacked, she came into my room and sat cross-legged on the bed next to me. In her hand was a picture of Grace, the baby she had come to China to adopt. She propped the picture against a lamp on the bedside table. I looked at the chubby child and the child smiled back at me.

"Where is she? Where is your baby?"

"I'm going to tell you. I'll tell you. I will." Lily picked up the brandy I'd ordered and swallowed it neat. "I'm OK. I'm OK now," she said, as if to persuade herself, and then she told me her story.

"Did you know they skin live monkeys in the market in Guangzhou?" Lily said. "Did you know that, Artie?"

22

That they skinned them alive and you could hear them scream from a mile away was the thing she remembered. As you got deeper into the market, the dust settling in your hair, the air clotted with pollution, sweat pouring off you, you heard the monkeys shriek at their own death.

Lily had not gone to Guangzhou first. She had first traveled to Beijing. She had had help getting the baby quickly, but now, now she knew she had Grace, as soon as she received notification the baby was waiting for her, she wanted to do it right. She could have pulled more strings, but she thought to herself, "No, I'll go through channels. I'll do it right."

At Beijing Airport, all she noticed was that two out of every three lightbulbs were burned out and the erratic sound system squawked out intermittent announcements and Paul McCartney tunes. The Chinese Beatle, people called Paulie. Otherwise, things went OK. Mostly, she remembered stupid things like the burned-out bulbs, that and the tour guide's white umbrella.

Mrs Ling was the official guide and she carried the white nylon umbrella everywhere. She refrained from expressing surprise when Lily arrived, but Lily always knew Mrs Ling was thinking that she, Lily, being a single woman, would not know how to care for a baby. It wasn't Mrs Ling's business to think, however, Lily calculated. Ministry apparatchiks appeared and whispered to Mrs Ling from time to time, and Lily enjoyed the spectacle of the guide's changing wardrobe, the diamanté spectacles, the sweet perfume, the perm that seemed to have been stamped into Mrs Ling's hair with a waffle iron. Mrs Ling was New China Woman, official-style. "Not to look pretty is to be a dumb bear" was Mrs Ling's motto, Lily decided.

Every detail of the trip became a diversion for Lily; she was thrilled but anxious; in a week she would have her child. In a week, in Guangzhou, she would meet Grace. Grace was from Guangzhou, or Canton as Lily always thought of it, but a visit to Beijing was required first for the acculturation of the adoptive parents, according to Mrs Ling. "This translates to the spending of much foreign currency," said Clare O'Mara, one of the other women on the trip.

At the hotel in Beijing, Lily met her group. The five middle-class couples were from the LA suburbs—Long Beach, Glendale, Northridge—and they were nice, decent people, Lily said, but they were uninterested in anything except the babies they had come to adopt. Clare was different. Clare and her husband, Les, were black. Clare was a lawyer and Les, who played jazz clarinet in a San Francisco trio, taught music at UC

239

Berkeley. Like Lily, they had no other children. Like her, they were thrilled, thrilled and scared and full of the adventure of it.

Lily said, "We palled around together once in a while, me and Les and Clare. I was the only person alone. I was so lonely."

Lily saw the Forbidden City and, on its north side, the million-dollar mansions of the new rich. She shopped at the Friendship store and bought aimlessly— porcelain boxes, straw baskets, silk jackets, toys. In Tiananmen Square, she stood where the tanks had rolled over the students. Was it seven years already since those heroic kids had stood up to the tanks on June 4th? It was one of the stories Lily was sorriest she had missed covering.

"I was so nervous, Artie. All the time we were in Beijing I was nervous, and excited," she said. "Then it was time to leave for Guangzhou. Remember I told you at home how it is. How the picture of the baby comes and she's yours. You think of her as your own. Grace was mine. As soon as I got her picture. Finally I was going to see her." Lily looked at her empty brandy glass. "Is there anything else to drink?"

I opened a bottle of duty-free Scotch. Outside the window of the hotel room, I could hear the boats in the Hong Kong harbor, the constant buzz and whistle of the ferry boats, cargo tugs and yachts as they criss-crossed the water. Lily didn't seem to notice any of it. She drank some Scotch greedily and went on talking. At first her words were stilted and she spoke in staccato bursts, but the whisky smoothed her out some.

The day Lily's group departed Beijing for southern China, everyone in the group got food poisoning.

"Take chopsticks," Lily's friends had told her. "Take your own. They wash chopsticks in a common washing bowl." But Lily considered it was patronizing; that was the stuff of the Ugly American, and she would do what the locals did. "We were all sick as parrots," she said. "Me, because I was a fool, the others because no one told them. Sick as parrots. Sicker."

A heatwave blanketed southern China the day the group arrived in Guangzhou. There were no porters at the airport, no toilet paper, either. It didn't matter because Mrs Ling, waving her white umbrella to call the group to attention, said, "You'll get your babies tomorrow evening."

Drinking her Scotch, Lily leaned on my shoulder. "God, I was so excited. That's what she said. "Tomorrow night you'll get your babies." I was so excited I couldn't sit still. We stayed at the White Swan, this huge palace of a hotel. It made me claustrophobic, and I had to get out. To kill time during the day I went sightseeing."

At the train station, Lily saw the migrant workers who squatted there, waiting for jobs, thousands of them. In the markets, she saw the babies begging, and they ran after her, chattering, getting hold of her hands, shoving plastic bowls at her.

A truck rattled by and the crowds in the street looked up because on the back of it were six young women with ropes around their necks. Lily found someone who spoke English and asked what it was. "An execution," the woman said. "A good thing too," she added with fierce insistence. The girls, who were prostitutes, had "lured railway workers to their death with sex", as the woman put it. It was right they should be executed; crime had to be punished. The government had executed ten thousand persons in the interest of destroying the criminal element, the woman said. As the truck disappeared, Lily saw the trembling girls were only kids of fifteen or sixteen and, as she watched, she heard the monkeys scream.

In the morning, Mrs Ling assembled the group over breakfast. "You have your money in a belt under your clothes?" Mrs Ling said. "When we get to the other hotel, you will make the donation to the orphanage," she said. "I will tell you when to hand it over. Only pay money when I say this: 'Pay now.'"

A minibus took the group to a Chinese-style hotel where all the chairs in the lobby were occupied by taxi drivers who all resembled Mao Tse Tung. "Like hotel porters in Moscow looked like Leonid Brezhnev," Lily said to me. "Remember? Remember that?"

A man from a ministry was waiting and Mrs Ling said to Lily's group, "Pay now."

"Except for me, the husbands were carrying the money," Lily said. "They went into the men's room to get it out. I didn't want to be alone, I went with them."

In the toilet with the cracked tiles, she thought: fifteen thousand dollars between us. We could all be killed in this toilet.

As they got their money out, they found the bills had stuck together in the heat. Lily got a battery-operated

242

hairdrier out of her shoulder bag. On the dank toilet floor, the men laid out the bills and Lily squatted and blew the money dry with her hairdrier. Everyone laughed. Les, the musician, pulled a bottle of Kaopectate out of his bag and passed it around; another guy had a pint of Scotch. They toasted Lily.

"To Lily," the husbands all said and, in the toilet in China, they clapped their hands for her and drank the Scotch.

That evening, the phone in Lily's room rang. "Come to Suite 1001," a voice said.

Mrs Ling, a nurse, foster parents, the couples were all in the suite, everyone milling, waiting, clutching gifts and baby clothes. Thirty people were in that room. In her arms, Lily held her old teddy bear. In the other room of the suite were the babies.

"Then they gave her to me," Lily said. "Without any ceremony. Some woman just brought Grace out and put her in my arms just like that. She was about five months old, very cute, like her photograph, and fat, like a little sumo wrestler. I gave her my old teddy bear. She didn't like it, but she was transfixed by some fancy gift paper I had and my colored rubber bands.

"At first I didn't feel anything much, it was too chaotic in the room, but I put my hand under her and she wasn't wearing a diaper. They put them in pants slit back to front, you know; when they have to go, they just open the slit. So I was actually touching her skin," Lily said. "That got to me.

"I took her back to my room. Late that night, Clare, the lawyer, came in with Maria—her baby was named

243

Maria—and said, "Does yours cry a lot?" I said I thought it was normal but Clare, who knew about children, said, "They think westerners like fat babies. They feed them up. Then the babies cry all the time because they're used to so much food." So we did what good American mommies do," Lily said. "We put on the television and we lay on the bed, me and Grace and Clare and Maria, and we watched TV, and the babies stopped crying, and I realized Grace had never seen TV. Then Clare took Maria back to her room, and I spent the whole night alone with my daughter. The whole night." She stopped, downed another drink, then put her hands over her face. Lily looked at me. "Followed by two weeks in hell."

When she applied for a passport for Grace, Lily discovered some of the paperwork was incomplete and she entered a hell that consisted of building after building of bureaucrats and offices, heat, noise, smoke, of parents yelling and babies crying.

On the third day or maybe the fifth, she could no longer remember, in one of the concrete buildings that had no windows and no air conditioning, a man in a white nylon shirt smoked in Lily's face. Grace in her lap, she sat opposite him and thought to herself, concentrate on the cigarette hanging from his mouth, concentrate on the big yellow stain on his nylon shirt, concentrate on the fact this man is nothing.

"Paperwork has to be completed in America," he said, and Lily thought, they're going to take her away from me. "I knew," Lily said. "Oh God, I knew."

In the hotel, Mrs Ling was waiting. "There has been

an error," she said to Lily. The child would be returned to foster care until Lily's papers and the baby's passport were properly arranged. A nurse appeared.

"They picked Grace up and took her away. I couldn't get anyone to listen." She took a cigarette from my pack and lit it, filling her lungs with nicotine. "I had quit smoking, you know. As soon as I heard about Grace I just quit, but what's the point now?"

She twisted her hair around a finger incessantly, then scraped it back and tied it with a rubber band she had in her pocket. Without make-up her face was white; the freckles showed. Her voice trailed off. "They gave her to me, Artie, they gave Grace to me for a whole night. Then they took her away."

23

It was almost five in the morning and Lily had talked through the night. Now, still on my bed, she was weeping as she said it over and over. "They took her away from me. They took Grace." Then, suddenly, her tears seemed to run out and she got up. "I'd like to walk a little. Can we go out?"

The hotel lobby was empty except for the cleaning women who were polishing the marble staircase and a couple of guys in striped pants who stood behind the desk yawning. As we left, one of them smiled politely and covered his mouth.

It was mild outside and the clammy air lay on my skin. Along the waterfront was a promenade. There was some milky gray light in the sky now, but the Hong Kong skyline across the water was hidden by fog. Lily leaned on the railing and looked out at the water.

"The group left China," she said. "I stayed. I went everywhere I could think of, I called everyone. It was like the shutters went up. Someone was punishing me, but for what? For what, Artie? There was too much flak, too many people averted their eyes. I thought I might crack up."

"What about Pete Leung? He helped you fix the adoption." I put my hand on her shoulder.

"It was the first thing I did. From Guangzhou. I called. I called his house. His office."

"And?"

"All I got was bullshit. Secretaries, assistants. He was away on business, they said. Somewhere in China." Lily held onto my arm. "When I left Guangzhou, I thought I could get help here in Hong Kong. I thought I'd look for Pete Leung." She stared at the water, her face dry as a bone and now as white. "I left him a million messages."

"Then you called me."

"No. First I tried TV people, I tried the papers. A Chinese woman I know at the BBC tried to help. I went to the consulate. Wherever I went I said I was a friend of Pete's. I thought it would carry some weight. Everyone was unavailable or furtive, worried or coy. I couldn't tell what was going on at first. Then I realized how delicate an issue adoption is. Hong Kong is trapped, you know. It's going to blow up when the Chinese get here in a few months. People I met all said, 'It's rough for you. We're sorry. But we're not that brave. We're not Harry Wu.' Then I didn't know who to call except you. I could give you the money for your ticket. The rooms are paid for. I fixed a deal. There's a guy in the hotel business I used to know. I hope you're not mad. I behaved like a jerk at home, it's just I want this baby so much."

"I'm not mad. Shit, Lily. I'm not mad. Is that what you think?"

"You're a nice man, Artie."

"What about Phil Frye?"

She turned her back to the water and faced me. "You were right all along. Phillip's a prick. He said he was OK with this. I went to London. I did go. I lied to you. I went to London on the way to Beijing. He played hard to get. He said that, in any case, the Chinese adoption system was exploitative. Phillip's very big on human rights. Not mine, maybe, but everyone else's." Lily laughed bitterly.

"Do you think it's because of him? Do you think they connected you to Frye and stopped the adoption?"

"God knows. But I'll tell you something. I had a friend who did a story that the Chinese didn't like. She moved to a different TV company and they knew, they knew she had moved, and when her new company wanted to do a story on China, they said no. And it was because my friend was there. They keep very close tabs on who gets in and who doesn't. I'm not saying it's anything to do with me or with Grace, I'm just saying that they know, Artie. The Chinese don't like us telling them their business."

A sultry little breeze came in off the water. The promenade was deserted except for two old women who practiced Tai Chi and a third who performed a self-obsessed foxtrot all by herself. Lily took a cigarette out of a pack in my shirt pocket. "You were jealous of Pete, weren't you?"

"Yeah."

"You saw him come out of my building, he told me that. I'm sorry. I couldn't tell you any more about it. He made me promise. He said, 'I'm a businessman, Lily, I don't want to look like some do-good jerk. If I make a lot of noise publicly, nothing works. I do what I do in private.' And he helped me."

"So where is he?" I lit the cigarette for her.

"Business, I guess. I saw him briefly in London and that was the last time I heard from him. But God knows he tried."

"Did you sleep with him?"

"Screw you." Lily laughed and punched my arm lightly. Then she inhaled a lungful of smoke and sighed. "I told you, no. But I think I would have done anything I'd been trying so hard to adopt. Then you introduced me to Pete at that awful club you worked at and it was some kind of miracle. He said, 'Maybe I can help.' He asked me not to say anything. Then, out of the blue, the picture of Grace arrived. I had something that mattered."

"More than me."

"Yes. More than Phillip. More than you. Yes." She tossed the cigarette she held into the water. "I think I need to sleep, Artie. I think maybe now I can get some sleep. Is that OK? Can we go back to the hotel?" She leaned in towards me.

My arm around her, we walked back to the hotel. It was light now, but the city was socked in by fog.

Lily began to walk faster and faster. "Artie, I think there's someone behind us."

But there wasn't. Even the dancing woman had disappeared. There wasn't anything except noise from the boats. I held Lily as tight as she let me.

"What do you want, sweetheart? Just tell me."

"I'm going to get Grace back. I'm going to get some sleep. And then, if it kills me, I swear to God, Artie, I'm going to get her back."

When I opened my eyes and swung my legs over the side of the bed, I wasn't sure where I was. I looked at my watch. It was ten to six. I fumbled with a TV remote. On TV people were dancing ballroom stuff, tango, foxtrot, two-step, faces rigid with effort. It was ten to six in the evening and I went and knocked on Lily's door, which was next to mine. She opened it, eyes half shut, kissed me and said she could sleep through the night, so I grabbed a shower, changed my clothes and went downstairs. I had been on the ground almost twenty-four hours; I was hungry.

The hotel lobby was immense. The bellboys in white criss-crossed the marble floor like the cargo tugs in the harbor, hefting luggage as guests checked in and out.

The Regent Hotel was at the very edge of the harbor as if floating on the water. The back wall of the lobby was made of glass and tourists, drinks in hand, stood there mesmerized by the city: the water, sky, the lighted skyscrapers against a dark mountain. The sky was thick with the humidity, and the sunset had left a streak of violent colors that appeared to fire up the night and the neon signs that blazed into orange and red. It was spectacular. It was Andrew Lloyd Webber: Hong Kong, the musical. In the lobby behind me, the piano player, foot glued to the pedal of a Steinway grand, switched from "A Whiter Shade of Pale" to "Memory".

A waiter brought me a beer. "What happens when there's a storm?" I asked him.

"We drop the typhoon nets, sir," he said, impassively, but I could tell he was pleased at my discomfort. "We drop the nets."

I carried my beer to a table in the bar area and slumped into an armchair, wondering if I should call Sonny Lippert even if it was only six in the morning back home in New York. I was here on Sonny's nickel and I better get busy, I thought, but there were cashews on the table. Looking for a waiter to order another beer, I was stuffing some nuts into my mouth when I felt a huge hand grab me from behind. I flew out of my chair and spun around, but I wasn't prepared for what I saw.

"Christ. Jesus Christ!"

"Sorry. Anatoly Sverdloff."

What could I say?

"So, Artemy Maximovich, you were not precisely expecting me?"

It really was Tolya. Goddamn Tolya Sverdloff picked me up in his arms and jumped up and down. I'm six one, but Tolya can pick me up like a pet. Around us, the tourists stared.

"Put me the fuck down."

"Sure. OK." He swung a snakeskin briefcase onto the table and sat. He stretched out his legs. On his feet, Tolya wore green suede Guccis with gold buckles the size of a sandwich. "Gold," he said. "Eighteen carat."

I wasn't going to admit how glad I was to see the son of a bitch looming over me in the hotel lobby, all six six, all three hundred pounds of him encased in a green linen jacket as big as a tent and a black silk shirt. In one ear, he wore an emerald stud and, with his square head, he resembled an Easter Island statue with an earring and dimples.

"Just like old days, Artie, just like old days."

"What old days?"

A little less than two years back, in New York, Tolya had entered my life. He drove me nuts, then he saved my ass and became a friend.

"Always I love Hong Kong," he said. "First taste capitalism." He said it lovingly, caressing the idea like a Moscow crooner with a big ballad. He was drunk. For Tolya's English to deteriorate, he had to be completely soused. With me, he always talked a crazy mix of his lovely purring Russian, the first class English, and gangster slang in both.

"You remember also, Artyom, I am Chinese expert."

It was all true. His father, Anatoly, Sr, was a famous actor, and everyone in the family was a brilliant mimic. Tolya's privileged youth had included the Moscow language schools. For Tolya, before the commie cocksuckers departed—the real commies, I mean, not imitation crud like Zhuganov—language was escape, the ticket out. He spoke Chinese. He could do dialects. As a result, he got a job as a DJ at Radio Moscow where, even before glasnost when rock became acceptable, he broadcast the news of Russian rock to the Chinese in Chinese.

"Half the time the scumbags in Moscow didn't know what I'm telling the Chinese. The Chinese officials didn't know shit about rock and roll," he told me once.

"We say whatever we want on air. Good times." Above all, Tolya was an operator; he could bargain your liver out of you.

"Hong Kong." He waved his arm to take possession of the whole lobby. "Last great grab on earth. MMMhmmm. You're hungry, Artyom? Yes? Come."

In the restaurant, the maitre d' practically kissed Tol's hand and led us to a table by a window. Several dozen oysters were set between us by a waiter who also opened a bottle of Champagne. "Krug Grande Cuvée." Tolya raised his glass. It made me think about Dawn Tae. She had been on my mind since I knew I was coming to Hong Kong, but I wasn't in a hurry to call her.

Between Sonny's brief and the business with Lily and the child, I had plenty on my mind. For me, Dawn had been trouble. Big trouble. And still I didn't know if I could resist her, if I was honest. I sipped the Champagne. In Russian, I made Tolya a toast that lasted five minutes and included good fortune for twenty generations of Sverdloffs. I really was pretty fucking glad to see him.

Wiping away tears of laughter, he said, "Russian stinks, Artyom. Rusty. You lost the habit. More oysters?"

I nodded and said, "How's the family?"

"Wife left," he said cheerfully. "Kids great. One already working in movies. Best teen actor at Mosfilm, Anatoly III." He beamed.

I had met Tolya's family during the only trip back to Moscow I ever made. It was more than a year and a half ago now that I had met them, his parents, his kids, and his cousin Svetlana, the woman I fell in love with and planned to marry; Svetlana, blown up by a car bomb outside Tolya's village on a balmy night in early fall when the woods crackled with Russians picking mushrooms. It was Svetlana who glued our friendship and we both knew it, me and Tolya; his eyes teared.

"Mom puts flowers for Svet every day," was all he said.

I changed the subject. "How did you find me? Sonny Lippert called you to babysit my ass?"

Did Tolya have connections with the KGB in the old days? With the Russian police now? I knew that once in a while, when Sonny Lippert needed help with the Russians in Brooklyn, Tolya and Sonny did business together.

"For Mr Sonny Lippert I do some times few phone calls now and then. Here, I am businessman, Artyom."

The waiter tied linen bibs around our necks, brought more Champagne and then some white Burgundy that tasted like nectar. Tolya sipped the wine and leaned over. "Not bad," he said, as another waiter delivered a two-foot mountain of crushed ice that cascaded shellfish—clams, crayfish, shrimp, sea urchins.

"Good, huh, Artie?" Tolya winked at me and I said, "Great," and went on eating.

A gaggle of suits, six of them, sat at the next table and Tolya bowed to them and they bowed back. Dark suited, white bibbed, the men ate oysters and read the time from half-million-dollar watches on their wrists.

"You like mine?" Seeing me look at the watches, he

stretched out his own massive hairy arm where a diamond Rolex was embedded. Then he patted his lips with his bib, took a sea urchin in his paw, swallowed it and watched the waiter serve us a crystal platter of baby lobsters. Silently, Tolya ate. I ate. Finally, he scrubbed his whole face with the bib and took it off. He didn't ask me about my business once. I think he knew. From the minute I saw him, I think he knew all of it, so I let him talk. Tolya did things his own way.

"Me, I have become rich Russian," Tolya said. "Business of Hong Kong is making money. Bedrock. Money machine, stainless steel. Money money money. Great." He looked out the window at the spectacle of lights and buildings and water. "My adorable pimple on ass of China, all up for grabs. Jewel in crown. Whatever. Also, you know what I love?"

"What?"

"No one is shy about this, no one shy about money. Here money is religion. Old rock and rollnik like me, now entrepreneur. Indian, Jew, Jap, Russki, Chink. All making money. Money for all." He whistled a few bars from "Fiddler on the Roof".

"So how did you make all these millions?" I asked.

"This and that. Real estate to start. Pop gave me a few acres at home. Near Moscow, dacha land selling very good to nouveauskis. Seed money, then China. Movie business. Casino business. Hotel in Macau. Several ball-rooms. This dancing thing is huge in Asia, the waltz, the tango. I take lessons. You will see. You want oysters again? Ice cream?"

"No oysters. No ice cream. Talk to me, Tolya. You

knew I was here, didn't you? You came to the hotel looking for me."

"Small town, Artie. I am big man." He laughed. It always got to me, his impersonation of a Russian thug.

"You know what I'd really like?"

"What you like? Artie? What we should do?" He got up and the suits bowed to him again and he bowed back.

"I'd like you to stop talking like some Brighton Beach loser."

Tolya pulled out a thick wad of bills, peeled some off and tossed them on the table.

"Come," he said, and I followed him through the lobby and out into the long driveway. Half a dozen Rolls Royces waited there for the hotel guests, and there were Mercedes and Jags by the score. There was also a customized Hummer. Next to it, a driver in a cap saluted Tolya. "You like it?" Tolya asked. "Like the one Schwarzenegger has."

"Nice," I said.

"Sure. Nice vehicle. Traffic sucks. Let's walk. Do you know why I came to Hong Kong, Artie?"

"Why's that?"

"In a way, because of you." As we plunged into the crowded street beyond the hotel, he switched to Russian. "You always thought that I was a greedy vulgarian, a Russian of the sort you had left behind long ago. Too loud. Too sentimental. Too idle. When my father gave me the land, I took it and I sold it and I made money. I became myself, Artyom. Every man has a certain size to his life, and he can refuse to fill it or he can use it all. I intend to use mine. I have become who I am.

256

Thanks to you." He smiled a melancholy smile, then changed back into his slangy self. "You got that, dick-brain? Huh? Art? Now, you need some help? You got troubles? Double troubles? Sonny Lippert? Women?"

"Yes. All."

"Here." From his pocket Tolya took a sleek cell-phone and handed it to me. "I told the hotel to forward your calls. In case anyone needs you."

"Like who?"

"Like Miss Lily Hanes."

"You know about Lily?"

"This is a small town, like I've been telling you. I knew because your friend Lily Hanes made noise. Too much noise, Artyom. Everyone talks about it. Screaming at people about this child. Calling consulates, TV stations. Saying she is best friend of Peter Leung."

"For Chrissake, Tolya, she lost a child," I said. "And Pete helped her with the adoption in the first place."

"Here, you talk too much, they cut out your tongue. Then kill you. Phone's OK?"

"Thanks."

"You also need a gun, Artie?"

"Do I? You tell me."

"I think yes."

Away from the hotel, the streets were festooned with neon signs and jammed with people. It was bright, hot, noisy, seductive. By comparison, New York in winter had been a bleak monochrome with people muffled in cold-weather clothes. Here, girls, their arms and legs bare, swirled by in glamorous colors. Boys with gold necklaces cruised the blazing shop windows. Families swarmed in and out of restaurants, and the pungent smells wafted through the ventilator shafts onto the night air. Making his way through the crowd was a man with a pole across his shoulders, baskets hanging from the pole. With him was a woman who pulled a handcart piled with suitcases. They moved through the crowd like characters from a period movie and no one turned to look.

"Moving day," said Tolya. "Everyone always moving here."

The shops, which were jammed with watches, cameras, electronics, furs, emitted the pulse and pop of phones and faxes, and on the street, people clutched their cellphones like cans of oxygen; the air literally crackled with them. In every doorway or bar or café, boys in stone-washed jeans slouched over their phones like a love object.

"My town," Tolya said in Russian. "Fast. But efficient, you know? Everything is illegal—whores, gambling, drugs. Everything is available." Around us the streets throbbed with people looking for action. The neon avenues went on for miles.

"Look. I will help you. I will help Lily Hanes. But it's late. Tomorrow, I will fix things officially. Where is Lily?"

"Asleep."

"Good," said Tolya. "I'll let my guy know. He'll be nearby. Just in case. So."

"So."

"So let's look around. Let's see if we can run into Pete

Leung who can perhaps help us over Lily's baby. Let's see if we can meet a few people who can help us with Sonny Lippert's requests."

"Sonny told you about the dead women? The fire? Some guy he calls the Debt Collector?"

"He told me some."

"Tolya?"

"Yes, Artyom darling, what?"

"You ever heard of a kind of smack with the name Hot Poppy?"

"If some new drug exists, I know where we can find out." Tolya winked. "Maybe even if it doesn't exist. Hot Poppy. I like it."

some who were paying tribute to Tolya Sverdloff. A
somed, laughing, bowing, eve
A scaled-down of a Rolls Royce was the equin
the foyer

24

Between two department stores, the windows crammed
with mannequins wearing leather and fur in spite of the
weather, was a nondescript hotel with a revolving door.
Tolya stopped in front of it, the doorman bowed us in
and spun the door for us. Down a winding flight of stairs,
I followed him to the foyer of a cavernous club that
heaved with shadowy figures. A blast of arctic air met us.
Hong Kong was a tropical city; the more luxurious the
environment indoors, the colder the air.

In the distance I could hear karaoke: on an ascending
note, someone warbled, "I Left My Heart in San
Francisco".

From the throbbing gloom, men emerged and
surrounded Tolya, laughing, bowing, a squad of men
paying some kind of tribute to Tolya Sverdloff in the
dark vestibule. Having claimed Hong Kong's nightlife as
his own, he thumped them all on the back and shook
their hands. Then I followed him over the threshold of
the club itself. A scaled-down Rolls Royce was parked
there, along with several other cars. Tolya clambered

into it and gestured for me to follow. The turquoise Rolls was the size of a golf cart.

After a few seconds, my eyes adjusted to the dark and I could make out that there was a track, like the track of a kid's train set, that ran into the club.

"A hostess club, they call it." Tolya chuckled as a girl came alongside the car and handed me a picnic basket with a bottle of Champagne and some glasses. I opened the wine and poured. Tolya pressed a button and we set off down the track into the club in our kiddie car.

"Hostess club run by—how you say?—not quite nice people." He had switched back to his own brand of English. "But friends. And many pretty women."

The club was as big as a football field. There were several dance floors, two restaurants, bars, mirrored doors that led to private rooms, a cabaret, conversation pits with plush purple sectional seating. Music played from behind mirrored ceilings: Barry Manilow, Janni, the Canto-pop I'd already heard on the local MTV.

The car track ran in and out of the various areas; in all of them, stupendous women lounged or danced. When the men in the cars saw a woman they wanted, they disembarked.

Tolya stopped the car a few yards from a bar where six or seven women danced, some naked, some still peeling. A disk jockey sat at the end of the bar, and now he was playing the Bee Gees. "Staying Alive," they warbled, and the women strutted up and down the surface of the mirrored bar, pubic hair shaved into a narrow strip, enormous tits like melons, but hard, shiny, smooth melons that never ever moved.

"Some knockers," Tolya exclaimed as we got out of the car. Instantly, a young guy hopped in and drove it away, back to base.

Tolya was sweaty with excitement as we sat down at a table near the bar. A girl in a G-string teetered by on spike heels and he slapped her on the ass, then tossed her a thick wad of bills. The Bee Gees went on singing.

Tolya ordered caviar and more Champagne. The club filled up. The air got colder. More girls got up on the bar and took their clothes off, and in an area a few yards away, on a curved sofa were a couple of guys with women on their laps. On their dicks to be more precise. The women wiggled and moved their hips. Just watching, Tolya grinned with pleasure. He quit drinking Champagne and ordered brandy.

"You always had an appreciation of artistic women, I recall," I said. "With unnatural tits."

"Yeah. The bigger the better," he agreed. In the corner, a guy getting a lap dance exploded. The woman looked relieved and jumped off him as fast as she could. But Tolya's attention was diverted.

"I've been waiting for you, darling." He rose to greet a woman clad in only a rhinestone G-string. She was over six feet tall. With her, she had a wolfhound on a leash.

"This is Catherine the Great." He kissed her hand. She held out her hand to me. I shook it.

"So, Katya, darling," he said in Russian. "You liked caviar I sent? And this?" Tolya put a fold of large bills in her G-string. "Best hookers in Hong Kong all Russian. Naturally." He patted her dog and fed him a spoonful of the caviar.

"Katya, listen. Mr Leung is a friend of yours?"

"No," she said quickly; Tolya pinched her thigh gently.

"That costs," she said, flicking his hand away.

"How is it you always need so much money?" Tolya chuckled, peeling off more bills.

"I would prefer American dollars, Anatoly, darling," she said. "I am saving up to go to America. When the communists arrive in Hong Kong, I am going. Communists are all cheap bastards. Which Mr Leung?" she asked.

"The son. Peter. Your boss told me it was OK for you to help me, darling. He wants you to help me."

"I never met the son. The father once. Before he died. A cousin. I heard the cousin uses girls to move dope over the border. I don't know the son. I know people who know the son."

"What kind of people, darling?"

"Girls," she said. "A lot of girls."

"Working girls? Some of them working here?"

"Yes."

"Where else?"

"I don't know."

"Don't lie." Tolya's smile faded. "Don't lie to me after what I gave you."

"Macau," she said. "Maybe China. Maybe across the border."

"What else?"

"You didn't ask me about the wife of the son." Sipping the Champagne with her pillowy lips, she flirted with the words, teasing us.

In Russian, I said, "You know the wife of Peter Leung?"

She smiled. "Not exactly. But I know about her."

"What do you know?"

She swept her impossibly long arms out to include all the women in the club then looked at Tolya, who said, "Tell him."

Katya let the lids fall over her pale blue almond-shaped eyes and the lashes were like spiders on the high-boned face; then, languidly, she opened them. "People say she is one of us," Katya purred. "A dancer," she added. "A whore."

"You're a liar," Tolya said. "Now tell me one more thing, darling, to make it worthwhile spending all my dollars. Tell me where can I get some Hot Poppy."

But Katya only shrugged. Until, as we started to leave, she ran after Tolya, her high-heeled mules going tippy-tap on the floor. She whispered something in his ear and he took some more money and pushed it under her G-string.

"She says she knows this Hot Poppy but she was lying," Tolya said when we were out in the street. "They all lie."

"I'm going back to the hotel."

"No, Artie. The night is—how do you say?—young. Come on." He hailed a cab.

In the taxi, while Tolya chattered at the driver in Chinese and we did ninety through a tunnel under the harbor, I used the cell-phone to check in with Sonny Lippert and with Lily. Sonny said he was faxing me. Lily

264

said all she wanted was sleep and I told her Tolya's guy was there for her—he was in the hotel parking lot. I gave her his number. I gave her mine. "I'll just sleep now," she said. "I'm glad you're here, Artie."

The taxi pulled up in front of a waterfront bar. I looked out and saw we were on the other side of the harbor from my hotel. We were on Hong Kong Island among the skyscrapers. For twenty-four hours, I had been looking at that skyline from across the harbor.

The drunker Tolya got, the more agile he was, and he navigated the night like a hippo in water. We went from bar to bar, hotel lounge to hostess club, stopping for drinks, for barbecued ribs, to buy the Monte Cristos Tolya adored. In Hong Kong, he had friends everywhere. Everywhere we went, people were edgy, anxious. "Shall I stay, Tolya?" an old British reporter said to him. "Should we go?" asked a retired Russian general. Like the humidity, anxiety seemed to have settled onto everyone.

"Anatoly Anatolyvitch, welcome!" Don Ho was not anxious. Don was making barrels of bread, he told me. Like everyone else, Don was an old pal of Tolya Sverdloff. With a string of Hawaiian theme pubs across Asia—Don had taken his idol's name as a kind of nom de guerre—he was making money hand over fist. Business was very very good, he said, as he seated us in his pub. On the stage, hula girls did their thing. I remembered that, by a weird coincidence, Don, who was Shanghai born, was a remote relative of the Taes. I asked about Dawn. Don held out his hands, palms up, wrinkled his nose and gave his grass skirt a shake. "We do not occupy same social scene." He offered us drinks in a coconut shell. We drank several of them. With the rum in me, I could barely see straight.

"I can't drink any more. I'm not sure if I can stand up any more. I'm tired, Tolya. It's one in the morning and I'm weary as fuck."

"One more for the road. Then I call driver," he said.

"It's all bullshit, you know. All this sniffing around is Russian melodrama."

"I am Russian, I do what I can, Artie, you know. I told you. OK, Sonny Lippert asked me. Help him, Tolya, he says. Help him help me before more girls die in New York City. This is how I know to help. Look around. Call me James Bondski. I call you Yankee Doodle Dandski. What do you want from me?"

"American Club," Tolya answered, as we emerged from an elevator on the forty-seventh floor of a skyscraper in the business district. "Home sweet home. America the beautiful. CIA. ABC."

At a Steinway grand, a guy played Cole Porter and he was good. Tolya chose a table near a window, went to the long bar himself and returned with three vodka martinis and a man in a suit.

"Chris Roy," Tolya said. "Artie Cohen. Chris is a friend of Pete Leung."

"Hi," Chris Roy said.

"Hi," I said, and we shook hands and the three of us settled into deep chairs. Chris Roy polished off his martini in one gulp. "Great view."

After a night out in Hong Kong, I was sick to death

of views. You got views with booze, views with food, views with strippers. Spectacular views. Panoramic views. Views of the skyline. Views of the peak or the water or the out islands or all of them at the same time. OK for a bird, but views don't tell you much about the town you're in. Some geography, maybe. Otherwise, not one fucking thing. For that, you need people in a landscape.

"So. You know Pete Leung a long time?"

"I was in grad school with Pete briefly," said Chris Roy.

"And Dawn?"

"No. No. I never met her then, not at the time," he said. "I went to the State Department; Pete stayed with money. We kept in touch. You know how that is. You're American."

I said, "Yes." Tolya raised an eyebrow and flicked an olive from a bowl on the table into his mouth.

"So. What can I do for you, Art? Any pal of Tolya's is a pal of mine. Tolya is Mr Hong Kong, of course, as you know, I'm sure. Everyone loves Tolya Sverdloff." He shot a faintly patronizing glance at Tolya, who was talking into his cellphone across the table. Tolya had let Chris Roy—and for all I knew, everyone else in Hong Kong—assume he was a clown.

"Christ, I remember what a trip it was when we started getting pally with the Russkis. What a time. So. What can I tell you about Hong Kong?"

"Whatever, Chris." I drank the martini. "What brought you over here?"

"Well, officially Hong Kong was British, of course.

267

But it's really been ours for years. Huge financial stakes here. Officially, being anti-imperialist, the US is for the return to the motherland." He signaled for a waiter.

"Reality is, we need the Chinese market. We need them to buy our shit, we need them to buy our cigarettes. Tobacco guys were desperate, they need markets, they leaned on George Bush. Reagan. Mrs Thatcher, too. Everyone was screaming back in '89, '90. With my help and our distinguished leaders, we have made this market our own. We've even got the Chinese girls smoking. They think it's way cool."

"What about the banking rules? They're pretty loose here, Chris, that right?"

"Sure are, Art. Secrecy in the banking trade here makes the Swiss look downright candid. Big banks. Private banks. Gang banks."

"Smugglers' banks?"

"Why not? Smugglers. Pirates. Russkis."

"I see. Very interesting. Tolya, could you get some more drinks?" I said, and when he had gone, I leaned over to Chris and lowered my voice. "So, uh, between us, could we talk about other types of smokes? Christ. I mean besides the tobacco trade, you know?"

By now, Chris was drunk. His watery blue eyes were rimmed with red. He looked to me like one of those CIA specimens who always stay on too long in a foreign country. For Chris I made like a spook. He was thrilled to talk business.

"Sure. Sure, Artie. I get the picture. You're talking something confidential."

"That's right, Chris. You know how it is. So, look,

did you ever meet anyone that scored some smack named Hot Poppy, Chris?"

"Why?"

"I have some interest, Chris."

Slowly, he smiled. "I'm surprised you know about it. It's hard to come by. Very rare. Specialty stuff for the rich and recherché." He was wrecked on booze. "You know someone, for instance, who's looking to score, Artie?"

"So to speak. Yeah. Someone."

"I'll give you a call if I can help your friend, OK?" He was knowing. "And shall I tell Pete you're looking for him? If I see him?"

"Do that, Chris. Tell him. Tell him I'm at the Regent Hotel for, let's say, another forty-eight hours."

Roy took a pill out of his pocket and ate it. "Heart. I'm thirty-six and I got heart stuff wrong." He looked out the window. "Fucking views," he said. "Who's going to run it all? How's it gonna be for the millions of poor bastards that ran away from the commies already and got themselves a life here, twenty-four grand per annum, in dollars, even a little nibble of democracy lately. You think the pricks from the People's Republic know how to run a railroad? You think the PRC is gonna care about a western education? You want your home town defended by the People's Liberation Army, Artie? The PLA guys that rolled the tanks over kids in Tiananmen Square? It sucks." Chris Roy took another pill out of his pocket. "What the hell. I'll be going home. Wherever that is. For now, Art, it's party time. Yes!" He punched the air with his fist. "Yes!"

Tolya, who was no clown, watched Chris go. "He's a jackass, but he's right, you know," Tolya said. We drank for a few minutes silently, watching the skyline and the harbor.

"Do you know, Artyom, that Hong Kong is one nine-thousandth the size of China?"

"You looked it up."

"I always liked school. Hong Kong Island is a tiny rock. Out there across the harbor is Kowloon, the New Territories, and then China. China all the way to Mongolia, to Tibet, to the Russian border. Think of it in terms of your New York City. Hong Kong Island as the Manhattan you love. Kowloon, the New Territories, are the boroughs, Brooklyn, Queens, Bronx. Worker housing, factories, airport, cargo terminal, power plants, water supply. Also beaches, universities, fishing villages. Like New York, right?"

"Sure."

"Borough of Bronx, it's connected with mainland of America, right?"

"Right."

"So imagine if on the border of Bronx is one billion Chinese. One fucking billion plus, all wanting to take a bite. Prada meets the People's Liberation Army. This is a city on the fucking edge of a nervous breakdown but you know what? End of last year, stocks soared, real estate went through the roof. You can make a shitload of money waiting for Armageddon."

Tolya had reserved himself a suite at my hotel, and when we got back, we stood in the lobby for a minute. In the wrinkled green suit, he looked terribly tired. "Tomorrow we begin. Tomorrow, we begin with Lily. The other thing, also."

"Tolya?"

"What?"

"You said Sonny told you about the dead girls in New York, the kidnapping, the extortion. You actually think they can pull the strings here in Hong Kong on stuff that goes down in New York?"

He kissed me on the cheeks three times, Russian-style.

"If there is money involved, you can pull any string." He held up his cell-phone. "The world is only about this big, Artyom. It's only about as big as your dick." He laughed. "And you can carry it in your pocket."

25

The next day, and most of the day after that, Tolya
turned on the juice. By the time Lily was up, he was
waiting for us in the coffee shop, dressed in a black
Armani suit, his guy at his side, a list of appointments in
one hand, his cellphone in the other.

Sober, Tolya's English was charming. He greeted Lily
and ordered breakfast for her. Unfurling her napkin, he
put it on her lap and then buttered her pancakes and
poured the maple syrup delicately between the layers.
"It's nice?" he asked.

"Yes," she said.

"Then eat some more." Tolya smiled and listened to
Lily talk.

After a while, he said gently, "I think, Lily, that you
should step out of the picture for a few days. People
know you have been making noises about Chinese.
Noises about adoption, about girl babies."

"So what?"

"This looks like the West," Tolya went on, "but is
not exactly the West. I told Artyom, a person could get

hurt here for talking too much. Please, Lily Hanes. Would you consider this, stepping out of the picture for a few days?"

"I can't do that."

In Russian, Tolya asked his guy to get the car. Then he got up. "I understand. Come. We'll try to fix something."

In the Hummer, we criss-crossed Hong Kong all day, visiting men and women in government offices, visiting consuls from three countries, also bankers, policemen, friends. Like the night before, Tolya was welcome everywhere; by day, though, Tolya was jolly but sober. This was a city built for business by day. With Lily he was lovely. He made her buy some clothes. At a restaurant he ordered snacks she found irresistible. He even got her to laugh.

For a day and a half, we were on the move or on the phone. I tried Pete Leung. Eventually, I tried Dawn. I came up empty handed. I took a call from Sonny Lippert, who gave me some names. While Tolya took Lily shopping, I introduced myself to Sonny's contacts who seemed like good cops. But they were busy men—trouble brewing, they all said, and I was unofficial.

For most of the day and most of the day after, I watched Lily suck hope out of all the activity; when she insisted on buying tiny outfits for Grace, I wanted to cry for her.

The official we were looking for, when Tolya finally tracked him down, was a middle-aged man with an ashen, drained face, and he sat at a desk in a government office on Ice House Street, a tensor lamp on his desk, feeding paper into a shredder. Between the thumb and forefinger of the other hand he held a cigarette. His short-sleeved white shirt was buttoned to the neck. He looked up. "What can I do for you?"

I was alone with Lily. Tolya had moved on to another appointment.

"I understand you might know what happened to this child." Lily pushed a photograph of Grace across his desk. He turned off the shredder and glanced at it, then snapped open a drawer in the metal desk and riffled a few thick manila files. Behind him was a pile of brown cartons. Books stood in stacks on the floor.

"Where is she?" I said.

"This child is no longer yours." Ignoring me, he picked up some more paper and spoke to Lily. "She will be placed with another family. Currently she is in a facility, probably in Guangzhou. Possibly in another city. I think you have been told before."

"When? When will she be placed?" Lily was very tight, very tense. I could see the skin on her neck pulse with rage.

"As soon as possible in order not to cause disruption in her life. There are always many families waiting."

"Show me the file. I want to talk to your boss."

"I am the boss," he said.

"What about trying again?" I said. "We have time."

"I have no time." The man had heard it all before. "I am leaving this job. This country if I can. Someone else will come. Someone from the new government."

"From China?"

"Yes. From the mainland."

"Is that why you're shredding your files?" I didn't care why, but I figured if I showed some interest, he might do a little extra work for Lily. She was restless and obsessed. I think she had forgotten everything except the child. I said to him, "You expect trouble?"

"Some of my employees have been involved in pro-democracy rallies."

"Where will you go?"

"Anywhere I can," he said as the shredder hummed.

Lily leaned over the man's desk, her face a few inches from us. "You don't care because Grace is a girl, isn't that right? In China, all the abandoned babies are girls. If they get lucky, if someone doesn't drown them. Ninety-seven per cent female it said on the adoption forms."

"Lily, let's go back to the hotel."

Lily turned to me, but the caustic words were for the man. "Did you know, Artie, that children in China, especially girls, can't be adopted? They have to be abandoned. Formally. *Then* they're put up for adoption. Grace was tossed on the sidewalk near a paint factory in some godforsaken village and left to die. Adoption is actually illegal. It's people like him who make the rules." To the man himself, she said, "Why don't you do something?"

Removing his wire-rimmed spectacles, the man behind the desk got up, walked to the door and opened it. "I don't make any rules. Now please go." Staring at Lily, face impassive, he added coldly, "I have three daughters."

By the time we got back to the hotel, Lily was wrung out. There was no more room for maneuvering, no more time. I think she knew it, too, but all she said was, "I want to take a shower, Artie. Then I'm going to sleep."

"I'll stay with you."

"Don't be silly. I'm not going to kill myself."

I stayed a while anyway.

Whatever shit's going on, it's better for me when Lily's around. That night, waiting for her to fall asleep, I brushed the hair away from her face and I thought, suddenly: I'd like to marry her. I wanted to marry Lily.

Later, in my room, I made some more calls. Tolya sat on the bed, his cellphone in his hand. On a table was the remains of the room-service dinner we had eaten. He looked up. "Tomorrow night I have to go to my place on Macau for a couple days. You and Lily must come with me."

"We'll see," I said. "Tolya?"

"Artyom?"

"Get me that gun."

26

The gun was delivered to my room along with a bottle of eighteen-year-old Scotch ten minutes after Tolya went to bed. He had wrapped the Gluck neatly in a hand towel, then placed it in a leather bag. Gucci, I think. A room-service waiter brought it on a tray. I felt better.

In the morning I left a note for Tolya and one for Lily. The gun in my pocket, I got a cab and gave the driver the address that Tolya had obtained for me.

The house itself, when we got there, was on the top of Hong Kong Island. The Peak, they call it. Thick morning mist swirled around the mossy green mountain and, from the road, I could barely see the front gate. The driver, an accommodating young guy, agreed to park behind a stand of trees, the cab hidden from the house by the foliage and the fog. I went up the rest of the way to the house on foot.

Beyond a low stone wall was the compound, an elegant sprawl that consisted of two houses and a swimming pool, a detached garage and a tennis court. Slowly, I made my way around the perimeter, glad for the enveloping fog. It was early Sunday morning and I wondered if everyone in the house was away or only asleep. The gardens were gauzy green and gray, and when I got a better look, I saw that the tiles in the pool were green, too. Chinese green. Celadon, they call it. It looked like old porcelain. There was a pool house and a gazebo. It had Dawn's mark on it. It was all very expensive, and even the security was subtle. It took me ten minutes to find the spy cameras; they were tucked into artificial birds' nests cunningly placed in ornamental trees.

"You know how much land costs on an island like this?" I could hear Tolya saying. But Tolya was down the mountain, across the harbor, asleep in bed. Me, I was up here, like a burglar on the prowl in this thick green fog.

Was Dawn in there, asleep, refusing to answer my calls? If she had vanished, I would find her and she could lead me to Pete Leung. But I had tried everything, every number in Tolya's book, every contact.

It was only instinct that made me lurk there at the edges of the house instead of ringing the bell. Somehow I thought the house might give up some kind of secret. But there was only the silence and the beautiful gardens and the cameras whirring in those silly little trees.

"She's one of us," the Russian hooker had said. "A whore." She was lying, Tolya said of the hooker. All I knew was Dawn was a junkie and they always lied, but I'd known that since the night in New York. And when she had pushed her leather skirt up over her hips, I had gone for her like a dog in heat.

The ancient bronze bell-pull at the low wrought-iron gate tinkled faintly, but it was enough.

The front door flew open, and a maid in slippers and a pink bathrobe appeared. Arms piled with clothes, she flapped furiously towards the gate, knocking into bushes, shouldering them away imperiously. "No one home," she shouted. "No one. Everyone vacation. Go away."

I turned as if to go. The maid retreated. I waited two, three, four minutes. Nothing moved. I was getting ready to leave when I thought about the clothes. What was the maid doing with all those fancy clothes in her arms?

Making my way slowly towards the garage—it was a hunch, but what else did I have?—I saw a black Jaguar parked outside. The maid appeared and so did an elderly man in a chauffeur's cap with a suitcase under his arm. He stowed it in the trunk of the car. The maid gave him the heap of clothes and he put them in the trunk, too. I waited. Clouds moved lower across the peak; it started to rain.

The branch of a cherry tree poked me in the eye. Sweat ran down my back, rain dripped on my head; like a rat in a puddle, dripping, I waited. Something crackled again. I got hold of the gun.

"Private property," a man screamed. I turned around. In one hand, the old chauffeur had a long rake. In the other hand, he had a gun and, as I turned, he pointed it at me. My gun was already in my hand. Somehow, it misfired. I never knew how.

The old man dropped his weapons like a couple of

hot potatoes and scuttled back to the house. He yelled plenty, but he could run, so I figured he wasn't hurt bad. At least I hadn't killed him, but I was deep in shit. Deep shit Hong-Kong style, and it smelled nasty.

It didn't take much to figure Hong Kong wasn't the kind of town where you could trespass on the rich and shoot up their servants without anyone noticing. I ran like fuck for my taxi, wondering if the driver had waited. Wait for me, I thought. Goddamn it, wait!

He was there. I jumped in and, as I shut the door, I saw the black Jaguar slide out of the gates of the house. In the driver's seat was the elderly chauffeur. He looked healthy enough. I had missed, thank Christ.

"Can you follow him without him seeing us?"

"Sure," said my cabbie. "Sure."

"Then go. Go!"

The old man drove the Jaguar for about half an hour doing fifty. We followed. At a palatial house somewhere off a coastal road, he picked up two women. We followed the Jag inland for maybe another twenty minutes, keeping a distance. The streets got poorer, the apartment houses were festooned with laundry, the shops run down.

In the middle of nowhere—it could have been Queens—the black car drew up in front of a low building with a tiled roof. Two women got out. As the Jag pulled away and the women walked into the building, I saw that one of them was small but with the elegant posture of a dancer. The other woman was Dawn Tae.

My driver was antsy. I gave him some money and a piece of paper. He copied down the sign on the front of the building and the name of the street. He hitched up his jeans and offered me a cigarette, then got into his cab.

"What is this place?" I said.

"It's an orphanage," he said.

Dawn was in the playground. The rain had let up. The sun was out. A dozen kids of five or six ran around, shouted, climbed up a jungle gym, rolled on the ground, jumped rope, kicked a soccer ball and tried to sock each other. Little girls pulled at Dawn's arms, kissing her. She kissed them back and laughed. It was a performance; it was as if she knew I was watching. She looked up at me.

"Hello, Artie. I'm glad you came." It was the same thing she had said that night in Riverdale and again in Ricky's apartment. She said it like a mantra. Dawn's allure was that she made you think you were the only guy on earth that could satisfy her, or save her, or both. There was also her appetite for raw sex.

"You look well."

"I feel better." She introduced me to Alice Wing.

The woman with the dancer's posture held out her hand. It was small, soft and perfectly dry, the most expensive hand I had ever touched.

Alice Wing wore a green jacket and black jeans, but the pearls she had tucked discreetly under the collar of her polo shirt were as big as cherries.

"Alice takes care of me. And the kids," Dawn said. "I

281

needed help, Alice got it for me. I've been staying at her house for a while. But you probably know that."

Alice put her arm around Dawn. "She's like my own."

"Who are these kids?"

"Local orphans," said Alice Wing. "A few from over the border, the lucky ones. The physical plant here may look a bit run down, but the staff is terrifically good. Well trained. Caring. Hong Kong has very good policies, very good facilities, like this one. I don't usually come out here on Sunday, but I wanted to check on one of the babies. Would you like to see the rest?"

"Sure."

"Dawn will show you."

I followed Dawn into the building where she showed me a school room and the dormitories. Road Runner grinned loonily from posters on the wall. The children Dawn passed chattered at her; she spoke to all of them. She knew their names. She had learned Chinese at school and in her parents' restaurant, a willing student. "It will come in handy," she used to say, "when I'm a big tycoon."

The masonry walls sweated in the heat, but in the nursery four nurses sat patiently in a circle, feeding the babies they held on their laps. In a large blue crib were three more infants. Two crawled and yelled, but it was the third child Dawn picked up.

"Ducks and geese, we call the babies. The geese are the fatties, the ducks are the skinny ones. I'm not sure why—ducks aren't really skinny, are they?" She bounced the child in her arms. "We'll make her fat too. We'll make her well. We will, you know."

"So how's Pete?"

"I don't see him much." Her tone changed. The smile disappeared. Dawn's face disengaged and became a mask.

"Where is he?"

"Away. Business as usual."

"Can we talk?"

"Now?"

"Why not now?"

"I wasn't expecting you yet. I have some things to do. I'll call you tonight. I promise."

"Yet?"

Dawn babbled on cheerfully. "It was a slip of the tongue, darling."

"Then aren't you going to ask where I'm staying?"

"So where are you staying, Artie?" It was a charade, of course. She knew exactly where I was staying. I had left her messages and she had obviously received them, but I said, "I'm at the Regent. Call me. OK?"

"I'm glad you found me." Dawn walked me to the front door. "I'm glad you couldn't resist. And Artie, darling?"

"What?"

"I'm thrilled you're here. But do me a favor. Don't go around taking pot shots at my chauffeur any more." She kissed my cheek. "If you do, I might have to turn you in."

She lifted her gorgeous face to look me in the eye and I had the feeling Dawn was what I was looking for. Volatile, impetuous, she was always high on something, dope, men, even this thing here with the orphans, and her fix, whichever it was, required money. Lots of money. In that split second when she looked in my eyes, I had the crazy idea it was Dawn Tae who was the Debt Collector.

27

"I am Ringo Chen," a polished British voice said. I was in the hotel coffee shop when a thinner, younger version of Jerry Chen appeared, unbuttoned his natty navy blue blazer and held out his hand. "Inspector Ringo Chen. May I sit down?"

"Look up my goody-two-shoes cousin, Ringo," Jerry Chen had said. "He's your kind of cop."

Seeing Ringo, I wondered if he knew about the shot I'd taken at Dawn's chauffeur. But he only shook my hand, and said, "Sonny Lippert asked me to get in touch. How can I help you?"

A waiter appeared and I ordered coffee and toast and a mango. "So how's Cousin Jerry?"

"Jeremy has taken some leave. Also leave of his senses." He tittered at his joke. "Before either, however, he told me about his case. He wanted my help. I avoided him, at least until Sonny Lippert called me in on it." He was clearly anxious to put some distance between himself and his scumbag of a relative.

"Coffee?"

"I'll get some tea." At the same time, Tolya and Lily arrived, Lily in a new shirt and pants, her hair washed.

She kissed me. "I behaved like a fool yesterday." She turned to Ringo. "Are you from Hong Kong?"

"Yes, I am. But I went to London as a teenager. I lived with some relations in a place called Milton Keynes. Horrible place. The Chinese love it. You can have a big modern house. We don't like old houses, most of us."

"And you became a cop over there?" Lily was curious.

"In our family, there had always been policemen. Jeremy was the hero. He became a heroic New York cop. To tell you the truth, I never liked him. His recent activities confirm my feelings." The tea came and Ringo splashed some milk into it. "I never cared for London myself."

"In what way?" Lily leaned forward, listening.

"When I was first a policeman in London, 'Boy,' they'd say, 'go and make the tea.' They called me Chink and Chow, they slashed my tires—I'm talking about London. I hated it. I hated the corruption. I could understand the corruption in third world countries, but in London it wasn't necessary. It was accepted, and I hated it. Egg the pudding, gild the lily, that's what they all thought."

"Perfidious Albion, my father always said."

Ringo put his cup down. "Was your father a policeman too?"

"In a way," I said, thinking about my pop, poor bastard, a star of the KGB in his youth, him and his pal

Gennadi. When they kicked him out I was only twelve. "In a way, he was. They're all dead."

"What's on for today?" Lily asked Tolya.

"I'm sorry," Ringo said to me. "I've been making chit-chat. How can I help you?"

"We have an appointment at some agency, don't we, Tolya?" Lily said, and showed Ringo Chen her picture of the baby.

"I don't think you should go into Central," Ringo said.

"Why not?"

"There was a deadline on emigration permits yesterday. Sometimes it gets sticky."

She tossed her napkin onto the table and looked at Tolya.

"Don't worry," he said. "It will be OK."

Ringo got up and walked towards the men's room; I followed.

"I can't help your friend over her baby, I'm afraid. It's way off my turf. She'd be better off going back to America."

"If I could find Pete Leung, I could help her," I said.

He turned his head sharply. "What's Leung got to do with it?"

"He helped her with the adoption."

"You're joking." He said it half to himself.

"Why should I be?"

"Let's just say Peter Leung's reputation is not as a warm and fuzzy chap. Still, your friend is obviously very well connected. The Leungs have a lot of power here. Very rich. Very social. Perhaps he's simply preoccupied."

Ringo was unconvincing. "Look, I'll do what I can. But things are tough, we're tight on manpower."

"On the other business, Ringo. Sonny put you in the loop? You're up to date?"

"That's actually why I came over. Sonny Lippert has put me in the picture. I have a few ideas. Get a visa for the mainland," he said. "Get a visa from the concierge. Double entry. It never hurts to have it. But first, do try to get your friend Miss Hanes to go home, if you can."

"What kind of sticky?" I asked.

"There have been demonstrations," he said. "Nothing much to worry about. Not yet. Just sticky."

"Why the visa?"

"It's always useful."

"Ringo? The cops here in Hong Kong. You guys are armed?"

"Yes, indeed." He buttoned the blazer. "Very much so," said Ringo Chen, and he strolled out of the room.

28

"Sticky!" Ringo's idea of sticky was a lot different from mine when the riot started later that afternoon.

After Ringo left the hotel, we took the Star Ferry to the Central District. There was an hour to kill until Lily's appointment. We strolled, her, me and Tolya, in the heart of the town.

The sun glinted off the massed skyscrapers, the gold and silver, the bronze and glass, the competitive architectural marvels bankers had built to testify to their god. Mammon never lived better and Hong Kong was his Olympus.

Pocket parks and gardens were tucked tight between the endless skyscrapers that then rose in stands up and up against the mossy green mountain. Down in front of the City Hall, a bride and groom, the boy in white tie, the girl in a dress like a pile of meringue pies, posed for a wedding picture.

Suddenly, the chatter of a thousand voices spiraled towards us from the main square. Hundreds, maybe thousands of women, awash in shopping bags, sat, stood, sprawled, sunned themselves in the square. Like birds, they flocked and twittered in the sunshine.

"What's the language?"

"Tagalog," Tolya said. "They're Filipinas. They're the housemaids. They get Sundays off, so they come here to see their friends."

I was mesmerized. Women sat on the edge of a fountain. They read newspapers and letters. A girl in red shorts rolled her friend's hair on pink plastic rollers. Transistor radios played and some of the women danced together. Others ate or swapped plastic casserole dishes; the spicy smells circulated towards us. A man appeared with a guitar and began to play. Before long he was joined by more musicians.

"I have heard rich women here say that a full-time maid is the ultimate Valium," Tolya laughed. "The guy with the guitar is very good. Let's listen." He took Lily's arm and we moved closer to the square. Lily looked at her watch. "It's all right," said Tolya. "We'll make the appointment. Don't worry."

In the square, the mood was festive, the women all laughing, the music growing louder. The whole town seemed to rumble with the noise and the music. I thought it was the music, but then Tolya looked at the sky and I heard the thunder, too.

"What is it?" Lily asked. The sky was still clear.

The noise got louder. A murmur of panic ran through the crowd as women started packing their belongings into the shopping bags. There were shouts. Women began to wail.

"What is it?"

"They think it's an earthquake." Nervously, Tolya flipped open his cell-phone. "I'll call my driver." It was too late. Much too late.

Police sirens screamed. Tolya held onto Lily, I took her other hand and we tried to move out of the square, away from the sound of the sirens. We made it half a block.

"Look," Lily cried. "Look!"

Coming down the avenue was a mass of bodies moving steadily. As they came closer, the noise grew, the thunder-like roar, the rumble that scared the Filipina maids, who even now flapped around like trapped birds.

"What's the time?" Lily shouted.

Tolya said, "You'll have to forget your appointment," and she replied, "I see. Yeah. I understand."

The crowds tried to get out of the way of the marchers. Above us, people came out on hotel balconies. Someone began dumping shredded paper. Covered in the stuff, as if for some macabre celebration, Tolya managed to get hold of a man in the crowd near us. For maybe thirty seconds, they talked intently to each other, then Tolya turned to us. He was very tense. He spoke to me in Russian.

"It's a pro-democracy demonstration. There are rumors the Chinese are planning to crack down even harder on free speech. Rumors of more corruption. Also, many people who tried to get exit visas yesterday failed. They were turned away. Hundreds. Thousands. I can't tell. It's bad. Very bad."

Lily said, "The white banners are for the color of death."

As the marchers came even closer—I could see the headbands they wore now and the slogans on their banners—a band of thuggish kids materialized from God knew where and began taunting them. They jeered and screamed, provoking the cops who streamed in from the other direction.

"Let's get the fuck out of here," I yelled.

"I want to see what's happening, Artie. Take Tolya and get out of here," Lily shouted, but I clutched her arm.

The marchers, the goons, the cops, the onlookers merged into a heaving mass, thousands of us, tens of thousands—I couldn't tell. The Filipina maids got caught in it. I could hear their shrill tweet as dozens of them went down. Shopping bags flapping, they stumbled and fell and the crowd trampled them. One woman reached for me and I felt her fingers on mine, but the crowd carried her away.

We were trapped, the three of us locked together in a nightmare. The nightmare where you're drowning in glue.

Like a movie shot out of focus at the wrong speed, the buildings moved by. At the intersections, the crowd broke apart, people crashed away into the narrow side streets, then the mob reformed. The noise was indescribable. The crowd roared its slogans. The cops screamed through loudspeakers. I heard glass break. Overhead, a fleet of helicopters buzzed in the humid afternoon. The heat was suffocating.

Suddenly, a banner flapped down on my face like some angry predator. I felt an elbow in my ribs and thought I heard a crack. We kept on moving. "Sticky," Ringo had said. Sticky! Christ!

Tolya towered over everyone. Sheer brute force on his side, he shoved through a wall of bodies into a smaller tributary of people, a breakaway demonstration that wound its way up a narrow hilly street, past a row of shops and stalls. We stumbled over rattan furniture. A cage full of snakes burst open.

All the time, I could feel Lily next to me. When she heard Tolya's nervous shouts, she yelled at him, "It will be OK," and I saw her face. She was flushed, but her eyes were bright, as if she was looking out at the world again instead of turning in.

Lily saw the gap in the crowd before I did. "Go. Go." She held Tolya's arm and my hand, and we ran like fuck into a narrow alleyway. Dipping in and out of back streets, moving in the opposite direction to the mob, Lily in control, somehow we got back to the middle of town where we shoved our way through the door of the Mandarin Hotel. From somewhere outside came the crack of a rifle shot. Then more sirens. The riot police massed in ferocious ranks.

The Mandarin lobby was jammed with reporters, camera crews, tourist and hotel guests, all of us milling, fretting, demanding service. Hotel guys in striped pants ran around reassuring everyone. Waiters hefted trays of booze and tea. Champagne corks popped. More rifle shots could be heard outside.

Tolya, who was drawn and ashy—the riot got to him bad—commandeered three chairs and ordered a bottle of brandy. Then he took both of Lily's hands in his.

She sat down. "I know. No appointment. Grace is gone for good. With all this, who has time? With riots and chaos and the Chinese settling in, who can think about one baby?" Her smile was wry. "And why the hell should they?" She looked at the lobby. "The cocktail party at the apocalypse, eh?" She rubbed her left temple. Her hand came away streaked with blood.

"Do you want a doctor?"

"It's nothing."

A cameraman in a flak jacket separated himself from the crowd in the lobby and began running towards us. "Lily? It's you? My God, Lily Hanes. How the fuck are you, man?"

Lily practically leaped out of her chair into his arms. She hugged him and, beaming, they pounded each other on the back. She dragged me out of my chair and introduced me. Cambodia, Salvador, Colombia, Moscow, East Berlin, Northern Ireland, Eritrea, they traded war stories and made plans to meet at the next revolution.

"We had a lot of fun," Lily said when her pal had gone.

"You were very cool out there in the streets. You were sensational, Lily."

As if she had reclaimed her old self, she grinned at me. "Toots, this is nothing compared to when we left Saigon."

"You were there?" Tolya, who had finished most of the brandy, was impressed.

"I used to be a reporter, didn't I? I was there the day

we lifted off from the embassy." I thought of Pansy. Pansy had been a baby that day in 1975 when the helicopters lifted off from the embassy roof in Saigon. Lily took my hand.

"I knew it was finished for me and Grace today, that I'd have to get over her or I'd be completely braindead. Somehow, out there, I realized having an obsession would never be the same as having Grace. And I'll never have her."

"If you want to keep on, I'm here for you."

"I'm going home."

"I'm so sorry about the baby." I put my arms around Lily.

She peered at the calendar on her watch. "It's four weeks and two days since I got Grace's picture in New York. She was mine for more than a month," she said. "I think that's all I'm going to get."

Tolya fixed Lily's flight home. Before he left for Macau, I told him about the gun going off and he took the pistol from me and stuffed it in his briefcase. "In case anyone comes looking for it," he said. "Just in case. I'll get you another one," he promised.

Later that day, I stood with Lily near the departure gate.

"I'm sorry I've been such a pain in the ass," she said. "I'm sorry I made you come to Hong Kong. It was for nothing."

"No it wasn't. Not for me. I'm not sorry. I'll be home soon, I swear. But I have to do something. I promised Sonny Lippert. It's about the dead women in New York.

I don't want to lie to you again. But I need to do this. Like you said, it's who I am. Will you be OK, on the plane I mean?"

Lily kissed me. "Sure I will. Hey, like I said, this is nothing compared to when we left Saigon."

They called her flight but all I did was to kiss her back. Then, hoisting her bag over her shoulder, Lily smoothed her red hair with the other hand and tugged her sweater down over her jeans. Straightening her back and shoulders like a schoolgirl, without turning around, she marched through to the departure gate. I should have run after her right then and told her I wanted us to get married, but I didn't.

Ringo Chen called me at the hotel and said, "There's a rumor you've been firing off an unregistered weapon."

"It was an accident."

"The gun or firing it?"

"Can you help me here, Ringo?"

"I'll do my best. We're all on overtime because of the demo today. Keep your head down. There's nothing I can do on a Sunday, but I'll sort it out. Leave it with me until tomorrow. And forget about carrying any weapons. You'll do what I say, won't you?" It wasn't a question. There was a steely side to Ringo Chen.

"By the way, Ringo, ever heard of Hot Poppy?"

"No. What is it?"

"Some kind of irradiated heroin."

Ringo chortled. "A fabulous name, but I don't think so. I honestly don't." Still laughing, he hung up.

After that I called Chris Roy and flattered him with

some spook talk; he promised he'd get hold of Pete Leung. Then the phone rang again and it was Sonny.

"Art? Hey? I got something for you. I think this is the information we've been looking for. I'm getting you an address, OK? It might take me a day to nail it, but I think it could be interesting. I'll fax you."

"What address? What are you talking about?"

"Just trust me, man. Hello?"

"I hear you."

"And get Ringo Chen to go with you, OK? I put him in the loop. I'll fax you. If this works, then you can think about coming home."

"You trust Ringo, Sonny?"

"A hundred ten per cent," he answered.

I hung up on Sonny, switched on CNN and watched the report of the riot. It had been contained. It was over. A hundred injured, none dead. On TV, the riot police looked like brutal bastards but they did the job.

That evening, it was as if nothing had happened. The riot had occurred just across the harbor, but here in Kowloon, eight minutes away by ferry, people strolled and shopped and went into Pizza Hut with their kids for a slice or grabbed a Big Mac up the block. It was just another Sunday night. Idly, I drifted into Nathan Road and considered buying a watch. I had been a jerk with the gun. It was hard to know if Dawn's maid had reported it or if Dawn herself called the cops. She had taunted me with it at the orphanage.

Was it a threat? *Was* Dawn the Debt Collector? Was she fronting for her husband, for Pete? If, as Ringo said, the Leungs were very rich and very social, why would Pete run dope? Why would he use hookers at a club to run in his shit? Unless it was a particular kind of shit, the kind his wife needed. The kind called Hot Poppy.

At the hostess club, I looked for the big Russian stripper. For a second, in the throbbing gloom, I thought I saw Dawn Tae. But then Katya materialized. She escorted me to a private room with gold plush pillows and soaked me for almost all the cash I had. For a minute, I thought about fucking her, which is what she expected, but I settled for a bottle of vodka and some talk.

"They use some of the girls here as mules," she said. "They carry the heroin in from China. Tolya doesn't believe me, but it is true," she added, and took the rest of my money. I wasn't convinced.

On the way back to the hotel, I stopped in a sleazy bar for a nightcap. In the light of the green strobes, a naked, middle-aged couple writhed listlessly on stage while three elderly jazz musicians played "Danny Boy". By the time I had had a third Scotch, I wondered what the hell I was doing there.

I was running out of options.

Go to Hong Kong, Sonny had said. Take this one on, see it through, find the money trail. Do it before more people die. What about the Fujianese? What about Fuzhou, I'd said, isn't that where it starts, isn't that where the snakeheads, the smugglers, are? Yes, he said. But the banks are in Hong Kong. And we can extradite in Hong Kong. We have a few more months, Artie.

A few more months. Find the Debt Collector. I didn't have a few days. I wanted something for Sonny Lippert so I could get the hell out of here and go home to Lily. I was beginning to grasp at straws.

29

The green Mercedes pulled up in front of the Regent the next afternoon. Dawn Tae got out. Her long slender legs were bare; she wore a pair of lavender Hush Puppies and she carried a little Vuitton shopping bag. I was in the Regent lobby, checking airline schedules with the concierge. I was getting antsy.

Alice Wing was with Dawn and she said, "Would you like to come racing some time, Mr Cohen? We have lovely racing here," she said. "I've got a couple of horses running on Wednesday night. It would be very nice indeed if you came."

"Oh please come, Artie. We'll all be there," Dawn said. "Say you'll come to the races."

"Sure," I said. "Wednesday. I'll be there."

"That's lovely." Alice Wing smiled. "I'll send round your badges. Give him the books, Dawn, and we'll go."

"I'm going to stay for a drink, Alice. You'll buy me a drink, won't you, Artie?"

Alice chimed in. "I'd rather you came home. Won't you come to supper with us?" she said to me.

"I'll be OK, Alice. Honest. I'm sick of staying home. I'll be fine with Artie, won't I, darling?"

It was almost dusk. Some rain had fallen, then stopped.

"What books?"

"It was an excuse. Can't I have a drink, Artie darling? I'd like a drink."

"Sure." I made for the bar.

"Not in the bar. I might have to kill the piano player if we sit in here." She had a point. He was playing "People" very loud. "What made you come to Hong Kong?" she asked. "You didn't come for me. I asked you to come to Hong Kong but you didn't. You dumped me." Dawn smiled. "After you fucked me, that is."

I told her about Lily and the baby and I was surprised when she said, "Men are bastards. Where is your friend, then? Where is Lily?"

"She went home."

"I see."

"I hear you've been telling people I've fired a gun at your chauffeur. Did you?"

"No," she said. I knew she was lying. "Of course I didn't tell on you, Artie. You know I wouldn't."

Dawn looked terrific, but she was even more brittle than before.

"Let's go to your room," she said.

"It's not a great idea."

"But why not?" she teased. "We already did it. I'm not exactly a virgin where you're concerned. You liked this skirt in New York. Didn't you? You remember?"

She took my hand and put it on the soft leather skirt. By then we were in the elevator.

In my room, Dawn found the Scotch and poured some for herself. I got hold of her hand. "I saw you, Dawn. I saw you in the hostess club, didn't I? It was you."

Dawn only laughed. "Do you want me to show you what I learned there, is that it? But I wasn't really in a club like that, was I, Artie? Is it all an illusion?" She pulled some clothes out of her bag. "I'm going to change. Then I'll take you out. Show you my town."

Dawn pulled off her skirt and sweater, then changed quickly into a short black dress and then slid her feet into high-heeled sandals. She tossed me a thin diamond necklace. "Fasten this for me, would you?" she said, turning her back to me. Dawn's back was soft and hot.

Briskly, she picked up a little satin bag with silver handles, and in front of my mirror, she inspected herself, touching herself, shifting her dress; I wanted to put my hands all over her. Instead, I tore a suit off a hanger and changed. In the mirror I saw the gold compact in Dawn's hand. She held it out to me. It was full of white powder.

"It's only a little coke, Artie. Think of it as Heroin Lite, darling," she said. "I never shoot up."

I shook my head. She put some delicately in her nostrils. "Lighten up, Artie. It's only a pinch. Consider this evening wear."

Waiters in Mao jackets and women in evening clothes padded softly across the floor at the China Club. Fans twirled languidly on the ceiling.

302

The club was in an old bank building in Central. As soon as we arrived, dozens of Dawn's friends appeared and exchanged little air kisses with Dawn. "We missed you so much," they all cried. "We missed you."

Silver spittoons, rosewood tables, lacy headrests on velvet armchairs, the whole place reeked of nostalgia. On one wall hung sepia photographs of men in pigtails and caps; from another, Mao and Michael Jackson beamed down from a large oil portrait. Sometimes I think all communism left behind was the misery, the corruption and the kitsch—Gorby toilet paper, busts of Lenin, Mao on watches and on walls.

"Shall I order for us?" Dawn said later when we were seated in a carved wooden booth with red silk cushions. She picked up a pair of silver chopsticks, then turned them over in her slim fingers. "Did you know the silver turns if the food is poisoned? Don't you think I've gone native, Artie?"

We ate. Between courses, Dawn tripped away to the bathroom, the gold compact in her hand. All evening, people sidled up to her, pressed her flesh. "How are you? How is Peter?" After a while, when I looked at her eyes, her pupils were dilated. She was ripped.

"Oh, darling, the party was a drag, but I'm off to Rome tomorrow," said one woman and Dawn shot me a secret sardonic grin as the woman drifted away. In a cage, a mynah bird sang opera.

Dawn looked at the bird. "Madame Butterfly," she said.

More food appeared, and more Bollinger.

The men were suited and buffed and polite. The

women were spectacular. Tough, velvety, seductive, these were top-of-the-line international babes and they looked like a billion bucks after taxes. As soon as they said hello, they were asking me where I lived, how much rent I paid, what kind of car I drove. They did it naturally, like asking if I preferred shrimp dumplings or pork. Money was like eating. It was not an embarrassment.

"She's the richest woman in Asia." Dawn watched a small woman flit from one table to the next. "Worth billions, more than Alice Wing even. She built the business herself. I asked how much her new shopping mall will cost. 'Two billion,' she says. How does she intend financing it? She says, 'Cash. Mostly cash.' Two billion, Artie.

"Hong Kong's the richest refugee camp in the world. The parents or grandparents all ran away from China, from the communists. Money's the only security, you can't have enough, you've got to keep piling it up." Dawn leaned her elbows on the table and played with her glass. Even when she was ironic about money, she purred.

"You really love the stuff, don't you?"

"It's better than being poor." Clasping her gold compact again, she got up. I put my hand on hers.

"That's enough, Dawn. I saw the marks on your arms."

"I told you I don't shoot up. Those weren't needle tracks."

"What were they?"

"Bruises."

"Sit down."

"They call us the Tai Tai." Dawn sat, but she couldn't stop talking. "The ladies who lunch. The dragon ladies, the iron butterflies. That's me, Artie, an airhead who does lunch and gets her hair done every day and, at night, when her husband's away, looks for some stray guy to screw." She reached for her glass. "Some of us, they call the Hong Kong *belles de jour*.

"I loved it when I got here. The women were the stars, it was all ours, we could strut across the city. At night, the lights would flick on, I'd head for another ball or dinner or cocktail party and I'd think: showtime! 'Must fly,' someone was always saying. 'Must pack.' People came and went, weekends in Sydney, summers in the south of France, ski houses in Colorado—they've all got ski houses near Vail, you know—I had to move to Hong Kong to learn to ski! Asia was one big party, Manila, Bali, Indonesia, Tokyo. Pete was even OK with it when I went to work. It had become fashionable for women to work. And I made lots of money."

All the time, her face growing more and more animated, Dawn scanned the crowd: she was waiting for someone. Suddenly, she tossed her napkin down and we went out onto the terrace.

It was a clear night. I leaned over the parapet and looked at Hong Kong. All that neon. All the lights. Hong Kong looked like it could burn itself up.

In the dark, the women, pale skinned, in silky dresses, moved like butterflies. I looked at Dawn. She was leaning against the wall, one hand on her hip, a cigarette in the other. The wind blew her dark hair across her

305

eyes. I swore to myself I wouldn't touch her. For me, she was trouble, like a drug.

More women spilled onto the terrace. One of them was Helen Wong. It was Helen Dawn had been waiting for and, in the corner of the terrace, the two leaned towards each other, whispering.

Helen Wong was about thirty-five with a serious pretty face and a lucid, quiet manner. She drew me into their conversation.

"I was telling Dawn to be careful," said Helen. "You know what happened to me. I challenged some laws to do with the lack of rights for women and children. Certain men threatened to cut my tongue off, or rape me, and a lot of people applauded. People went on radio and said, 'She needs to be raped, this sexless woman.' Because I had had an American education, I thought I had certain rights. To speak up, for instance. Then some men came to my flat. They held my arms. They bashed all my teeth in. 'You talk too much,' they said."

"Help Artie, Helen. Whatever he needs, help him." Dawn hurried to the ladies room, and Helen said to me, "Is she using?"

"Yes."

"Help you how?"

"I have a friend who tried to adopt a baby."

"In Hong Kong?"

"China."

"I don't think there's much I can do. I haven't any authority over there. Here either, for that matter. It wasn't Lily Hanes, was it?"

306

"How come everybody knows about one woman in a town of six million?"

"It's not six million, Artie. Can I call you that? This is a very small, very provincial society. It's how it was when the British were top of the heap and how it still is. There's not much culture. We all dine off the tiniest scandal or scrap of gossip. We pick it over like jackals."

Reaching into my jacket for cigarettes, I found the fax Sonny had finally sent. "Does this address mean anything to you at all?"

Helen looked at it. "Yes, it does. Does this have to do with Dawn?"

"No," I said too quickly. "No, this is a case I'm working. Where is it, this place?"

"It's a village way out in the New Territories. A housing project. I know this one. I had some clients when I was practicing law. Illegals sometimes wash up there."

"You have some time tomorrow?"

"I'll arrange something, if I can. I'll do what I can. But forget the baby. Miss Hanes' baby."

"She's already gone home."

"Good. Look, Mr Cohen. Artie. Take Dawn back to Alice's before it gets any later. Take Dawn home if she'll let you."

"It's not easy."

"I know. And God knows, I sympathize. But I have some sympathy for her husband, too. Dawn behaves very badly. I wish you'd take her back to Alice Wing's now. Better still, take her home to New York. Dawn Tae is in terrible trouble," she said, and I was going to ask her what kind, what kind of trouble, when Dawn reappeared on the terrace.

Naked, Dawn lay on my bed an hour later, drinking Champagne. "Nice," she said, putting the iced bottle on her breasts. "Very nice." Raising her head, she looked around the room. "What is it, four days since you've been here, Artie, darling? Five?"

"You knew I was in Hong Kong all the time. You knew. All the time I was calling you, looking for you, you knew. What are you, Dawn? What's happened to you?"

"So I knew."

"Why didn't you call me back?"

"It's hard. People listen in on cell-phones."

"That's bullshit. You have drivers, you have errand boys."

"I thought if you were looking for me, you might find out something."

"What kind of something?"

"I don't know."

"Don't play games with me."

"Why not? I like games. I like it when you follow me," she said. "It makes me hot. Can I have a bath?"

"Sure." I lit a cigarette and watched her get up.

She saw me look, put her hands on her hips and giggled. "Come in the tub with me," she said, but I let her go and when she was in the bathroom, the tub running, I looked through her bag.

What was I looking for? I don't know, but what I found was the gold box with cocaine in it, some credit cards and cash, and a pink enamel lipstick. It was the same shape as the lipstick that Babe Vanelli had carried, and when I twisted the tube, like Babe's lipstick, a knife popped out.

"Artie!"

Half an hour later, we were up to our neck in bubbles and I couldn't keep my hands off Dawn and I felt shitty about it, but not shitty enough to stop. Not scared enough, either, which was bad. Stupid.

Guys all lie about how crappy they feel, how the low hum of guilt keeps them up nights; maybe it does. Like me, they'd put up with the low hum—or the high howl—in exchange for this.

She ducked back under the water; I didn't know Dawn could do stuff like that with her tongue. When she surfaced, hair streaming, she reached over the edge of the tub, retrieved a joint she'd put in an ashtray on a stool, then sucked up the pot with long delicate drags. It smelled very sweet. She passed it to me and I sucked some up, too.

"Pete was lovely, at first, you know." Dawn leaned back, arms behind her head. "He showed me around, he gave me all the money in the world for cars, clothes. We played games. Sometimes, we'd go out to dinners at Government House, I'd put my hand in the lap of some guy next to me, some ambassador, some cabinet minister from London, some princeling, and I'd look at Pete and he'd know what I was doing and he'd put his hand in some woman's lap, and we'd get off on each other. It was so much fun." For a while she lay dreamily in the tub smoking the pot, then slowly she climbed out and, still naked, started drying her hair.

I scrambled out after her and grabbed one of the plush hotel robes. "So where is Pete?"

"Who knows? Who cares? China. Taiwan. North Korea. Cuba. Making deals. AKs from Deng's arms factory. New kinds of burgers. Sell. Buy. He's the new China man, my husband. The new comprador class, they call it. Like the men who brought the opium once upon a time."

"What about the orphanage where I saw you?"

She picked up a towel and wrapped herself in it. Her tone sharpened up. "It's just a thing I do. I help out. Give some money. It's nothing. I don't want to talk about it."

"Who are you so frightened of? Why are you holed up at Alice Wing's?"

"Stop interrogating me. I'm not afraid," she said. "Peter doesn't like me working is all." She was lying and she knew I knew.

"You ever hear of someone called the Debt Collector, Dawn? Is there an Eiffel Tower around here? Dawn?"

"What is this, the third degree? You miss being a cop? You want some handcuffs, darling? Would you like that?" Dawn went into the bedroom and I followed. Laughing now, she pushed me onto the bed. "Should I show you more of what I learned since I got here, Artie?"

She took off the towel, stretched out on my bed on her back and wrapped her legs around me. "Like this, Artie, darling? Or you want me to put the leather skirt back on?"

310

"What about the Eiffel Tower?" I said again, but she held me tighter and said, "Don't be silly, darling, everyone knows the Eiffel Tower is in Paris."

She was like a drug. All I could think about was getting more. For a few hours after Dawn left, I slept badly, woke up, watched TV, slept again, then went downstairs to get my passport from the concierge. The visa wasn't ready.

"I'm sorry, sir," he said. "It's not back yet. It will be back tonight."

"I need it now. You said morning."

"I'm sorry," he said.

"What if I have to get to China?"

"I don't think it would be wise to go without your passport. You have a special need to get there today?"

Whatever answer I gave would be in a whispering gallery before long. "No. I'm just doing some sight-seeing is all."

"Would you care to look at some brochures? Various packages for visiting the mainland." He handed me a sheaf of slick tourist brochures; I handed him some money. His expression was polite.

"So, you know anything about some Eiffel Tower?"

"Yes, of course. You'd be talking about Shenzhen. The theme park. Small-scale replicas of all the great buildings of the world. It wouldn't be of interest. It's mostly for Chinese tourists, sir. If you want to go, however, you can take a train, if you don't want a package tour or a private car. You would get off at Wo Lu and cross the border."

Pansy had said, "Look for the Eiffel Tower." I had thought it was a hallucination. "The Eiffel Tower is in Paris," Dawn had said.

"Is that something everyone would know? About the Eiffel Tower? Locals, I mean."

"Probably they would, sir. Yes."

After that, I killed time waiting for Ringo Chen and Helen Wong and wondered why Dawn had lied to me. The whole business was beginning to stink from all the lies.

30

There was a stink of fish and sewage as Ringo pulled off the highway onto a feeder road that night. Most of the day, I'd done what I could, but it was scraps. Scraps from cops and bankers I talked to. Some from Chris Roy. Names of enforcers and errand boys, most of them in China beyond our reach. Anecdotes. Everyone was polite but distracted. Like Tolya said, Hong Kong was a town on the verge of a nervous breakdown.

In these godforsaken suburbs and villages around the border, hide-and-seek would be real easy for the creeps. You could almost taste the corruption that already leaked over that border, like fall-out from a nuclear melt-down.

"Christ, it really does reek," I said to Ringo who was driving a snappy red BMW roadster.

Pollution was suspended on the air like a layer of grease and Ringo put up the top of his car. Helen Wong was in the back seat. "She does good work, but she offends a lot of people," Ringo had said when I told him Helen was coming with us. I didn't care. Helen Wong knew her way around the New Territories.

Ten miles north of the hotel, the village of Tai Po was close enough to the coast to account for the fishy stench. We bumped around muddy roads looking for the address on Sonny's fax. Hulking jerry-built apartment buildings stood on tracts of raw ground so barren there weren't even weeds, only empty cans, dead dogs, and sewage. Forests had thrived here a few years earlier, Ringo said. It was the ugliest place I'd ever seen.

Leaning over my shoulder, Helen peered through the front window at a group of buildings. "I think this is it," she said.

Ringo stepped on the brakes, I snuffed out my cigarette. We all got out of the car and I looked at my watch. I had lost all sense of time and place. Millions of people inhabited these buildings: they had kids, got married, went to work, celebrated their birthdays. They aspired, lived, died, but I couldn't see it. All I could see was air so thick you could chop it up with a meat cleaver. My own paranoia, the feeling things had gone off the rails, made it feel like a dead zone. The three of us walked towards one of the buildings. Only the whine of traffic kept us company.

"Tell me about the illegals at this end," I said to Ringo.

"There's a million stories." Ringo walked faster, eyes clicking right, then left. "Some go overland to the old Soviet bloc. Some go in container ships to America, which means six months at sea, packed in like sardines, or slaves. There's big unemployment on the mainland now. In certain regions, the government encourages the smugglers. It's an old story here," Ringo said. "When

314

the communists took over China, in '48, '49, the bravest boys would jump into Mirs Bay and race the sharks to Hong Kong. Later on, when there was bad famine, the Chinese let people go if they could bribe or finagle their way out. So they walked to the border. The Hong Kong guards played another kind of game. If you could make it through the barbed wire and avoid the guns, you could stay. Mirs Bay is a few miles from here," he said, pointing into the dark. I thought of Henry Liu in Chinatown, who had raced those sharks.

"Hong Kong has always been a gateway, the first stop on an illegal's route to paradise. Look, we deal a case at a time, when we can; we try to put some connections together. It can take years." He looked at the building in front of us and then at me. "We haven't got years any more. We've hardly got months. We haven't got anything."

"But who's the money in Hong Kong? Where's the beef? Who's the Debt Collector?"

Ringo grimaced. "I don't know."

"Quiet! Quiet!" Helen put her finger over her mouth as a pair of men passed us. Then she stopped. "It's here. I'm sure this is the building."

The apartment was on the nineteenth floor, and while the elevator slipped and shuddered on its cables, I jammed my hands in my pockets, sweating.

Helen Wong found the door and knocked and an old man opened it. The two of them talked rapidly, gesticulating, pointing. Helen shook his hand and turned to me. "Come on. I know where to go," she said and I had the chilling sense that it was all too easy, too smooth.

315

Everyone was too accommodating. The old man shut the door but not before he took a good hard look at us.

"We'll walk." Helen was in charge. We walked away from the building. Ten minutes later, we reached the site of a half-demolished building. Next to it was an old silver Windstream jacked up on concrete blocks. It must have been someone's vacation home once; now the trailer was webbed with dirt, rust, dead bugs.

"Let me go first." She knocked on the trailer. Her knuckles made a hollow metallic noise. "I'm going to have a look." She went inside, then stuck her head back out.

"It is the right place. Give me five minutes, then you come in."

We squatted on a pile of tires near the trailer, me and Ringo, and smoked. From the near distance came the sound of sirens. "Your guys?"

"When there's trouble, like the riot yesterday in Central, we show our colors. We put up roadblocks. Papers get checked. But this never was a democracy."

"How far to the Chinese border?"

"Five miles. About five." Ringo tossed me a fresh pack of cigarettes, the Dunhills that his cousin Jerry always smoked.

"Sonny Lippert thinks he can pin something on Jerry, that he's screwed."

Ringo looked at the sky, then at me, and said, "Good."

On that pile of used tires on a piece of waste ground somewhere near China, we sat, smoking and staring out into the dark. A stray puppy leaped at us suddenly, but Ringo caught it and held it between his hands.

"I fixed it about the gun for you, Artie. For now."

"Thanks. Thank you."

"I wouldn't stick around too long. They know your name. If there are more riots, and there will be more riots, things will get very tough. Less than half of us Hong Kongers want reunification with the mainland. It's an empire of corruption over there." He waved his hand in the direction of the border. "We are very skittish. We have to show our new masters we can police ourselves, or they'll do it for us. I won't be able to help you much after tonight. Certain Chinese dignitaries are expected. Cops like me are required, so my boss says. He already suspects me."

"What of?"

"A touch of sedition, you could say." He laughed bitterly. "I can't help you, Artie. I can't even help myself. I'm a lame duck."

"How's that?"

"I'll be heading to Sydney before July."

"With Mrs Chen? Is there a Mrs Chen?"

Ringo's tone turned scathing. "There is no Mrs Chen. That's why I'm leaving. Did you know that criminal sanctions on homosexuality were only lifted in 1991? That's why I came back from London. You know how the People's Republic treat gays? Do you?" He tossed his cigarette away. "God knows why I'm telling you this. Just don't stick around Hong Kong too long, Artie, not if things go bad. They have your name at headquarters."

"I am Mrs Moy. My daughter was murdered in New York City one month ago plus one week." The woman in the trailer sat on a ragtag sofa that obviously doubled as a bed, Helen Wong at her side. Helen did the translating and she was very deft. After a few minutes, I forgot she was there.

Mrs Moy held out her hand. In the other hand, she held a cigarette stiffly between two fingers. In jeans and a yellow T-shirt, Mrs Moy looked about forty. She would have been handsome if she ever smiled, but she never did. The trailer itself was cramped, the window covered with a dark plastic shade, the air stuffy, thick with exhaust fumes and fear.

I noticed Ringo's eyes were fixed on the door. "Please go on," I said to Mrs Moy.

She was from the southern part of Fujian Province, she said. Her husband was a mechanic and she herself sewed when she could get the work. Sewing, she could make about fifteen cents a day.

She had had one child, but it was a daughter and she wanted a boy, so she tried again. She miscarried late and had to go to the hospital, she said, so it became known that she had defied the one-child policy and she was sterilized. Then her husband died of cancer.

The suffering seemed medieval and I said I was sorry for her troubles, but Mrs Moy said it was normal. There were tens of thousands of women like her. There were many women much worse off, she added, and put out the cigarette, then took another one from the crumpled pack in her lap.

In her village, several of her cousins had gone to America. Everyone saw how much money came back to the village. Mrs Moy's daughter had been married when she was very young and her husband had died. Now, the daughter wanted to go to America. Mrs Moy helped her put out the word that she was looking for a passage. In a matter of days, the snakeheads showed up and offered to deliver the girl to America for $35,000. With help from some relatives and from a money-lender, Mrs Moy raised $10,000. The moneylenders took forty per cent a year, but Mrs Moy said she had accepted that it was the down-payment for her daughter's journey to the Golden Mountain.

"We knew it was possible," said Mrs Moy. "The snakeheads spread news of the Golden Mountain and how, if you went, you would find money almost on the streets. Girls who went sent back pictures of themselves with big cars. It was well known. We believed. There was nothing in the village, no work, nothing." She paused. "We had to believe. And there were the pictures."

It took six months. She took the bus to Fuzhou with her daughter and saw her leave for the airport for a flight to Guangzhou where she was to receive a passport with her name and picture in it and then to board a ship. "After eight months, I became desperate," said Mrs Moy. "Then I heard she had arrived. I was called to the home of a wealthy cousin who had a telephone and she was on the phone. 'Hello, Mommy,' she said. 'I'm in America.' She was at the Golden Mountain." For the first time, Mrs Moy smiled. Very softly, she said, "I was happy."

Ringo stayed at the door. I sat. Helen produced Cokes and passed them around and then Mrs Moy resumed her story.

From America there were phone calls from time to time. And although her daughter sent less money than she had hoped for, Mrs Moy believed she was doing well. Until one morning, she was summoned to her cousin's to take a call from a man in New York City. Her daughter had been kidnapped and was being held.

"Four hours," Mrs Moy said. "They gave me four hours to raise ten thousand dollars. Or they would kill her. They put her on the phone and she cried, 'Help me, Mommy.' How could I help her? Where would I find so much money so fast?"

Miraculously, the girl was released and Mrs Moy received several phone calls from her to say she was well and happy and that she had, in fact, met a man. But Mrs Moy had a premonition. It would happen again. It had happened to other families. The snakeheads had become greedy. The price was going up.

"I had to do something. My brother had come here to Tai Po years ago, he had fled the communists and he offered to help me. So I became an immigrant, too."

For ten dollars, Mrs Moy got herself smuggled into Tai Po in a fishing boat. She kept house for her brother who was prepared to help with money if it became necessary. She let her daughter know how to find her, but no one else.

"One evening my brother's phone rang suddenly. I wasn't expecting it, It was the news that she was dead. No one even called for the money. I had the money

320

ready this time, but no one called me. They killed her without even calling me." Silently, she wept. "After that I still had to pay the moneylenders. Even after she was dead they came to me for the money. They came to collect."

I didn't ask because I already knew, so it was Ringo who said, "What was your daughter's name?"

"She was called Rose. Her name was Rose."

For a few minutes, Mrs Moy sobbed. Then, from her pocket, she took a picture and handed it to me. It was a duplicate of the picture of Rose I knew by heart—smiling face, pink jacket, the white car. The story that began on Hillel Abramsky's floor on 47th Street ended on the other side of the world in a rusty trailer on a derelict tract of land in China.

Even through her tears, Mrs Moy watched me. When she spoke again it sounded like a script. "But there are bad people everywhere. Rose met some bad people in New York. I thought to myself, if only the officials back home had known, if only they knew in time. At least she made it to the Golden Mountain," she said.

I turned to Helen. "Is that Mrs Moy's brother in the apartment?"

"Yes."

"Why doesn't she stay there?"

"She says she's frightened of being trapped on the nineteenth floor. She is scared of heights. She feels safer out here. But she can't stay." Helen helped Mrs Moy gather up her bag and the picture of Rose. "They're tearing all this down. I'll take her back. I'll talk to her. I'll meet you at the car."

The women set off from the trailer before I could stop them.

"What's her brother's job?" Ringo called out.

Helen turned around. "He's a local official. Quite rich. Quite important. I won't be long," she added, and disappeared into the dark wasteland.

Something was wrong with the whole set-up.

"Ringo?"

He fastened the door of the trailer with a padlock.

"Ringo, she's told that story before. More than once."

"That's what I thought. You got this address from Sonny Lippert, didn't you?"

"Yeah?"

"How did Sonny get it?"

"I don't know. How did she expect to help her daughter if she didn't tell anyone else? How did the money-lenders know where to find her? What's going on here?"

We were already running. "Didn't you wonder why she's still a believer? Why she laid the blame off on bad men in America? I thought, if only Stalin knew. They used to say it on the way to the Gulag. If only Stalin knew . . . when Stalin had ordered the whole thing."

"Or Mao. Christ." Ringo ran faster. "She *had* told the story before. It's an old Chinese trick. And it only makes sense if the smugglers and the officials are complicit."

I tried to catch my breath. "What trick?"

The soft terrain pulled at my feet, the mud and shit pouring into my shoes as we ran.

Ringo was breathing hard, talking fast while we ran.

322

"In the story the officials are good. It's only a few bad people who are to blame. Usually foreign dogs. Say some Western reporter is nosing around, or a cop from New York like you. You wheel in Mrs Moy. She pours out her heart. Who wouldn't believe her? She is telling the truth, more or less. The foreigners are satisfied. The reporter writes the story, people in the West are shocked, but nothing happens. The story goes away. You're right. She has told it before and her brother is an official. It's a set-up."

"So people know we're here. Us. Helen."

"Christ, yes!" was all Ringo said. Gun in hand, he reached the apartment building ahead of me. "Where is she? Where's Helen?"

When we found Helen Wong in the playground behind the building, she was hardly breathing, her face covered with blood.

"Mrs Moy said she would go upstairs alone." Helen spoke haltingly. "Mrs Moy. Said her brother didn't like strangers. I let her. I came out. They were . . . waiting . . ."

"Stay with her. I'll get help." Ringo ran.

I was alone with Helen, her head in my lap. "Animals. Waiting. Held my arms," she gasped. "Used my face . . . a punching bag. Bare hands. A knife. Knives."

"Don't talk."

"Have to tell you . . ."

"Later."

There was blood everywhere. Helen's white shirt was sodden with fresh blood.

"Artie?"

"What is it?" I leaned down. Her breathing became more irregular as she whispered, "Unstable . . . Dawn . . . dangerous," and then it stopped completely.

All I could do was sit on the raw ground in the dark, the ugly buildings looming over us, and hold her hand, but by the time Ringo appeared and an ambulance came, Helen was dead.

"She's dead, Sonny. You happy? She's fucking dead." I was yelling into the phone from my hotel room. I told him about Rose's mother and Helen's death. "Who gave you the address? Who?"

"Pansy gave it to me."

"Where is she?"

"She's still in the hospital. But she's started talking. That's what I was waiting for. As soon as she started talking, I got the mother's phone number and we traced the address. So we know that the contacts run from Fuzhou into Hong Kong. We know that for sure now. We got Pansy's brother, too. He was the enforcer, he ran the errand boys in Chinatown."

"Yeah, and I bet he's already got one of OJ's lawyers on the case. Was it really worth it, Sonny? Was it worth another woman dying?"

31

In the morning, the invitation was under my door. It was from Alice Wing for the races and a cocktail party beforehand. I had promised and then I forgot. It was Wednesday. I called Alice Wing and thanked her and asked for Dawn. She picked up the phone. "I'll see you tonight," I said.

Flirting, she said she wasn't sure and did I really want her; I could barely keep from snarling. "Be there. OK? Dawn?"

Then I did the one thing I had resisted. I called the Taes. I almost fell off the chair when Ricky answered.

"Ricky? Rick, is that you?" I was shouting.

"Yeah," he said. "I'm better, Artie. I'm getting better. It shook me up, Dawn leaving, you know? It really got me that I wasn't here for her. She's OK, isn't she? You're there for her if she needs you, aren't you?" he said and so I couldn't ask him what I needed to ask. I couldn't ask if he knew what his sister really was.

"Good," I said. "Everything's good. I'll be home soon. You take care, Rick. I'll be back soon and we'll go raise some hell."

The races would be perfect. I wanted a confrontation with Dawn in a public place because I didn't trust myself alone with her. I *had* to know if it was her—the Debt Collector. Then I could leave her to her husband or Ringo Chen and I could go home. There was a late flight out of Hong Kong. I reserved a seat on it. Then I packed.

To clear my head and get death off my brain, I got a ferry to Cheung Chau Island about an hour from Hong Kong and found a café where I ordered a beer and watched the banners on the fishing boats in the harbor. It was a gorgeous day. I inhaled some unnaturally clean air; the sun felt good on my face. At the next table, an old man, a crumpled straw hat on his head, sat sketching the harbor. We got to talking—he was British—and he ordered a beer and invited me to join him. He had been in Hong Kong for sixty-five years, he said. He was a professor of some arcane form of Chinese art.

"When I first arrived, no Englishman spoke Chinese," he said. "Not even the government." I asked if he would be leaving when the Chinese came. "Where would I go?" He turned his face to the sun. "Where on earth would I go?" We finished our beers and I mentioned Pete Leung.

"I knew the father," he said. "I knew the grandfather. The Leungs were very raffish men," he said. "Adventurers, all of them. But decent in their way and extraordinarily charming."

For a while we chatted. The colorful banners snapped merrily in the breeze, the sun got hotter and it was like balm after the nightmare with Helen Wong. When I got up to go, the old man asked me my name. "Did you know that Sun Yat Sen had a bodyguard named Morris "Two-Gun" Cohen?" he said. He tipped his hat, saluted me with his Chinese newspaper and watched me as I walked away towards the ferry.

I wasn't any "Two-Gun" Cohen, but I had fallen for Hong Kong. The water was full of sampans and yachts, cargo tugs and container ships, not to mention the ferry boats. I loved the ferries, loved sitting on the water, the sun on my face. I took off my jacket.

Hong Kong. Fragrant Harbour. The Pearl River Estuary. China. The romance of it. The crime. As far back as I could remember, China was everything exotic to us Soviet kids. And big. Mao was never afraid of nuclear war because he could afford for millions of Chinese to die.

Whatever went on in Chinatown in New York was only part of the game. If you looked at it from China, we were only bit players.

It had never been a murder with a plot you could puzzle out or piece together. Rose's murder was a by-product, so was the dead woman at the sports complex, and Babe Vanelli. Helen Wong. Sonny Lippert could arrest the errand boys, he could fry the enforcers like Pansy Loh's brother, he could hammer half the criminal element in Chinatown. It was only the tip. The ties to China were indestructible. And China was endless. It could squander millions of people and survive.

But where did I fit in? Sure, I went to help out Hillel that morning the blizzard began. Sure, I found myself with some kind of stake in Pansy's survival. It wasn't enough. Neither was this Hot Poppy, Dawn's drug of choice. Almost no one had heard of it. Not Sonny Lippert or Ringo Chen, only a Russian stripper who lied for money and a pathetic ex-spook like Chris Roy.

Dawn had been in New York. Now, she was in Hong Kong. Everywhere I went she was just ahead of me, or just behind. She was ambitious, she loved money and power. Dawn was a junkie, and maybe the drug made her a killer.

I thought back. Had Dawn really been in love with me years before, like she said? Wasn't it something she invented? She knew she could divert me. She knew she could seduce me and I would let her. Had let her. The Leungs were adventurers, the old man had said. Adventurers but not killers. It was Dawn I had to confront.

The ferry docked and I went back to the hotel feeling that the morning in Cheung Chau had been a brief lull before, one way or another, all hell broke loose.

"Hi, Artie? Pete Leung. Lunch?" I was in my room at the hotel when the call came. "I hear you've been looking for me. Look, I'm really sorry, pal. It's been a hell of a week. Lunch? Drinks? Or see you at the races perhaps?"

I got ready for the races. I didn't call Sonny Lippert before I went. Ringo Chen was busy. I was on my own. Anyway, Dawn was mine.

I found her in a private room at the Happy Valley Racecourse. About fifty people swirled around Alice

Wing who was the host of the party. Dressed to the nines, smiling, chattering about parties and horses, everyone drank pink Champagne. There were faces I had seen at Dawn's club. "How are you? Are you enjoying yourself? Are you going to pick a winner? Will you come to the ball?" I smiled back at all the hospitable, beautiful, charming people and all the time I was looking for Pete Leung.

"You came." In a yellow silk suit and diamond earrings, Dawn put her arm around my shoulder, kissed me and clinked her glass against mine. "Couldn't resist me, eh? Good." I smiled back. I couldn't show my hand until I had some kind of evidence. I told her Helen Wong was dead. Dawn barely said a word. She was a cold fish.

"Let it all be, Artie," she said.

"I can't do that." Just then, Tolya entered the room. Adjusting his blazer, he strolled towards me. Dawn walked away.

"I have something for you." Tolya patted his pocket.

"Thanks. How's tricks, Tol?"

"Not so good. I worked on this thing, Artyom, since I saw you. I thought to myself I would give it one more try. But Lily's child has been assigned to another family. At least she will know. At least she will have the certainty. I'm so sorry."

"Thank you."

"You are welcome." He slipped the gun into my pocket. The racing hadn't begun, but the noise in the room grew as more people arrived. Waiters served hors d'oeuvres from large silver trays. Dawn took my hand

329

and we found our way to an open balcony where we could look down at the track and the crowd in the stands. Unstable, Helen Wong had said.

"Do you think Pete is down there?" Dawn looked into the sea of faces. "I asked Alice to invite him." She was playing games with Pete, too, I thought. Sipping Champagne, she scanned the crowd. "I feel he's here, Artie."

I followed her gaze. "Why did you ask Alice to invite him?" I asked, but all she said was, "Well, let him come or not. What time is it?"

"Six-thirty."

"I have to go soon."

"I'll come with you. Whatever you have to do, I'll do it with you. You asked me to come here, Dawn. Stop jerking me around. OK?"

She finished her Champagne. Then she looked at me, tossed her hair back, hesitated. "OK," she said finally. "OK. If I decide to let you come, it will be on my terms. I'll tell you how and where we do this. Did you pick a horse, Artie? Pick a horse. For luck."

We went back to the party. Dawn drank another glass of Champagne and looked at the crowd with wistful longing. "I used to love all this so much." She put her hand on mine. "If you want to come, come. But don't fuck around. You do what I say. I'll give you some instructions and you can meet me. You can't bring a gun, either. They'll stop you if you do."

"Fine."

"Do you have a visa?"

"Yes. Where am I going?"

330

"You make like a tourist, Artie. Or a bozo business guy. There's a regular train from Kowloon Station. It's safest. Get a train. Get out at the last stop. I'll write everything down."

"What about you?"

"I need my car. I'll meet you. As soon as it's dark. Look, if something goes wrong, you'll bring the car back? Promise me. Just say yes. If they bother you at the border, make like a dumb American."

"What's this about?"

"It's about a thing I have to do."

Dawn glanced across the room to where Tolya stood. "And tell him to keep away. You pushed me, Artie. That's why I'm doing this, you understand? I'm doing this so you'll know exactly who I am."

At first, I had no intention of following her instructions. I had no intention of letting Dawn out of my sight. She was playing games. Then I saw that I had to gamble. If I didn't play the game her way, three hours from now, we'd still be in this room full of laughing people drinking pink Champagne. Without some kind of proof, how could I pin anything on Dawn?

"Where the fuck are we going, Dawn?"

"We're going to Shenzhen."

"You knew about the Eiffel Tower, didn't you?"

"Yes. I lied." Dawn looked grim. "I couldn't afford to have you messing around over there by yourself."

32

"Please mind the gaps in the platform. Please alight on the right." An English voice that could crack glass played through the loudspeaker on the commuter train from Kowloon to Wo Lu. On the train, workers hugged duffel bags, suitcases and babies. Others crammed into seats, folded up Chinese-style and went to sleep in tiny places. We passed Tai Po where I'd been with Helen Wong the night she died there. Was I a fool? If I had insisted on staying with Dawn, she would have refused to budge. This way, if I got her, I'd have something else on her. Or I'd be spending a lot more time in China than I planned.

Periodically, as the electric train buzzed slowly away from Kowloon toward the Chinese border, this voice delivered instructions. "Please mind the gaps when alighting."

I had left the racecourse, stopped at the hotel to change my air ticket home and to call Lily. I left her a message on her machine in New York to say that I loved her and I'd be back soon.

"Please mind the gaps." We stopped at Wo Lu. I got off the train. The trip had taken twenty-nine minutes. I was on the Chinese border.

In seconds, I was into the station. Dawn had fixed our meeting for ten. It was 8.45. I was in good shape.

"Take a taxi when you come out of the station," Dawn had said. "Walk across the square to the Shangri La Hotel and get an English-speaking driver."

Jogging through the station, I turned a corner and hit a wall of bodies.

It was human gridlock, a tidal wave of bodies jammed together. There was a covered bridge that formed the actual border. I looked ahead of me. All I had to do was get over the bridge.

Pushing against the human wall, I got onto the bridge and shoved my way to the railings at the side. Below the railing, crap floated in the stream. Cola cans, human waste, dead dogs and cats, all of them drifted in the water. On a wall at the far end of the bridge, looking over the sewer of a stream, was Jack Nicklaus. "Jack Nicklaus Golf Course, Mission Hills, China", the poster said, and Jack beamed at us and at the crappy stream.

Around me, people shoved at each other with chickens, bicycles, strollers and toilets. A few yards away, another American waved. He wore a yellow button-down shirt. He frowned and held his hands up in despair.

"What's going on?"

"Factory workers. Going home. Use your elbows. Good luck," he yelled as he was carried away in the crowd. I saw his arms flail over his head, a camera in one

333

hand, before he disappeared, like a man caught in a tide pool.

"Fuck off," I screamed at a boy who banged into me with a bike he carried over his head.

"Fuck you," he answered, the international English that worked a lot better than Esperanto. Then, like a dam breaking, the crowd broke. Ten thousand people ran. I ran.

It was completely dark when I came out of the station. A little boy grabbed onto my sleeve, chattering at me, begging. He was barefoot and carried a naked baby. I tossed them some coins and started for the Shangri La, but a taxi pulled up in front of me and I dove into it and gave the driver Dawn's piece of paper. He looked at the address and took off. I was in Shenzhen. A million people and pollution so thick you could see it. It was a gruesome, unreal city; I was heading for an unreal encounter, and I wondered if Dawn would be there at all or if I had let her get away.

Ten minutes later, I saw the Eiffel Tower.

A three-storey-high billboard floated out of the dark. "Window of Wonders," it read. "Theme Park. Seventy great buildings, the Eiffel Tower, the Statue of Liberty, all in exact replica." The Eiffel Tower, like Pansy Loh said it would be, was in China, after all.

The taxi turned into a side street, then the driver put his foot on the brake, scratched his head, looked around and reread Dawn's instructions. Slowly, he lit a cigarette and peered out of the window. It was getting late.

"Go," I yelled. "Go." He didn't understand.

Leaning over him, I scanned the horizon for landmarks.

"A large building," Dawn had said. "A large building at the end of a narrow road. Two blocks past Kentucky Fried Chicken."

"There. It's there." I pounded the taxi driver on the shoulder, pointing, yelling. He moved off, stopped again. I threw money at him and fell out of the cab.

Dawn Tae had been my friend. Whatever she was doing, whoever she was, it wasn't my business. When I tried to breathe, I choked. I thought about Rose and Babe Vanelli and Helen Wong. If this was the bank, if this was where money from the trade in illegals was laundered, I needed the proof. If it was something else— and I already figured there was something much worse than dirty money waiting for me behind those walls—I had to know. I put my hand on the gun and opened the gate.

"You're late."

Dawn was waiting for me on the other side of the wall. She wore jeans and a man's shirt. The sunglasses were pushed on top of her head and her hair was braided. She looked tense but calm. There was no sign of drugs.

"Come on." We were in a courtyard. The three-storey building that surrounded it on three sides was a patchwork of concrete blocks, cheap masonry and aluminum siding. A piece of lawn looked ragged and yellow in the light from a lamp stuck over the main door of the building. Some of the windows were half shuttered. A few had air conditioners in them. Laundry hung heavy and limp from others. There was no breeze. Close to the door was a brown Volvo station wagon.

"Wait," Dawn said.

A security guard emerged and greeted her warmly. She gave him some money and he disappeared swiftly through the gate. Clearly, Dawn was in control here. This was her turf.

"You seem right at home here."

"Sure, Artie. They all know me here."

Dawn reached for the door. "What did you think, darling? That I was the bad guy?"

"What is this place, Dawn? What are we doing here?" She pulled the door open, but I grabbed her hand. "No more games."

One more time, she glanced over her shoulder towards the courtyard. "It's not a game. And you can put the gun away for now, if you wouldn't mind."

"Then what the fuck are we doing here?"

Dawn started through the door. "We're going to steal a baby."

33

Even in the hallway where an old woman sat, a sentry on a stool, I could hear the sound of babies crying. The veins on the woman's legs were thick, raised and purple, but when she saw Dawn she made to get up. Dawn patted her shoulder, gave her some money and smiled.

"She's the matron," Dawn said. "She's a Christian. She likes to think she helps me for love, not just for money. I encourage her."

There was a flight of stairs and I followed Dawn up it. She opened a door and shone the flashlight she had in her bag on the floor. Squinting, I could see a few cots and on them, fast asleep, girls of seventeen or eighteen. One of them snored lightly. Another muttered in her sleep. Dawn closed the door and we moved on, climbing another flight of stairs. "I'm sorry. It was the wrong room."

"Who were they?"

"Some young women who help out here."

Pansy, I thought. Pansy had been one of them.

"Illegals?"

"Yes."

We climbed another flight. The sound of crying grew louder and more insistent. Dawn opened a door. A blast of air conditioning hit us and a young woman greeted us, then hurriedly picked up a milk bottle and resumed feeding a baby in a crib. She murmured something to Dawn. From the other cribs in the room, more babies yowled.

"What's she saying?"

"She says the geese are always hungry. The fat babies. Remember? I told you. They fatten up the babies before adoption. They feed them around the clock."

The room was large and freshly painted. The air conditioner rattled in the window and toys that dangled over the babies' cribs danced in the breeze. There were six babies all in cribs of their own, all of them fat, all with skin like silk. The helpers, three of them now, ran from crib to crib to feed the bawling infants, feeding them and making soothing noises.

"Fat babies!" Lily's Mrs Ling had said. Lily's baby had been fat like a little sumo wrestler. I was beginning to understand.

Outside, rain splattered the windows, clattered on a tin roof. The sound of an engine came from the courtyard. I gestured to Dawn, to the stairs. "Come on," I said, silently, mouthing the words.

"We'll be all right for a few minutes. I paid him off. You saw the station wagon?"

"Yes."

"It's mine. It's registered in my name. And yours. I fixed some spare papers before I left."

"Spare papers?"

"It doesn't matter. I couldn't tell you before. I couldn't risk it. I'm sorry." Dawn was self-possessed and brisk now. "Everything's in order. In the glove compartment, there are the names of a couple of border guards. Decent guys. There's a can of extra gas in the back in case you get stuck on this side. But you won't get stuck. Go back to Hong Kong. Go straight to Alice Wing. Do you understand?"

I waited.

"In case I don't make it back, I need you to know something. I'm not the bad guy, Artie. I have to tell you. The drugs make me weird sometimes. I'm trying to stop. Sometimes I have to put people off the track, OK? I'm sorry if I hurt you, but I'm still me. More than for a long time, in fact." Dawn hugged me and started downstairs.

In the back of the building was an annex. I had to duck to get inside. The ceilings were low, there was no air conditioning. The place stank, the air was hot and dead. Rain clattered on the windows. Clink clink clink. The floors, the walls, the ceilings leaked humidity like an abscess leaks pus.

Dawn turned the flashlight on. The floor was raw concrete. There were cribs, seven of them jammed into the space, but they had no sheets, no mattresses. The stink that came from them almost made me gag.

In one of the cribs, two babies were wedged together so that they could barely move. Bottles of milk stood on the ground out of reach. There was no way the babies could get to the milk or feed themselves.

Against a wall was an iron cot with a baby on it. "Girl or boy?" I said.

"Don't you get it?" Dawn whispered. "They're all girls here." She shone the light on the infant, who looked about four months old. "She's two," Dawn said.

"Two months?"

"She's two years old."

Her legs were like sticks, like children in the Nazi camps or the Ethiopian famine. Stick legs. Dawn lifted the child's shirt gently and showed me her skeletal ribs.

Water dripped into a tin basin in a corner. Plaster had fallen off the ceiling. Water dripped through it. Paint chips came down with the water. Plink plink plink, the noise was insistent, unrelenting. Dawn turned her flashlight on the other side of the stinking room.

A few feet from the basin was a row of crude three-legged stools, a baby on each, heads lolling as if they were drugged. Under the stools were more chipped metal bowls. The babies were dressed in thick pants and shirts. One of them opened her eyes and seemed to see us. She made a mewling kind of noise. Like the others, she was tied down to her stool, she was its prisoner, tied to it by her legs.

Gently, Dawn touched the little girl. "I'm going to take this one."

"She looks all right. She doesn't look sick."

"She will be soon. 'Summary resolution', they call it."

"What?"

Dawn picked the child up and wrapped her in a blanket she had in her bag.

"'Summary resolution'. Death by starvation. They don't have to be sick. There are state orphanages where it's completely random. Babies are starved and beaten. For a while, people thought it was only the big orphanage in Shanghai, the one that made all the papers. State orphanages, private ones like this. It's all over the place. The idea is to reduce the number of babies and let westerners adopt the others. Adoption involves a hefty contribution. If you run an orphanage properly, you get a bonus. That's how I gather it works. That's how it works here, anyway, Artie. It took me some time to find out. Can you take her, do you think?"

I took the baby and held her. She wasn't heavy but she was warm.

"Sometimes, if a baby is simply considered too unattractive, they let her starve. They think this one is funny-looking. She's not pretty. That's her crime. Do you want to see the rest? It's pretty tough stuff." Dawn crossed the room to a rough wooden door that swung open on a rusty hinge.

In the next room, there were only two bare plank benches. It was dark except for Dawn's flashlight. What could be tougher than this? What? I followed her into the next room.

"They call it the waiting for death room," Dawn said. "The babies that are diagnosed as having congenital maldevelopment of the brain—which is often double-speak for bullshit—are starved, then they put them in here. They leave them on those benches to die."

For a few seconds we stood in the doorway. I looked at the benches. Seemed to see a baby on the bare plank.

"We have to go now." Dawn closed the door to the dying room behind us. "Now you know what I do, Artie. I take them one at a time. I pay for as many as I can or, if they won't let me, I steal them. I take them to Hong Kong, to the orphanage. We have to move fast. In a few months, it will be impossible to get in here, or anywhere else."

"Why can't you just take them all if no one wants them? You're not short of cash."

"It would ruin the system. There'd be evidence. Don't talk now, Artie. There isn't much time." Dawn looked at the baby in my arms. "Are you all right with her?"

Dragging her leg heavily, the matron found us outside the room. She whispered to Dawn.

"Something's not right. Someone's been making phone calls. Let me put the baby back," Dawn said.

The baby smelled terrible but she had attached herself to my shoulder. She was easy to carry. I didn't want to put her back. I said, "I'm taking her."

"Put her in the car then. Everything is in the back. Clothes. Papers. If you have to go without me, just go. OK? Promise me."

Carrying the baby, I followed Dawn. As we turned a corner in the corridor in the main building, I could see a man in the hall. He had on a shiny green suit and he cracked his knuckles and yawned. Then he hurried away through a door. To the toilet, maybe. We had a couple of minutes' grace time.

I thought I could hear the rain water and the fat babies crying upstairs. Mine was wet. My shirt was soaking. It would have been funny any other place.

"Let's just go," I said softly to Dawn. "Let's just keep going."

The man in the suit never reappeared. He was probably on the phone to the cops already. Maybe he was a cop. I didn't wait to find out.

There was an infant's seat in the back of the car and we put the baby into it. We got in. Dawn locked the doors, turned the key and drove slowly out of the courtyard, lights off, waiting, listening, peering out through the sweaty rain.

"It happens," she said. "Sometimes they call an official to check. Usually, I tell them I'm just visiting."

"And they leave you alone? Why?"

"Sure they do. After all, I'm Mrs Peter Leung."

Dawn drove the Volvo into the street. "You still don't get it, do you? This, you see, is my husband's business."

Negotiating the outskirts of the city, Dawn checked her rear-view mirror constantly. "You thought it was me."

"I thought about it."

"You thought I was doing business with illegals. You could say I am, I guess."

"That's not what I meant."

Suddenly, Dawn pulled into the parking lot of a Japanese fast fishburger restaurant. It was shut. The garbage piled out back stank of fish.

"Why are we stopping?"

"I heard something. Let's wait a minute. Maybe it's nothing. Maybe it's a cop."

"How did you find out about Pete?"

Dawn tied a black cotton scarf around her head. "Pete did a lot of business in Shenzhen. In Fuzhou. It didn't make sense. Pete's a banker. And he likes the high life. Beijing, Shanghai are his kind of places. Listen, Artie. It's quiet now. There's nothing. You hear anything?"

"No."

"You know how to change a baby?" Dawn chuckled. "You don't, do you?" She crawled into the back seat and got out some diapers, glancing out at the street every few seconds. "When I went to work with Alice at the Children's Center in Hong Kong, Pete got crazy. I couldn't figure it out. We were rich women doing a little light charity work. But Pete was already furious that we didn't have a baby. I'd had a miscarriage. He got angry. I started doing pills, uppers, downers, tranqs, ludes. Pete got me whatever I needed. I even tried shooting up. Sometimes I can get straight these days. Sometimes not. I guess you noticed." Dawn got back into the driver's seat.

"Do you want me to drive?"

"I'm all right." She turned the car and drove carefully through Shenzhen and onto the highway.

"What about Lily?"

"I told you. He likes games. Maybe he had the hots for her. Perhaps it was a sort of quid pro quo. You and me. Pete and Lily. Maybe it was just to spite me because we didn't have a child."

"Couldn't you adopt?"

Dawn laughed and took some gum out of her pocket. "Pete wanted his own child. His own blood. A son. Is it hot in here?"

"Yes." I rolled down the window.

"But in New York, Pete was nervous. I didn't see him much, but I could sense he knew I was on to something. You showed up. I had an idea that a girl you knew in New York had been here, as a helper. She was an illegal en route to America, they told me. Somehow I got the idea that she had connected it all up for you, the babies, the illegals, the whole business."

"A girl named Pansy Loh?"

"I never knew her name."

"I wish you'd said something."

"What was there to say? I wasn't sure until I got back to Hong Kong. You couldn't help me. I couldn't help myself. I'd quit my real job, I was too strung out. I scored some bad stuff. I got a hole in my gut. How the fuck did I get from there to here? I would think. For a while I thought I was going to die, so I decided I'd do something useful. High drama, huh, Artie? One of life's little epiphanies. Alice saved my life. By the way, I was telling the truth, darling, when I said I was crazy about you. I'm sorry."

"I'm not."

It was raining harder. The highway was slick. Massive long-haul trucks carried their loads of electronics and livestock. Their windshield wipers swept away water in a frenzy.

"We're almost there," Dawn said. "Oh shit," she added a moment later. "Look at that."

Ahead of us, running up to the border, trucks jammed the road. We inched forward.

A border guard on a motorcycle drove up and down

the line of cars and trucks, stopping here and there to peer inside, tapping on windows. I reached in back and covered the baby with my jacket. She was fast asleep.

We were second in line now. To the right, through the blur of rain and fog, I could make out buildings—customs sheds, I assumed. Then the guard knocked on the window of the Volvo. Dawn rolled it down, delivered her most seductive smile, pulled a cigarette out of her purse and asked sweetly, in English, for a light.

He didn't understand English but he got the message. He produced a lighter, cupped his other hand around it and held it for Dawn. He looked through our passports.

Ahead of us, I thought I could see the glow from Hong Kong's lights in the sky. Shoulders hunched, Dawn smoked, but her face was calm, impassive, like a mask. There was one car in front of us now. In her sleep, the baby whimpered.

"We're almost there," Dawn said. "The other side will be a piece of cake. A few more minutes." She stuffed her cigarette into the ashtray.

Border crossings still get to me. It was the banality that scared me: the grey concrete building. The wet black road. The guards in their lousy uniforms. It wasn't sinister. It was drab. The worst places I've ever been were always drab, the bright lights always just out of reach.

As a kid, I'd been taken to East Berlin. The place had a concrete soul. In the Alexanderplatz, Aunt Birdie took me up to the top of the television tower that looked like a flying saucer.

"Look," she cried. I looked. Even on a clear day, the lights in West Berlin were on. Loads of lights. I could see right into West Berlin, could almost touch the buildings. It was so close. And I thought: this is for me. But how would I get there, me, a boy from Moscow? I could almost touch it, but I couldn't get across the wall.

Now, I thought I could see Hong Kong's red glow. But it was all taking too long. "I don't want to be here, Artie." Dawn peered out of the window.

"Is the baby OK?"

"She's fine."

"Why don't you get in the back seat with her?"

Dawn didn't argue. She slid out of the driver's seat into the back and I moved into her place.

The guard returned. He signaled us to pull out of the line. He waved in the direction of the buildings at the side of the road.

"Do what he says," Dawn whispered. "And Artie?"

"What?"

"In case I don't make it."

"Don't even think it."

"You don't understand. They think of me as Chinese. They think I belong to them. I need to tell you something."

I pulled up in front of the building. "What is it?"

"Pete has a lot of influence. Pete can cut any deal he wants. He can do what he likes. He's American. He's Chinese. No one can touch him. He has dozens of businesses, he has hundreds of ways of moving money. He can buy anyone anywhere. And he has absolutely no scruples. Do you understand? He isn't really a human being."

"It will be OK," I said, as Dawn picked up the baby and we got out of the car.

"Please listen to me. Listen to what I'm trying to tell you." Her voice shook with rage and increasing panic. "What I'm trying to tell you is that it's my husband who they call the Debt Collector."

34

"Hello, darling. Hiya, Artie."

Pete Leung entered the room where we sat waiting for our passports. With him were two other men, their thuggish bodies only barely concealed by the suits. Like every room at every border crossing, it had a few benches, plastic chairs, a table, peeling paint and official notices on the wall. Pete spoke briefly to the bodyguards and they left the room and shut the door. I knew they would be outside. The official border guards never came in. Maybe Pete had bribed them. Maybe he didn't need to. He was in charge.

But the charming man who rode a bike in the snow and loved the movies was gone along with the corduroy pants and the raffish smile. Pete Leung wore a suit.

"I'll take the gun, by the way, Artie, if you've got one. It wouldn't be at all popular with our friends here in the PRC if you shot me. The folks here are real big on squashing crime, and there's no extradition with your country." I tossed him the weapon.

"I want to go," Dawn said, the baby in her arms. "I want to get out of here."

"I don't think that's such a great idea, sweetheart. Don't look at your watch, Artie. We have all night. Is that one of my babies you've got, Dawn?"

"One less for you to kill."

"Don't be ridiculous. You don't suppose I'm personally involved, do you? It's just the way things are. Drugs have become difficult to move, I'm told. In the West, officials have to pay attention to drugs." He pulled some cigarettes out of his pocket, tossed them on a table and sat down. "I can see you need a lesson in the new economics of the free market. Cigarette?" I reached for my own. "Leave your hands on the table, if you don't mind. So. In the new world order, you can move people cheaper than any other resource. Women especially. Illegals for cheap labor. Hookers for export. Wives for Chinese village men who have none because the one-child-family rule means that too many girl babies have been aborted or killed. Ironic, isn't it? It's cheap and it's easy and there are huge profits. In the next century, it will be the great resource," he said. "Body parts is also quite lucrative. Time consuming, though. A fresh liver has to be delivered in twenty-four hours." He looked at us. "You've both lost your sense of humor. I've heard much sicker jokes at New York parties and so have you."

Holding the baby, Dawn looked around. He would kill her if she tried to leave. Leaning his elbows on the table, Pete flicked the collar of his white shirt nervously. He ran his hand through his hair, lit a cigarette, tossed it into the cheap tin ashtray. He took a handkerchief out of his pocket and wiped his glasses on it. He was jumpy; Dawn made him jumpy.

I looked at the window. It was small and there were bars on it. Beyond it was the highway and the border guards. Pete didn't miss a thing, neither would his thugs.

"What about the illegals? What about the illegals your people ship to New York? The people they extort," I said.

"You think it's better to spend the rest of your life in a shitty village with no work, no hope, no money? They know the risk. It costs. It always costs to get to America. They call it the Golden Mountain."

"And the murders ?"

"Perhaps someone forgot to pay. If they don't pay, well, a deal's a deal, or so I'm told."

"And the sweatshops?"

"It's a business. We're not talking *Schindler's List* here."

"How come you're telling me all this?"

"Why not? No one's going anywhere tonight." His laugh was corrosive. "Maybe not tomorrow either."

"But for Shenzhen, Pete?" I said. "For that one shithole."

"No, no, Artie. Hundreds. Dawn, make that baby stop crying, will you? Listen, in the next century, when borders are irrelevant and people expendable, the trade will explode. Look at the map. The old borders are gone."

"Why are you here? What do you want?"

"To see my wife, of course. I'm sorry I couldn't make

351

it to the races. You thought you'd keep me in Hong Kong and away from Shenzhen, did you, darling? I was amused that you put Alice Wing up to asking me, though."

"What about Lily Hanes?" I said.

"God, I'm bored with Lily Hanes." He looked at his watch. "Swatch," he said. "Sharp. I hate expensive watches. As for you, Artie Cohen. You got in the way. That's all."

"And the babies? The ones you let die?"

"No one wants a sick baby. Or an ugly one. Do they, Artie? Do you?"

The baby in Dawn's arms was fast asleep, and she handed her to me, then reached for a cigarette in the pack that lay on the table. Slowly, she lit one, inhaled and blew out the smoke. "He calls the babies Poppies," she said. "Like opium poppies. Like the irradiated opium poppies in the heroin he got for me. If they get too big or too ugly or too sick, they must be cut down. Hot Poppies is what he calls the babies he kills. It's his joke. Pete's a real poet."

Except for the dull roar of the trucks passing outside, it was deadly quiet in the room. There was only the one door. There was no other way out.

Pete reached over and, lightly, with the tips of his fingers, he stroked Dawn's face.

"You didn't have to fuck him, did you?"

Before I could put the baby down and make a move, Leung pulled Dawn to her feet and grabbed Dawn's wrists. He held them behind her back. Twisted them.

"I'm not so small as my brothers in China, perhaps.

But I'm the same. I went to Oxford. To Harvard. Penn. I sound like you. I sound better. Different brain, though. The Chinese are different. We don't like our wives screwing around." His expression changed. "I loved Dawn. I really did. But she was a fake."

The baby was heavy. Pete had Dawn's hands twisted behind her. The door opened a crack and one of the thugs looked in, but Pete shook his head and the door closed again,

"When Dawn couldn't carry a baby to term, my mother said, 'Get her medical records, perhaps we can help.' I got the records from New York. Something bothered me. A note from a pediatrician." Dawn's face remained blank. Slowly, his voice full of vitriol, Pete Leung continued. "Dawn isn't the Taes' real daughter. My wife, Dawn, is trash. She betrayed me in every way."

"You're crazy," she said. "Let me go."

"You've heard of the Walled City? It's gone now, but it was an outlaw nation in the middle of Hong Kong. On the border of Kowloon and the New Territories, actually. The buildings were so close together, there was no light even in the daytime. It was a slum run by gangsters."

"So?"

"Shut up, Artie. In the courtyard which was surrounded by the tenements there was a kind of temple. People threw whatever crap they didn't want onto the temple roof. They found Dawn there with the other shit."

Panic showed on Dawn's face now and I saw her look

towards the window. Don't do it, I thought. Crying now, the baby clung to me.

"The Taes found her in an orphanage and took her to America and passed her off as their own. No one told me. I was in love with her. It was all perfect. But she was garbage." A muscle twitched in Pete's neck, the tendons stood out hard against his collar. "You're the only guy who ever made me sweat, Artie. The only one, and I resent that. And that you fucked my wife."

The rain sluiced down. The traffic thinned out. I could hear the baby's heart and my own. I had to gamble. "This is insanity, Pete. This is how the goons behave. Someone told me your father was a decent man. You were a decent man. Let her go."

Dawn looked at her husband, then at me. "His father was a bastard. Literally. He has to punish everyone for it."

Suddenly, Pete Leung called out to the thugs. The men came into the room and stood, backs to the door, a solid wall of muscle and weaponry.

Still holding Dawn's wrists, Pete forced her onto a chair. He moved his hands to her shoulders. She was his prisoner.

"I can do anything I like. I have an American passport like you. And I am Chinese." Pete echoed what Dawn had said earlier. "The Americans like me because I'm one of them but I can cut a deal with the Chinese. The Chinese like me because I know how to behave myself. I speak their language, whatever it happens to be. This is about business. You see Artie, no one is going to raise a stink about me, whatever I do."

"Don't be too fucking sure."

"Who's going to rescue you? Your fat Russian?" He snorted. "Your faggot policeman? No one is going to rescue you, although I suppose I might let *you* go. No point in killing an American." He slipped his hands around Dawn's neck. 'My wife, however, I could kill with real pleasure. I'll let you keep the baby, Artie. I'll keep my wife."

"Do it," Dawn gasped. "Do it, Artie. He won't dare hurt me. I'm his wife. He's too proud."

At the door Pete's men shifted their weight. The floor creaked. The lights of the passing trucks made shadows on the ceiling. The baby began to wail.

Pete's body suddenly twitched. He pressed down hard on Dawn's neck, harder and harder, until she was gasping. She swayed on her chair. Then, as abruptly, he let her go. He let go of her and slapped her face once, very hard. It cracked like a rifle going off. He called out to the thugs. One of them opened the door.

"I'm bored," Pete said. "I'm bored with both of you. I really did think of killing you, Dawn. But it's not worth it. You're not worth it. I can always find you, can't I? It's more fun that way."

Halfway out the door, Pete Leung turned. "See you around," he said, and then he left and was driven away into the Chinese night.

EPILOGUE

New York

Sonny Lippert was sitting in the window of Mike Rizzi's coffee shop when I got out of the cab a week later. The sun was out. It was spring.

I had stayed on in Hong Kong after Tolya picked us up from the border crossing in his Hummer. Ricky Tae flew into Hong Kong, said he was feeling great and that it was his turn to look after his sister. "My turn," he said, and moved into the new flat Dawn rented. But Dawn was busy. She and Tolya had warmed up to each other. Tolya put his guys on permanent duty looking after Dawn. The two of them did a lot of shopping. Still, Ricky stayed on. I wasn't sure, but I got the feeling he met someone in Hong Kong. It was weeks before I discovered it was Ringo Chen.

I stuck around Hong Kong until Alice Wing had fixed some things for me. Then I called Lily and left a message to say I was coming home. "Come to dinner. Come tomorrow night."

"I wish you'd stay, Artie." Dawn kissed me on the cheek. I kissed her back and went home.

From the window of the coffee shop, Sonny saluted me, then he and Mike ran into the street to help me get everything out of the cab and into my apartment.

I asked about Hillel Abramsky. Mike said, "He's going to shrink school, Artie. He's going to be OK."

Pete Leung was missing in China, Sonny told me. The orphanage in Shenzhen had been shut down. Sonny had already collared a number of sweatshop owners. At least a few of the enforcers would fry if he had his way. Things would get better for a while. Then the cockroaches would return.

"You can nuke 'em and they always come back," Sonny said as we stood in front of my door. "I'm glad you're home safe, Artie." Me too, I thought. Me too.

When they left, I called Lily up. "Come tonight."

She said she was tired.

"Oh just do it, OK? Just this once, do it for me, don't say anything, just come, don't argue, don't give me sixteen reasons why. Just come. Six o'clock. Six. Be here."

By the time she got to my place, I think she had guessed. Instinct. Something in my voice.

Under one arm, she had my copy of the Tony Bennett album, the vinyl I'd lent her and she'd given to Phil Frye. "I stole it back," she grinned. In the other hand she held the teddy bear whose eyes her mother had removed when Lily was a baby.

Lured by the sound of *The Lion King* and maybe the chuckling noises, Lily headed straight to the bedroom. At the door, she turned and, looking beautiful, said, "I thought you only asked me over for dinner."

"Yeah, well, dinner and to tell you I brought you something from China."